PURSUIT OF JUSTICE

NEIL SANDS

First Edition

First printed in the United Kingdom

Published by MYRAR Publishing

This book is dedicated to the memory of;

Archie Sawyer
1912-1995

A voracious reader - I hope he would be proud.

"The first request of civilization... is that of justice."

Sigmund Freud

CHAPTER 1

The hand hit him with a loud crack across his face. "Stop crying! The sooner you do as you're told and realise you're never leaving here, the better!" With that he was hit again.

The light was shining too brightly in his face; he couldn't see the man stood next to it, only his silhouette. His mind was trying to block out the man's shouting. He didn't like it. He never liked shouting of any sort – it hurt him, upset him and made him cry. He was crying now, he didn't want to be here. The man had said he was a friend taking him on an adventure, but it wasn't an adventure, it wasn't nice. He wanted to go back home – he was safe there.

He had lost count of how many days he had been here as time had confused him, but at least he had enough sense to look at the man's phone when he left it lying there. He had learnt his mum's phone number by heart, but she hadn't answered by the time the man returned, tearing the phone from his hand and knocking him to the floor. He had been tied to the chair with the light in his face since then.

It was a damp, dark night, as Tom Windsor sped across the Cambridgeshire Fens in his Audi RS Q8, Carbon Black. The destination was a small farm off the beaten track, between Peterborough and King's Lynn.

He had secretly been monitoring Jean Terry's phone ever since he first found out about her son, Sammy, going missing two days ago. In the faintest chance he called her, or there was a ransom demand involved, she had contacted the police and told them he suffered from a development disorder and had the mind of a seven-year-old child. A PC had taken details and said he would pass the information on to the right department. She had heard nothing more from them.

He had been taking note of the growing number of missing persons recently. Over the past eighteen months he had worked tirelessly, building his expertise as a hacker. Using the dark web, he was now able to place a worm into the Police National Computer (PCN) and was receiving updates of any missing persons cases that fitted his criteria. Tracking where the call had been made from was now child's play, thanks to the programmes that were loaded onto the hard drives he had stolen in Baghdad two years ago.

He turned off the main A47, passing many small villages with either Saint or Drove in their names. He wound along B roads with water-filled dikes alongside them and further onto unmade dirt tracks where he turned the lights off and finished the journey in darkness. He stopped about four hundred metres away from the farm dressed in all-black, with his new PIG Full Dexterity Tactical gloves and a balaclava rolled up like a beanie hat. He pulled his night-vision goggles down over his eyes and made his way stealthily towards the farm. Tom had swiftly studied the farm on Google Earth before leaving his base in Northamptonshire and knew, as with all the recent cases he had been dealing with, that there could well be a violent outcome. He had made a pledge, however, to continue to seek justice for those unable to get it for themselves and therefore he was happy to be as violent as necessary to bring Sammy home.

Getting closer he heard dogs barking, but suspected they were either chained up or in a pen. Circling the empty-looking, dark house, he spotted a typical traveller's chrome caravan with a Nissan drop-side flatbed truck linked to it. Silently passing one of the outbuildings, he paused as he heard shouting and crying inside. There were no windows and only one door. Tom retrieved both his Glock 19 with a silencer fitted and his Taser from his backpack. Sliding the gun in his belt, he removed the night-vision goggles and pulled the balaclava over his face, took a deep breath and opened the door.

The first thing he saw was a man with his back to the door about to hit Sammy. Turning around in shock, he yelled, "Who the fuck are you? What do you want?"

Tom aimed his high-powered Axon Taser at the man and shouted, "Move away from the boy and kneel on the floor now! I won't give you another warning!"

Brendan Boswell was a big man although, only standing at about 5-feet 10-inch in his muddy boots, he must have weighed almost eighteen stone. The sleeves of his checked shirt were rolled up over huge forearms Popeye would have been proud of. He certainly had that look of strength so many farmers and ground workers have. With a couple of days' growth on his face and his unkempt ginger hair, he was the archetype Irish traveller.

He looked at the man stood before him all in black with a balaclava over his face. He knew he wasn't a copper – he would have announced that – so who the hell was he and what did he want with him?

Tom yelled again. "Your last chance – get on the floor!" but Boswell was a fighting man. He started to charge at Tom, but was stopped in his tracks by fifty thousand volts, like running into a brick wall. Every muscle in his body cramped and he fell to the ground, shaking.

Tom quickly made his way to Sammy, untying the ropes around his wrists and said soothingly, "Hello, Sammy. Don't be scared; you're safe now. I'm taking you home."

Sammy was still crying and was just repeating, "Taking me home, taking me home."

Tom put the gun and the Taser back into his backpack and walked across to Boswell lying on the floor. "You evil bastard, treating the kid like this. You will pay for it!" He then stepped back and aimed his size ten Oakley assault boot into the traveller's stomach, forcing all the air out and making him wheeze. But Tom wasn't finished – he stepped back again, this time kicking him viciously in the head, knocking him unconscious. He deftly tied the man's hands together with cable ties.

Tom turned towards Sammy and said, "Sammy, I'm going to take you into my car and then back to your mum." Leading him out of the building, he put the goggles on again to enable him to see clearly and to return to the car as fast as possible. He unlocked the car and sat Sammy in it. "Now, listen carefully, Sammy. I have to go back to the farm but I won't be long. Stay here in the car and *do not* get out. I will soon be taking you home to your mum; do you understand?"

Sammy nodded and replied, "Yes, understand."

The rain had started to fall as he made his way back to the farm. Before returning to the man he did a recce of the rest of the prefab-style, derelict buildings and wasn't totally surprised, looking through the window to see five or six men lying on the floor asleep, most of them snoring. *Just as I thought, this really is modern day slavery*, which he knew had been on the increase for years. There was nothing he could do for them now, he had to get Sammy back to his mum, but he would make sure they would get looked after.

Removing his night-vision goggles again, he opened the door, but Boswell, who had come round by now, had somehow got to his feet and charged at him rather comically, still with his hands tied behind his back. It was a fruitless move with Tom managing to easily sidestep away, grabbing him by the back of his head and driving it into the wall. Boswell grunted and fell to the floor with a large gash now visible on his head. Searching him first and pocketing his mobile phone, Tom took the gaffer tape from his backpack and bound Boswell's feet, legs and arms and, lastly, covered tape over his mouth. There was a doorway in the back wall leading to a storage cupboard, so Tom dragged him into it and then wedged the chair under the door handle to hopefully keep him in there. Finally, using Boswell's mobile and thankful that the gloves were touch screen conductive, he called 999, telling the police, "Come quick! There's been a murder at South Drove Farm. We need help." Afterwards he turned the phone off and stamped onto it, smashing it.

Remembering Sammy, he ran back to the car to find that Sammy had dozed off. He woke him gently, asking, "Sammy, are you OK, mate?"

Yawning, he then smiled. "Yes, thank you, mister. Am I going home?"

"Yes, you are, young man," and they set off. The roads were clear and Tom decided to take the A47, A1 and M11, the longest route in miles, but at the speed he was driving, by far the fastest.

Sammy soon fell asleep again. Tom knew he needed to call Mrs Terry and had a cover story ready that he'd used before. She answered on the third ring. He asked if it was Mrs Terry, who replied in a nervous voice, "Yes, who is it?"

"You don't know me and I am afraid I can't give you my name as I work for a government department that dislikes publicity, but I thought you would like to know that Sammy will be home with you safe and sound in less than an hour. He hadn't been treated very nicely, but I can assure you the person who took him has now been treated far worse. I will tell you more shortly, but have to ask for the utmost discretion – as I say, my department dislikes publicity."

"Thank you! Thank you so much, I don't know what else to say."

"You don't need to say anything. I will see you shortly."

Under sixty minutes later he was pulling up outside the Terrys' house. He woke Sammy and led him to the front door, which opened as he got to it. Sammy was still half-asleep but was quickly hugged by his mum, who had tears of joy streaming down her face.

"How can I ever thank you? I don't even know your name."

"Mrs Terry, there is no need to thank me, but this is an ongoing case, so if you say anything about what has happened, it would jeopardise it, so please, again, just be happy Sammy is safe and leave it at that. If the police ask, I would suggest you say that he was out wandering, got confused and couldn't find his way back home, that he found shelter in a derelict building but fortunately the confusion cleared and he was able to find his way home. It's a bit weak but as he is home safe and sound I'm sure they won't question it."

After a quick goodbye he jogged back to his car, knowing it had been a good night and justice had been accomplished.

CHAPTER 2

Dan woke a second or two before the alarm went off at 6.30 am. It was to be his first day back at work after his honeymoon.

A fortnight at the Sandals resort in Antigua, a beautiful island that boasted a beach for every day of the year, had done them both the power of good. They'd been swimming in the crystal clear, blue sea, walking on the powdery white sand and exploring each other's bodies every night – it was the perfect honeymoon.

It had been a crazy year, with him being first made CIO of the Vigilante Murders, as they became called by the press, which had led to him finding the murderer, only to end up joining *with* him to avenge the murder of his fiancée Catherine and then both of them brutally killing the culprits.

At first, he found the aftermath very hard to deal with; he had killed before when he was a paratrooper in Kosovo and Sierra Leone, but that was for the service of his country. This was different – on the downside he felt he had betrayed his oath as a police officer and he hated lying to his work colleagues and friends. But, on the plus side, he knew that he had taken the lives of evil terrorists who had killed innocent people and would no doubt have killed more. Plus, it had finally given him emotional closure and allowed him to move on with his life and marry Sue.

Dan stirred with the feeling of a fly landing on his cheek. Slowly opening his eyes, he took a second to focus on the blonde hair over his face. He smiled and sighed with pleasure, still feeling this fluttering on his cheek. He quietly whispered, "Sue, what are you doing?"

"Giving you butterfly kisses, my gorgeous, sexy husband. I love you so much, I could eat you and I know just where I'd start. Do you think we have time, lover boy?" she laughed, rubbing her hand over his chest under the duvet.

He roared back with laughter, taking her face in both hands and kissing her gently. "Mrs Hooper, you should be ashamed of yourself, trying it on with a detective chief inspector, especially while your son is downstairs having breakfast and we both need to get to work. Now, let me get up and hold that thought until tonight."

"Tonight? How about a quick one in the canteen kitchen after lunch?" she enquired teasingly, with a huge grin on her beautiful face.

Dan rolled out of bed, saying, "You are incorrigible, you really are, but I love you so much – just wait until tonight."

He made his way to the nick, arriving just before 8 am. He was amazed as he walked past incident room 2 to see all his team already there. As soon as they saw him, they all began to clap and cheer. DC Stan Jones was the first to call out, "Must be nice to be back on your feet again after two weeks in bed," which received a groan from everyone else.

"It was great, thanks everyone, and we did get out of bed once in a while, thanks, Stan. It felt much longer than two weeks away, but it's good to be back and I look forward to being brought up to speed, once I've checked my e-mails and post."

Sitting at his desk, he was going through his mail and picked up a postcard from his DS, 'Bronco' Laine, who was on holiday himself in Belgium. The picture on the front was of the Menin Gate Memorial to the Missing in Ypres, that bears the names of the fifty-four thousand British and

Commonwealth soldiers who gave their lives in the First World War, whose bodies were never found. Turning it over, Bronco had just written, 'What a place, you really need to come here one day, you will never forget it'.

As he finished reading it, his phone rang. It was his boss, Chief Superintendent Arthur Jackson.

"Morning Dan, welcome back. Could you pop up? I have some news for you."

Dan made his way to the Chief's office. "Come in, Dan, how are you? How's Sue? I guess you had a great honeymoon."

"We are both fine, thanks, Chief and, yes, it was paradise and she makes me laugh every day, it's brilliant. How are you?"

"Yes, all good, thanks, and I couldn't be happier for you, but we are having some changes. First of all, DI Roberts has got her promotion to DCI. It was always on the cards and I am pleased for Jane. I think we all know she is headed for the top, but the bad news is she is being transferred to MET Ops Covert Policing (*MO3*) with immediate effect. I think it's part of their long-term plan for her to work as many departments as possible. The other bit of bad news is, she's not being replaced here due to cutbacks, but we are getting another newly promoted DS and I think you will be impressed." Passing a file across the desk, he said, "Here is her file. It will do her the world of good working with you, but I also want Bronco, when he gets back, to take her under his wing. She's due to report to you at 9.00 this morning. Once you've had a chat, bring her up to meet me."

After that news, Dan couldn't wait to open her file as soon as he was back in his office. The Chief Super was right – he was impressed. Letitia Makubuya was 26 years old, born of Ugandan parents in Streatham, South London. She gained a master's degree in criminology from the University of Surrey in Guildford and was fast-tracked into the Met's

Operation Trident, a police unit set up to combat gun crime. She was an All-England School's pole vault champion, holding a Black Belt 2nd Dan in Brazilian jiu-jitsu and, as a hobby, fights in mixed martial arts.

Dan was still reading the file when Letitia was shown to his office. Dan was stunned; she looked more like a supermodel than a detective. She was standing at around 5-feet 10-inches, with her hair impeccably neat in cornrows, wearing black Nike trainers and a smart blue G-Star RAW jumpsuit over a white vest. Walking forward with a huge smile to shake hands, she said, "Good morning, sir, it's lovely to meet you."

Dan returned the greeting, saying, "Good morning, Letitia, and likewise, but first things first, there's no need for sir; I am quite happy with Dan if we are alone or Guv, in company."

She kept smiling. "Thank you, Guv. Well, in that case – second things being second – Tish is fine. I always think Letitia is too much of a mouthful and it really is good to meet you. I've heard lots about you."

They both sat down. "And where have you heard that from, then, Tish?"

"From Julie Burton, Guv. We are old friends and are both in the same club," and with a wink she added, "if you get what I mean, Guv. She said you would understand."

Dan had been friends with his Chief Crime of Scenes Officer, Julie Burton, for some years and, along with Sue, both understood she was part of the *LGBT* community.

Dan smiled again. "Did she, indeed? Well, yes, Julie is a colleague and a very good friend, as I am sure you know. I most certainly do understand and couldn't be happier to welcome you to the team."

"Thank you, sir; I mean, Dan or Guv," she chuckled. "In fact, Julie is one reason why I was happy to be transferred here as we are thinking of moving in together. I'm well pleased you're kosher with it." Her cockney accent was getting stronger as she relaxed.

"That's good. Julie is great friends with my wife, Sue; in fact, she was her maid of honour, so when you're settled you must both come over for dinner."

At that moment his phone rang. Picking it up, his part of the conversation went something like, "Yes, yes… Where? OK, we're on our way." To Tish he said, "Right, time to start. There's been an armed robbery at Bezenstocks Jewellers in town. Let's go."

They took Dan's Freelander, stopping in the High Street behind two patrol cars that still had their blue lights flashing. Two PCSOs were putting a tape barrier up across the High Street to keep a large crowd of nosey bystanders back. Getting out of the car, the first officer Dan spotted was one of the younger PCs, Jimmy Edmunds, who Dan knew from previous cases and had great respect for.

Walking towards the shop, he said, "Good morning, Jimmy. What have you got for us?"

Striding alongside him, Jimmy replied, "Morning, sir. I was the first one to get here. I was down the street and heard the alarm go off. Mr Bezenstock is a nice, old chap. He said that a tall, IC-3, dressed in all-black, black cap and had a mask over this mouth – I think he means a bandanna – entered the shop, grabbed the young, twenty-two-year-old assistant, Chelsea, and held a knife to her throat, demanding cash out of the till. This was a waste of time as the shop had only just opened and almost all their transactions these days are on card, so he made the old gent take four Rolex watches out of the window and, pushing the girl to the floor, he grabbed them and fled."

Inside the jewellery shop, Dan nodded to the two PCs already there, who were talking to the girl. He introduced himself and Tish to Mr Bezenstock who was visibly shaken.

"What is the world coming to, Chief Inspector? I have been here for almost fifty years and I have been robbed more times in the last five years than the previous forty-five. I'm getting too old for this, it upsets me and especially to see young Chelsea put through all this. I'm starting to think it's time to sell up and retire."

Dan nodded and said, "I totally understand, sir–"

Tish interrupted. "Excuse me, Guv, Mr Bezenstock – could you describe the man again?" and then, turning to Chelsea, she asked, "And could I hear your description, as well?"

The jeweller seemed unsure what to say. "Well, he was… ah, how do you say? Hmm… ah…"

She grinned. "It's OK, you can say black. I have heard it all before."

He seemed relieved. "Yes, he was black," and then went on to give the same description PC Edmunds had just provided. Tish turned towards the young woman. "Chelsea, have you got anyfin' else to add to that?"

She stood up from the chair, placing a half-empty glass of water on the counter. "Well, yes. Although you couldn't see much of his face he had two eyebrow slits above his left eye and a tattoo on the back of his right hand between his thumb and first finger."

Tish nodded. "That's great, Chelsea. Thanks, babe, you're a star." And then to Dan, she added, "Guv, we need to go outside; I think I clocked him when we arrived."

Walking out, her eyes searched the crowd until she saw him standing across to her right. Their eyes met and it was like he knew that she knew. He turned to walk away but quickly started to sprint. He was fast, but she was soon after him. He was knocking people out of the way and she was dodging them. Dan and PC Edmunds were trying to keep up but couldn't. They turned off the High Street into Fore Street, a long, straight, tree-lined road, but he soon realised, no matter how quick he was, this girl was quickly catching him up. Turning into a side alley, he pulled out the knife from his pocket, turned it towards her and said, "Fuck off, bitch, else I plug ya!"

She didn't pause. In a heartbeat her right leg shot out, connecting with a crack on his wrist and sending the knife flying. In one continuous movement she spun in a full circle and the next kick hit him hard in his solar plexus, doubling him over, at the same moment that Dan and the PC arrived. With a single pace forward she took his right arm, turning it against the joint and pushing him flat into the ground. "You couldn't plug in a kettle, you wanker! You're nicked," and with that she handcuffed him and read him his rights.

She looked up to see the DCI and the PC standing there open-mouthed with hands on hips. "Alright, Guv, I think he's the one," and she pulled out the Rolex watches from his pockets. Pulling him up to his feet and pushing him towards PC Edmunds, she said, "He's all yours, Jimmy, don't lose him. Not a bad start, eh, Guv? Another case solved. I guess the coffees are on you." Still grinning, she pointed across the road to the Starbucks.

"I guess they must be, Tish, then it's back to the nick. You haven't met the Chief Super yet; isn't *he* in for a treat?"

"OK, Guv, in that case, can I have a cupcake, as well?"

Tish finished the cupcake in seconds as they drove back to the nick. When they walked past the main office, Stan Jones stood up in a jokey kung fu pose and started singing, "Everybody was kung fu fighting..."

They all chuckled in amusement as Dan said, "Another word from you, DC Jones, and I will set our new secret weapon on you." Dan then introduced Tish to the rest of the team including Brenda Shaw, the office manager, before taking her up to meet the Chief Superintendent, with a huge smile on his face, thinking, *Working with this girl is going to be some adventure!*

CHAPTER 3

Chief Superintendent Arthur Jackson stood up, smiling, as Dan walked into his office with Tish. "DS Makubuya, I'm pleased to welcome you here and from what I understand, you already have your first arrest for us under your belt – I am very impressed."

"Thanks, sir, but it's no big deal."

"If the man was holding a knife and, from all accounts, was disarmed very quickly, I think it *is* a big deal. Hopefully he will go away for a few years, but I have a question for you... Reading your file, I know what jiu-jitsu is, but what is Brazilian jiu-jitsu?"

"BJJ is a slightly different form of martial art, founded by a man called Carlos Gracie and his family. It has more takedowns and submissions than normal jiu-jitsu. It is used a lot these days in mixed martial arts like the UFC; it's very effective on the street, sir."

"Ah, yes, it seems it is very effective. OK, well, thank you for that; you learn something new every day. I will let you get on. As I said to DCI Hooper, I think you will benefit from working alongside DS Laine when he returns from holiday next week. He is an officer with great experience."

Both Dan and Tish thanked him and returned to Dan's office.

Once Tish had sorted out her new desk, they went down to visit the custody sergeant who told Dan that the suspect's fingerprints, which were on file with a long record of petty crime, showed him to be twenty-two-year-old Caden Smith, currently of no fixed abode.

Handing the details over to Dan, he informed him that the duty solicitor had arrived and so he went to bring him up from the cells to interview room 1.

Smith was brought in with Angus McMichael, a sixty-year-old veteran solicitor, who was known to be serving his time, as easily as possible, before retiring in a few years.

Dan started the double-system recorder, which was still used even in this modern digital age. It was generally thought as being more tamper-proof than any other method. After going through all the formalities of naming everyone in the room, he paused, glancing at his notes before looking up.

"Well, Mr Smith, you've really messed up this time, haven't you?"

"No comment."

"I mean, this record of yours is littered with petty crime."

"No comment."

"But now, armed robbery."

"No comment."

"Assault with a deadly weapon."

"No comment."

"Attacking a police officer with a knife."

Smith, who had been looking down at the table, looked up. "Attacking a police officer? She fucking attacked me, the bitch! I should have plugged her. I ain't done nuffin', this is police brutality."

Tish laughed and answered in patois slang, more Kingston Town than Kentish Town, "Babylon brutality, mi ass; yuh a battyman. Wait til yuh friends kno, yuh fight like a gyal, yuh a guh jail."

Both Dan and the duty solicitor, Mr McMichael, laughed out loud as Smith sat there open-mouthed.

"Well, I didn't get all of that, but I think you did, Caden. Mr Bezenstock and his assistant both identified you and noticed your tattoo, plus, with all the CCTV in the High Street, I am sure we can find you on that, going in and out of the shop. You were arrested with the stolen items on you along with a knife, as well as the bandana and cap you wore for the robbery in your pocket. As they say, you are bang to rights; what do you say to that?"

Looking back down Smith just replied, "No comment."

Mr McMichael looked across at Dan and said, "I'd like a quiet word with my client but there is no need for you to leave the room." With that, he turned to his client, speaking quietly into his ear, "My advice to you, Mr Smith, is that you plead guilty. At the moment, you are possibly looking at a life sentence and hopefully, by pleading guilty and with us finding some mitigating circumstances, we could get that reduced, but if you take up time in court with a 'not guilty' plea you will go down for a long time."

"OK, yes, it was me, but I got mental probs and mitigating things."

Dan left Tish to write out a statement for Smith to sign before taking him back to the custody sergeant who charged him, remanding him in custody for a court appearance the next day. She met the DCI on the stairs heading back to his office. "Let's have an early lunch and you can meet my wife," he said, leading Tish to the canteen. Sue was clearing a table as they walked in and she turned to greet them. "Good morning again, DCI Hooper, at least this time you're awake and you must be Tish, I've heard loads about you from Julie." She gave her a hug, kissing both cheeks.

Tish hugged Sue back. "Likewise, Sue, it's great to finally meet you."

Giving Dan a quick kiss before returning behind the counter, she said, "So, I hope you are going to keep my husband out of trouble then, Tish?"

"Well, if he runs as slow as he did this morning, then you will have nothing to worry about."

"Yes, bless him, I think he's slowing down with age; he *is* getting on a bit, isn't he?"

"Hey, you two, I *am* still here, you know! I can see you two will get along just fine," and they all laughed.

Tish and Dan ordered their lunch, both going for the homemade shepherd's pie and had just finished when a PC came in and said, "Sorry to disturb you, sir, but a body has been found on the Millfield Estate and here are the details. Scenes of Crime are on their way; we have one car there and two more on the way."

"Thank you, we will be on our way directly. The bloody Millfield again, they should pull the place down." Letting Sue know he may be late home, they both made their way down to the car park.

CHAPTER 4

BATMAN, TURKEY, SIX MONTHS AGO

It was the end of another almost perfect day in Turkey; he'd been up early and had run five miles over the hilly terrain as the sun was rising. He dressed in a plain white Valentino shirt, Ralph Lauren tan cotton chinos, Hugs & Co penny brown loafers and a Hublot Classic Fusion Titanium Blue 45mm watch. He checked himself in the mirror realising that he would never have dreamt when he was growing up in Dr Barnardo's or, indeed, his time in the army and the SAS, that expensive clothes would please him, but they now reminded him of what it was like to wear hand-me-downs every day as a kid and where his life had taken him. They were also the perfect look for the wealthy oil executive role he always played while he was here.

He drove into town, stopping on the busy tree-lined Turgut Ozal Boulevard for his favourite slow-roasted Turkish coffee and a freshly baked Şekerpare, the sweet smelling, semolina-based traditional biscuit.

From there he had an appointment at the letting agent for the farmhouse that he had rented while still working for Coeus, a private military company (PMC) in Baghdad. He had rented it, thinking that he might need a bolthole if things went wrong there and they certainly did. He agreed to rent the place for another year and paid the fifteen thousand dollars on a card in one of the five names he had passports and bank accounts for.

Back at the farmhouse he was quickly into his usual routine of spending hours on-line, using much of the knowledge he had gained over the past year or so, delving into the dark web and researching what he planned to do when he shortly returned to England. Having seen a UN report that human trafficking was not only on the rise but taking on 'horrific dimensions', with sexual exploitation of victims the main driver, he also learned that children now accounted for thirty percent of those being trafficked and far more girls than boys. He knew it was something he should look more closely at to see if he could help stop any of this hideous trade.

After cooking a light dinner of sea bass and salad he sat under the stars, enjoying a large glass of single malt Glenmorangie. As the whiskey warmed his throat, his mind drifted back over his journey here and the life changing events, which had started almost two years previously

He often wondered what his life would be like if he hadn't taken up the offer to join Coeus in Baghdad, but the fact was that he had, and his life had changed forever. He knew from the first day that they weren't just another PMC but had to be some kind of mercenary black ops, set up either by the CIA's Special Activities Center (SAC), or some other more secretive department at Langley. Their code was that they must never leave witnesses, however, killing for no reason went against all he had ever stood for. But finally, the raping of his friend Sunny who ran the computer tech office, a girl whom he had grown close to, was the final straw. It started an unstoppable rage where he killed the rapists and the rest of the unit, all of which set him on his path of murdering the guilty, to bring justice for those who couldn't get it for themselves. He thought of his escape from Iraq to Turkey, setting himself up in Batman and then going back to the UK a year ago, searching for cases that he could bring justice to. He came across the case of Catherine, the fiancée of a former paratrooper, Captain Dan Hooper, now a DCI, who had been killed in a terrorist attack along with seventeen others – run over by a truck in London's West End. The amazing thing was that he actually remembered Dan from a joint SAS Paratrooper operation in Africa some years before and that had sealed this case, making it his top choice. In dealing with this, it meant more killings along the way, being confronted by Dan, saving his life and, in turn, Dan saving *his* life as they both dealt out justice to those responsible for Catherine's death.

He had returned to Turkey two days after the final 'Vigilante' murders, still suffering with the injuries he received from the hands of the Muslim extremist father, son and their co-conspirator. His bruised and battered face gained him some inquisitive looks at airport security, but the explanation of a car crash quelled any suspicion. It was, in fact, the stab wound in his shoulder that caused him the most concern and needed a visit to the local clinic to get proper treatment for. Thankfully, stabbings are commonplace in Turkey and it didn't raise any difficult questions but it did require a couple of weeks' rest to heal properly before he slowly rehabbed it to get himself returned to full strength.

The next few days were spent preparing to travel back to the UK. In the meantime he had also thought a lot about human trafficking. He still felt duty-bound to continue his crusade, bringing justice to those who couldn't get it for themselves and perhaps that was an area he needed to check out. But, he also knew it would be wrong to start another murder spree, like the vigilante killer one. This time, if he killed in the name of justice, there would be no 'guilty' signature left behind.

CHAPTER 5

Dan brought Tish up to speed on the goings-on at the notorious Millfield Estate, which consisted of five six-storey blocks, built after the Second World War and had fallen into disrepair over the years, no matter what political party was in power. It had almost been made a no-go area for police a couple of years back, where the powers that be complained that stop-and-search was being used against too many black teens. But since the vigilante killing of the area's main drugs dealer, along with a spate of old age pensioners being mugged, one fatally, which led to the vigilante striking again, killing two and seriously injuring two more of the culprits, things had recently appeared to have quietened down – until this.

As Dan pulled in, he saw the police vehicles parked next to the large communal rubbish bins by the third block. Screens were being erected around the bins and floodlights set up. Crime Scene Manager, Julie Burton, saw them getting out of Dan's Freelander and removing their Tyvek coverall suits from the boot, waiting for them to walk over. She looked a bit worried and noticed Tish raising her eyebrows in a questioning way.

Tish smiled. "It's OK, he knows and he's cool, babe."

Dan grinned back. "Yes, I know, and I *am* cool, babe. Now, what have we got?"

Now it was Julie's turn to smile. "It's the body of a young female found by Mrs Jenson who lives up on the fourth floor. She had brought some bin bags down, opened the lid of the wheelie bin and saw her. She called us immediately. The body hasn't been there long, but I can't do much until the Doc gets here. We're just fingerprinting the lid and the rim of the bin and making the place secure. Do you want to take a look?"

"Yes please, Julie." The lid had been tied back to keep it open and two sets of steps were placed in front it. They both climbed onto the steps to get a good look inside the bin.

The body was lying almost twisted in half where it had been tipped into the bin. They could see the bleached blonde shoulder length hair coated with dried blood and what they could make of the girl's face looked like it had been badly beaten. She was wearing a skimpy, white crop top over a black bra and a short, leather skirt with stockings and suspenders showing underneath. It would be difficult to see much more until the body was removed.

As they climbed back down, the crime scene photographer then climbed up, taking pictures from every possible angle. He was just finishing when 'The Doc' arrived.

Gareth Hew Evans was a large man, standing a bit over 6-feet tall; his ruddy complexion slightly hidden by a full beard and handlebar moustache that he had been growing for the past few months. He was born in Llanelli over sixty years ago and, at one time, played front row for their famous rugby team alongside the legendary Jonathan Davies. He was a very experienced Home Office pathologist and a great friend of Dan's.

"Good afternoon, Ms Burton; how are you, young Daniel, and who have we here?"

"Hello Gareth, this is our new DS, Letitia Makubuya, but I'm sure you can call her Tish."

"Lovely to meet you, my dear; I'm sure you will enjoy working with this wonderful team."

"Thank you, sir," she smiled.

Gareth climbed up the steps next to look in. "Hmm, that's not very nice, is it? If I get in I'm going to disturb things so I think, if we can, Julie, let's get her out as carefully as possible."

Between Gareth, Julie and another of the CSIs, they slowly lifted the corpse out, laying it onto a sheet on the ground.

Gareth slowly turned the body over onto its back and, gently removing the hair from her face, revealed the state of her injuries.

Shaking his head, he said, "The poor thing has taken a nasty beating around her face, but I doubt that killed her. There are various track marks on her arms, so I suspect some drug abuse." Turning her, he saw a large gash in the back of her head.

"That's more like it – blunt force trauma to the back of the head. Yes, I'd say that did it and before you ask me time of death, Daniel, I will tell you that from the rigor mortis and temperature, I would take a wild guess at twelve hours, which would take you back to the early hours of the morning, but judging by how the blood has dried and that there doesn't appear to be much in the bin, I am confident that this is just the dump site and she was killed elsewhere. If you can bag her hands just in case she has anything under her nails, I think I am clear for this afternoon, so the sooner you can get her back to me, the sooner I can give you more answers."

"Thanks, Gareth, that's great. Julie, any belongings found – purse, bag or phone?"

"Sorry, Guv, no, but we will need to get the bin emptied along with the others here, just in case."

"Right, thanks. Tish, any thoughts?"

Looking straight at him she replied, "Loads, Guv, how long have you got?"

"As long as you need – fire away."

"Well, first of all, I think she's a brass, a working girl – I've seen so many just like her – similar looks, size, age, cheap clothes and I would stake a year of your wages on the fact that she's Eastern European, either Romanian or more likely Albanian and she's been beaten up by her pimp. The Albanian mafia is huge over here now; they are vicious bastards and are known for treating their working girls badly."

"Well, thanks for betting my year's wages but, seriously, how do know so much about them?"

"I was seconded to SCO35, Covert Intelligence Command, and we had an operation against a gang of them called Hellbanianz, based in Barking and Dagenham. They have no fear of the law, or anyone else and they even post videos of themselves on YouTube with gold Rolexes, new Bentleys and Lamborghinis. They are into drugs, prostitution, people trafficking and slavery – you name it and they are into it – killing anyone in their way. Thousands arrived here in the 1990s during a refugee crisis, claiming to be Kosovan. They say it was the biggest case of nationality switching ever in the UK. Some took jobs as door staff in the sex and vice trade in Soho, which used to be controlled by the Maltese mafia. At first, Albanians began working alongside the Maltese but they soon killed them off and took over London's prostitution rackets.

They advertise their girls as Polish and Romanian but ninety percent are Albanian. They are often kidnapped from school, some as young as eleven and twelve and smuggled from the port of Vlorë in southern Albania, across the Adriatic Sea to the Italian coast. The girls are moved all around the country into brothels and often moved on every month or so. They are kept drugged and if they don't do as they are told or cause problems, they are murdered without a thought.

I am amazed she was dumped here; I think it's rare to let a body be found, which might help us."

"Thanks for that. I knew what a problem they were becoming, but I didn't realise they were that big. Could you call Stan Jones and get him to organise a team to start door-to-door? I'll call the Super and we need to get CCTV checked. I doubt she was carried here. We will know more once we hear back from Gareth."

CHAPTER 6

NORTHAMPTONSHIRE – PRESENT DAY

Tom's early morning run through the Northamptonshire countryside took him on a circular route from his house, down country lanes, along footpaths, through open farmland, and around the edge of the Althorp Estate, the resting place of Princess Diana. It was just over six miles; enough to get him wide awake and give him time to recap over the previous night's events and getting Sammy back to his mum.

His house was a modern five-bedroomed, three-storey house in a small cul-de-sac, off the main road through a quaint village. It had been built ten years ago with traditional stone under a slate roof and leaded windows. He had purchased it via a shell company in Grand Cayman, set up by Swiss Bank Corporation, in the name of Tom Greensted, one of his five aliases. To his neighbours, he used the cover of an IT consultant who often had to work away, a cover which now fitted him well with his increased knowledge of computers, especially hacking.

After a shower and light breakfast, he went up to his office on the top floor, first checking on the news channels for anything about the previous night and was pleased to see that Brendan Boswell had been arrested after an anonymous phone call had alerted police who found ten malnourished men being held in modern slavery.

Logging into the dark web via Cyber Ghost VPN to hide his IP address and the Tor Browser, he was keen to check out the updates on a thread he had been following of some people traffickers using boats to the East Anglian coast.

It was a well-known fact that many illegal immigrants tried to cross the English Channel to the Kent coast, these often being refugees from places like Afghanistan and Syria who have paid traffickers to bring them to the UK. The other way many of these unfortunate people try to reach our shores is in container lorries or trucks.

Tom was less concerned about those who had paid, sometimes with their life savings, to travel here to try and gain a better life – who could blame anyone for trying to get away from the horrors of countries like Syria?

His concern was for those who are brought here with the sole intention of being held in modern slavery. Their passports are taken away and they're told they need to pay off the debt before they can leave. Violence and threats are common. They are trapped here with no possessions, no means to return and are totally reliant on their traffickers. Many are drugged and forced to be sex workers, both male and female, some still in their early teens, others used in construction, manufacturing, nail bars and car washes.

Reading down the thread, he could see that a 'shipment' was arriving early the following morning at 02.00 hours at 'the place to catch crabs'. A quick on-line search of the Suffolk coast confirmed that it must mean the strangely named village of Walberswick on the south bank of the mouth of the river Blyth, about 11 miles south of Lowestoft and 28 miles north of Ipswich. It is the home of the British Open Crabbing Championship and it would seem that many families visit throughout the year to enjoy catching thousands of small crabs, all of which are safely returned to the water to be re-caught time and time again.

Checking the 140-mile journey on Google Maps, he then used Street View to get an idea of the area. He decided to leave early afternoon to give himself plenty of time to recce the area. He went into his garage where he had a workshop set up and to prepare some equipment he might need for the night's work.

Tom's journey took him across country on the A14, past the everlasting roadworks around Cambridge and into Suffolk. He then passed through the small village of Dennington, which was slowly becoming infamous as the home of music star, Ed Sheeran. The road continued to wind for a few more miles before finally joining the slow running A12. Driving past a large pig farm, he turned right and made his way into Walberswick. The narrow road led through the village with a sharp left turn, passing a pub on the right and the village green on the left, before leading down to the river's edge. There were open car parks on both sides of the road while to the left, a couple of traditional fisherman's wooden cottages and to the right, a small group of buildings standing a foot off the ground on blocks, some looking like holiday lets and one, a larger brick conversion.

Getting out the Audi, he strolled past families walking with buckets and nets, fresh from their crabbing, to the slipway into the river and a small jetty where he assumed the ferry crossed to Southwold, well known as the home of the Adnams brewery.

He walked along the edge of the river inland where moorings for single boats stretched for almost 100 yards and saw another half-dozen wooden huts. Heading back past the slipway, past the holiday lets and then over a small bridge that crossed an inlet and then onto the marshland and dunes, it finally led to the beach. He tried to assess where he thought the boat would dock and, just as important, where the pick-up vehicle would park. He came up with four scenarios. It was getting dark but he had plenty of time before the boats arrival time to put his plans together.

By midnight he was ready. He had left his car parked by the Bell Inn, having changed out of his day clothes into a black, Italian-made Gravity Zero neoprene wetsuit with hood and neoprene boots. Carrying his backpack that contained all he needed for the night, he silently made his way to the right-hand side of the slipway. By sliding under one of the empty buildings that was raised on blocks, it gave him a good view of the road in, along with the slipway and moorings. The time on his Garmin Tactix Delta watch showed 12.05 am as he settled down for the wait.

It was just before 1.30 am when he first heard the sound of a large vehicle approaching. Shielding his eyes from the full beamed headlights, he waited until the black, long-wheelbase Mercedes-Benz Sprinter van had pulled up by the slipway. Putting on his night-vision goggles, he could see two men sat in the cab. One of them lit a cigarette and wound down the window to let the smoke out; he looked to be Eastern European or from one of the Balkan countries, which tied in with the info Tom had managed to retrieve from the dark web, of this being an Albanian gang.

Tom lay very still, watching the man finish his smoke, wind the window up and rest his head against it, taking time for a nap before the boat arrived. Reaching into his backpack, he removed his Fairbairn-Sykes knife, which he placed in the strap on his wetsuit, along with a small package. Crawling backwards to slip out of the rear of his hiding place, he circled around behind the other buildings to approach the van from the back. He kept crawling slowly and ensuring he was keeping out of the sight line of the wing mirrors. Inch by inch he continued to move incredibly slowly on the ground until he was under the back doors. He was just about to attach the package to the underside of the vehicle when the passenger door swiftly opened and someone stepped out. He slid stealthily further under the vehicle, watching the footsteps walk towards the back and stopping by the rear wheels. Tom heard the man unzip his jeans before relieving himself against the wheel. The stream of steaming, hot urine splashed against the wheel and ran under the van towards Tom. *Great*, he thought, although pleased he was wearing a wetsuit. The man finished, coughed, spat on the floor and climbed back in. Tom slid backwards, attaching the package to the inside of the rear wheel arch, slowly slipping away and back to his hiding place under the building.

It was just before 2 am that Tom noticed the driver of the van answer his phone because it lit up the cab. He guessed the boat was due to arrive shortly. The van started up and turned, reversing towards the reinforced river wall.

He took a couple more packages out of his backpack before crawling out again. He made his way to the river's edge, slipped into the inlet and waited for the boat to dock.

CHAPTER 7

Aart De Vries had been a fisherman all his adult life.

He slowly guided the 40-foot trawler with two of the Dutch gang on board, to a stop at the riverbank, just before the slipway.

As this was happening, the two men were out of the van, one opening the back doors and the other catching a rope from the boat to moor it. There was hushed but urgent shouting as bodies emerged from below the deck. They were swiftly being offloaded and shoved violently towards the back of the van. One young man tried to make a run for it but was chased by the van driver; he was caught in just a few paces, knocked to the ground and kicked a half-dozen times to his body and head. Then the man was dragged back and thrown into the back of the van.

Tom watched the boat glide past the inlet and quietly swam out and along the river bank until he was under the stern of the hull. Taking the cover off the package he was holding, he turned a dial to set a timer, took a deep breath, dived under the boat and attached the package to the bottom of the hull next to the fuel tank.

By the time he had swum back to the inlet, the van's back doors were closing, the mooring untied and the boat began to pull away from the bank and stopped when it was in the middle of the river. Reversing a single inboard engine boat is a very tricky job but with a lifetime of sailing, Aart had no problem reversing the boat, in what would have been a perfect three-point turn, before setting out again into the North Sea for his journey back to Holland.

Tom was out of the water as soon as the boat had moved off. Keeping low, he saw the van drive away and ran back to his car. He wasted no time in getting out of the wetsuit and back into his day clothes. Checking his watch, he drove without lights onto the car park by the river – he was watching the clock count down, while at the same time turning on the master unit for the tracker he had placed on the van to see that it was making its way back up towards the A12. He would be able to follow its route with no problems. He wanted to track it back to its base and hoped it would lead, in time, to those behind this evil trade.

In ten minutes the timer had almost counted down to zero. Tom climbed out of the car and stood with his binoculars focused on the boat, now a few miles out to sea. His watch gave a loud bleep and a second later he watched the boat rise in the air on what looked like a waterspout, before a huge explosion lit the night sky. Wreckage and debris flew through the air. As the boat disintegrated into small pieces, he doubted anyone on board would ever smuggle a human slave again.

He returned to his car, setting off at a flying pace. With the night-time roads empty he was soon speeding down the A12, checking the van's route and was really surprised to see they had turned off the main road at a place called Friday Street, then onto a B road. Pressing his foot down even harder and, at times, touching a ton, he was soon on the B road and gaining fast. He could see the van's speed had slowed considerably as was now almost right behind it. Slowing to a stop, he noticed it had turned into a business park and industrial area, built near the old American air base at RAF Rendlesham, famous for what some believe was a UFO sighting in 1980. But he had no time for such thoughts as he could see the van had stopped. He pulled off the road between some trees and grabbing his camera, he quickly made his way through to the perimeter fence where he could see the van outside a large warehouse with the name International Trans Logistics emblazoned on it.

Dan snapped away and counted eighteen civilians being dragged from the van and pushed into the warehouse. There were more women than men and two children. He waited for about half an hour, but no one appeared outside, so he rapidly returned to his car to fetch a battery-powered Wi-Fi video camera, similar to those used by bird watchers but the special ops version. Attaching the camouflaged case to the trunk of a tree, being perfectly hidden, he returned to his car, pulling over further off the road into the trees so it was completely concealed. Opening the app on his iPhone, he could see the van and the building clearly – the motion sensor would bleep an alarm if any movement were detected. He then set the alarm on his watch for two hours ahead, closed his eyes and was asleep in less than a minute.

CHAPTER 8

Tom woke after just an hour's sleep when the alarm signalled a movement at the warehouse. Two men had come out to the van and were stood next to it as a container lorry pulled up. Tom knew the SD card in the camera would be recording this, but he still crept through the trees to watch first-hand. As the lorry stopped, the two men opened the back of the container and the driver walked around to the back. They then opened the warehouse door and started to bring people out, forcing them up and into the back of the container. Tom counted again; this time there were over thirty people, a mixture of male and female, mostly under thirty and a few in their early teens. In less than five minutes the doors of the container were shut. Tom quickly made his way back to the car and grabbed another tracker from the boot. Running out to the roadside, he waited until he saw the lorry approaching. Stepping out slowly into the road, pretending to be talking on his phone, oblivious to the lorry, he faked a trip and fell down, causing the lorry to screech to a stop. Tom scrambled to his feet, waving to the lorry driver to continue. As it began to pull away, he walked behind it and attached the tracker on the inside of its back bumper.

Next, he waited until it was out of sight, before returning to his car. Checking the camera's app as he walked, he saw the two men locking the warehouse door and approaching the van.

During this time, Tom sat in the car and continued to watch the tracker following the movements of the two vehicles as they made their way onto the A12, heading south.

Taking his backpack, he walked back to the fence to collect his Wi-Fi camera and then, taking out a pair of bolt cutters, he cut away a section of the wire chain-link fence. Squeezing through, he made his way to the warehouse. Unsure if anyone were in there, he knocked loudly on the door first and received no answer. He had noticed an alarm box on the outside wall and would have to try and disable it quickly if it was set. It took him less than a minute to pick the lock on the front door. Once he was opening it slowly, he was relieved that he didn't hear an alarm ticking.

Finding the light switch, he walked past an office into the main warehouse that was stacked with crates of Albanian shoes and clothes and he took various pictures. As he made his way to the back of the warehouse, he travelled through another door and was hit by a putrid smell. There, he found two steel cages littered with empty plastic water bottles, some dirty old blankets and buckets that had been used as toilets. There was also a large pool of dried blood. He made his way back to the office and carefully looked through all the papers and files to take more photos. He had seen enough by now and wished to get back to monitor where the van and lorry were now headed.

The lorry had turned on to the A14 at Ipswich and was heading west, while the van was continuing south on the A12. He decided he would follow the lorry, but first, he opened his MacBook Pro, downloaded pictures from his camera, took the SD card from the video camera and downloaded the footage of the prisoners being pushed into the container. Having put all of that onto one zipped file, he transferred it to a new burner phone and sent it, along with the van's registration number, as an attachment to an e-mail to the UK Border Force and Suffolk Police HQ, thinking that it should stir some interest, both here and in Albania.

He was soon onto and then off the A12 and onto the A14, speeding past Bury St Edmunds, Newmarket, and crawling past Cambridge. He saw that the lorry was now heading up the A1 and he wanted to get closer to it. Knowing the lorry could only do 60 mph, he put his foot down, often topping 90 mph and was close to 100 mph as he joined the A1 on the three-lane stretch up to Peterborough. By the time he passed the former Harrier Jump Jet base at RAF Wittering, he was only a couple of miles behind and had the lorry in sight as he passed the closed down Ram Jam Inn. Keeping his distance, with a few vehicles in-between, he followed as the lorry turned off at the Colsterworth junction. Dropping back more, he let them get further down the road. Watching the tracker, he saw them turn right onto a farm track, which took them into some woods.

Stopping quickly in a lay-by, he grabbed his jacket and backpack and, jumping over a ditch and climbing through a hedge, he set off through a field to the edge of the woods. Walking through the trees and bushes as quietly as he could, he was soon on the edge of the trees looking out on to a flat, concreted area with three large barns. One was open on all sides storing hay, one had side walls containing farm vehicles and the nearest one was a fully enclosed barn with large, double doors and a small, single door entrance. They were all only about a hundred metres away from him.

There was a fuel tank set high on a brick plinth next to the barn housing the farm vehicles and alongside the side wall was an area used to wash the vehicles down.

Four men were lining the prisoners up against the wall and they were shouting, some with foreign accents and some sounded English. They pushed and shoved the poor souls into line and then told them to strip off. Some didn't understand and those that did didn't want to do it and so they were hit. A few men began pulling their clothes off. When two of the men pulled out guns, one holding his against a young one's head, they all did as they were told. Most tried to cover their nakedness until a high-powered hose, normally used to clean trucks, was turned on. The power knocked some to the floor and the man who appeared to be in charge told them to turn the power down. They sprayed all of them making them lift their arms in the air before turning to face the wall, opening the cheeks of their backsides. The hose was turned off, they were told to pick up their clothes and were herded, still naked, into the nearest barn.

Tom had filmed much of this on his phone and stayed to watch for a short while as he wanted to learn more about the farm before doing anything else. Then he returned to his car.

He drove back, crossing the A1 and into the truckers' service area. Once he'd checked the tracker for the Sprinter van, he saw that it had stopped on a council estate in Basildon, Essex. Making a note of the address, he then realised he hadn't eaten for almost twenty-four hours, so he went into the cafe and enjoyed a truckers' special – a full English breakfast with a couple of large mugs of strong coffee. Checking the details of the farm on his phone while he was eating, he soon made his mind up what to do next. Driving back to the same lay-by, he made his way to the same spot, taking with him the Wi-Fi camera that he had linked up with another burner phone and fixed them to a tree facing the barns. He would get at least five or six hours' worth out of the batteries, which was more than enough time for him to do what he needed.

They were easily fixed in place and, in no time, he was back in the car making his way the fifty or so miles back to his house to get what he needed for his plans that night. He took a quick, hot shower to wash away the tiredness from only an hour's sleep and went to his workshop to get everything ready.

CHAPTER 9

Dan spoke with Chief Superintendent Jackson on his way back to the nick, explaining what they had found and passing on what Tish had said. The Chief listened carefully and said, "I'm fully aware of the Albanian problem; they make up ten percent of all foreign prisoners in our jails, even though a deal was set up to send them back to serve their sentences. I think we have been lucky to not have been bothered by them too much here, but with the County Lines' drugs problems everywhere now, I guess we need to expect it. Keep me up-to-date, Dan, and thank the DS for her input."

Once back, Dan logged onto the NPC to look closer into Albanian gangs and prostitution. Scrolling through, he felt the familiar buzz in the pit of his stomach that he hadn't felt in months, in fact, not since the vigilante murders and his dealings with Tom Windsor. He stopped for a while and wondered what Tom would be up to now. He still kept the card with his phone number on him that he had given him at Dan's wedding, telling him to call if he ever needed him.

His thoughts were broken by the old-fashioned alarm clock ring tone on his phone. "DCI Hooper," he answered.

"Hello, sir, its PC Edmunds. Sorry to trouble you, but I heard about the body on the Millfield, and over the past few months I have made a few good contacts there. I was chatting with one just now and he says that he was coming home very late last night and, as he drove in, he saw a guy come out from the stairs carrying something big. He thought perhaps the lights may have startled him, but by the time he had parked the bloke was walking from the bins, but not carrying anything any more and got into a black BMW 5 Series. He described the man as thirty to thirty-five, about 5-feet 10-inches tall and looking tough. He didn't look like he came from around here, he only saw him from a distance though, but thought he may have seen him somewhere before, but couldn't think where. I just thought it might help, sir."

"How trustworthy is he, Jimmy? It *is* the Millfield, after all."

"I think he's OK, Guv; he's a DJ, so he works late at night. A few months ago he left some of his vinyl in his car and they got nicked, but I got them back for him the next day, so he feels like he owes me one."

"That's brilliant, Jimmy. Well done, yet again. Could you write it up and get it to Brenda? She can enter it into HOLMES."

"Will do, sir. Pleased to have helped."

He had only just put the phone down when it rang again; this time the caller ID showed as Stan Jones. "Yes, Stan, any news?"

"Yes, Guv. You might want to buy me a deerstalker hat and a briar pipe and just call me Sherlock! Using my devastating chat up charms, I have managed to find out that a young foreign brass was using one of the flats that had been boarded up, to ply her trade. I've checked it out and it looks like it's the killing site – it's a right mess. Julie was still on the scene so I've let her know and she's on her way up now."

"OK, did you say to call you Sherlock or Shirley? It was a bad line," which caused Stan to laugh. Dan continued, "I'll get Tish and we will be straight over."

They were there in less than ten minutes. The area around the bins was still taped off, as was the staircase close to them. Two SOCOs were doing a fingertip search of the stairs and had put markers on some blood droplets. Donning their

Tyvek coveralls, Tish and Dan made their way carefully up to the flat. Lights had been set up on the landing and inside, which made the scene look in even more of a state than it was, if that were possible. Julie met them at the door and said, "Well, we have a job and a half here – it had been a squat, then a crack house and the council boarded it up but didn't really clean it out before and then next it was used as a knocking shop. I hate to think how many different DNA samples we might find, not to mention the cost and time of checking them. There are a half- dozen used condoms, but I doubt a punter did this. There are blood stains on the bed, splatters on the wall and spots of it across the floor, which must be the victims'. But, there is one bit of good news," and with that she led them into the bedroom.

It was dirty, smelt of smoke, body odour and various other unimaginable smells. Paper was peeling from the walls, the ceiling was yellow with nicotine and the floor was covered with filthy, cracked lino. The bed was half turned on its side and the dirty mattress had half slipped off onto the floor.

Tish looked around, commenting, "You would need to be very desperate to come here as a punter, but even more desperate to use this as a hooker. Perhaps she had set up on her own and was trying to keep a low profile."

"I was thinking the same," Dan commented.

Julie picked up an evidence bag and handed it to Dan. "I think it's the murder weapon, Guv, it's a leg off of the bed. There's blood and hair on it; we will check it for prints once we get it back to the lab."

"OK, well done, Jules. Any sign of a purse, phone or ID?"

"Not yet, Guv, the murderer may have taken it all."

Tish was slowly looking around the room and said, "Has anyone looked in the dressing table? Jules?"

"Yes, we've gone over that – why?"

"Can I take a look?"

"Yeah, go for it."

Tish carefully slid each drawer out. One contained a pack of condoms and some make-up, while the others were empty. She turned each one over, looking underneath, tapping the inside, but found nothing. She then tipped them up on end, looking underneath, but still nothing.

"Is it OK to look in the other rooms, Jules?"

"Yeah, just call us if you see anything."

Walking around from room to room, looking everywhere, the CSIs had done a good job, considering the mess the place was in. When Tish finally reached the filthy bathroom she saw the bath was smashed with a hole in the bottom and the toilet was stained and it stunk. One tap on the sink was also broken.

Tish called out, "Has anyone checked the U-bend under the sink?"

A CSI replied, "No, I'll do it now." Unscrewing the yellow, dirty piping that had once been white, some water ran out onto the floor. As he pulled the lower pipe away, something was poking out from the bottom of the top pipe. The CSI photographed it first and then removed it. He lifted it up to show Tish a condom filled with bank notes.

They called Dan and Julie in and Dan inspected it. "Well done, but we don't know if that was the victim's or if it had been left by a previous drug user. We will know more once you check for prints."

After scanning round for another five minutes, Dan decided to get back to the nick; there wasn't much they could do at the flat and he had to set up the first briefing for the next morning.

CHAPTER 10

Tom was back in the car within a couple of hours; he had been keeping watch on the app linked to the camera and there had been nothing to see apart from the men, coming outside at times, to speak on their phones. The journey back to the farm took him just over an hour. He didn't want his car to be seen on the main road, so he drove past the driveway this time, taking the next turning right up a narrow country lane where he pulled off the road, hiding the car in a small coppice. He loaded up with all he needed, carrying his trusty backpack. There was a tree-lined ditch not far from the coppice that took off in the right direction. After a few hundred yards he had to turn right keeping low behind a thorn hedge, before getting back to the woods, where his camera was still recording.

He set about making a better hide for himself as he planned to be there for a while. Going back into the woods, he cut down a few branches and carefully dragged them into place to give him good coverage. Extracting his flask and a Ration-X 24 hour ration kit from the kit bag, he tipped the contents of a pack of cooked and dried Bolognese into his mess tin, gave it a good stir and ate it quickly and heartily. Stuffing a couple of energy bars into his pocket, he settled down to wait for the time to be right. At dusk, he began to clear things up and packed away the Wi-Fi camera.

He waited until it had been dark for half an hour before pulling on a balaclava, black tactical gloves and night-vision goggles. He was soon ready, slowly slipped out of his hiding place and started creeping stealthily around the concrete area to get to the furthest barn that was storing the dry hay. Once there, he pushed a small package into the centre of the hay, before crossing the gap to the barn containing the farm vehicles. Here he placed a package under a new Massey Ferguson tractor and then, reaching the fuel tank, he was about to attach one to it when he saw car lights approaching. Swiftly moving to the rear of the barn and crawling under an old combine harvester, he watched the car, a black Mercedes-Maybach S 650, worth almost two hundred grand, drive in and stop by the first barn.

A tall, well built, dark haired man slowly got out and stretched, easing a crick in his neck. The small barn door opened and the four men he had seen earlier all appeared and all looking very happy to see the newcomer. The first two hugged him, speaking in a language Tom didn't understand but guessed was Albanian. He turned to the other two and shook hands, speaking in English and then they all returned to the barn, closing the door behind them.

Tom quickly placed the package on the fuel tank and put the others on the container lorry and the Mercedes. He was back to his hideout in no time. He laid out five burner phones in a line on the ground, all colour-coded with LX tape.

Placing everything in either his backpack or kit bag, he picked up the first burner and called the police. "You need to get to Cringle Farm, west of Colsterworth, ASAP. There has been gun fire and explosions and you need to get Border Force involved; there are a lot of trafficked prisoners there who need your help." He ended the call, removed the SIM card and broke it in two.

He then pressed the call button on the next colour-coded burner and, instantly, the fuel tank erupted with a loud bang and a fireball of an explosion lit the night sky with flaming fuel shooting everywhere. The five men ran out the barn, three of them drawing guns, looking everywhere to see what was happening. Tom pressed call on the next burner and three things happened at once: the hay barn exploded into flames and the Massey Ferguson disintegrated, splintering into a hundred pieces of razor sharp shrapnel; the two English-speaking men, who he assumed were farmers, were stood right by it and had no chance – one crushed by a huge tractor wheel and the other almost decapitated by a length of flying metal and also, the boss wasted no time running to the Merc and climbing in as the other two dived under the container lorry for cover. But at the same time that Tom had pressed the call button on the next phone, it sent a couple of hundred grand's worth of German engineering up into the air, landing almost in one piece for just for a split second as the fuel tank exploded, blowing the doors off and flipping the car onto its roof, crushing what was left of the driver. A second later, the blast under the container lorry didn't lift it but blew it onto its side, crushing the two hiding under it.

Tom ran quickly towards the first barn with his Glock 19 in his hand, sweeping his eyes across the flames and debris. Still wearing the balaclava, he looked inside the barn and could see that the prisoners were all locked in metal cages. As much as he wanted to, he couldn't release them all, there were just too many and he had to be on his way. "Who speaks English?" he called out. They all looked so scared. "Quickly – someone must; I am here to help you."

"I do," a skinny teenage boy called out.

"OK; you need to know you are safe now. I can't let you out myself, but someone will be here soon to help you."

With that, he turned to run back to his car and drove away slowly, using back roads until he was over ten miles away, before going back onto the main road on the route to home, pleased with a good couple of days' work and hopefully helping some people escape from modern slavery.

CHAPTER 11

It was exactly 8 am as Dan walked into briefing room 2. Brenda had put some pictures of the dead girl and the flat up on the whiteboard. Although so many detectives now preferred to use computers and their Toughpads, Dan felt that having it all up in front of everybody to see gave more chance to brainstorm things. The room was only barely half full, with just two other detectives, a few PCs, PCSOs and Julie Burton.

"Good morning, everyone. This is the first briefing of Operation Silverfern, the murder of an, as yet, unknown female found dumped in a waste refuge bin on the Millfield Estate. I think most of you have been brought up to speed with the basic facts sent to your Toughpads, by Brenda. I have received the pathologist's report and it confirms death by blunt force trauma to the back of the head and he confirmed that the weapon was the leg from the bed found at the flat. There was also some other DNA found under the victim's fingernails but, so far, no match to anything we have. The report confirms excessive drug use, but the tox reports will take another day. It's good to see Head of Crime Scenes Officer, Julie Burton, here. So, what have you got for us?"

Julie walked to the front of the room. "Thank you, sir. Well, we are still working on the flat and because of the state of it and previous uses – we just can't attempt to check the entire DNA that might be sitting there. But we have found ten sets of prints on the lid of the rubbish bin – none show up on our database, but it may help if we find a suspect. All of the bins have been emptied and we are still going through all of the rubbish. Fortunately, it was only halfway through the collection week – a couple of days more would have given us much more to sort, but that's about all for now."

"OK, thanks, Julie. DC Jones, anything from you and the door-to-door?"

"No, Guv, not really, apart from my amazing find of the girl's flat and I would like to quash any of the comments that I knew where it was because I was one of her customers," he added with a grin and a look around the room for a response. "Things have changed a lot on the Millfield since last year and what the vigilante did appears to have quietened the place down and we can get a few answers, but I genuinely think no one saw or heard anything."

"OK, Stan, and it's nice to know you're not wasting your pocket money where you shouldn't. Has anyone else got anything?"

PC Jimmy Edmunds stood up and said, "Yes, sir. The person I mentioned to you who thought he may have seen the suspect and recognised him has come back to me as he remembers where it was. It would appear he goes to the North Essex Country Club on a Thursday night, which is a popular night with females. He has offered to try and get a picture if he sees him, but I wasn't sure what to say about that."

"Well done, again, Jimmy, we can't have him taking that chance, but we need to look into it. Right – Tish will hand out individual jobs; we need to have someone on CCTV and, Stan, if you don't mind, you are our expert on that. Jimmy, could you come to my office? Thanks, everyone, let's get this sorted nice and quickly."

Dan had just sat down at his desk when Jimmy Edmunds knocked on his door and said, "Come in, Jimmy, sit down.

First of all, I wanted to say well done yet again; you are doing really well and it's good to see. As you perhaps know, we are very short staffed at the moment, what with cutbacks and DS Laine being on holiday, I could really do with an extra pair of hands, so if I OK it with the Chief, how would you like to be seconded to CID for a short while? I know you haven't served the normal two years yet, but if it works well for you and I think it will, as there's no reason why when your two years has been served, you can't come straight in. I would certainly back you for that."

Jimmy's face was beaming. "Thank you, sir, I don't know what to say. Yes, of course, I would jump at a chance like that and thank you for having faith in me."

"OK, I will go and see the Chief now and sort it. Stay here at the nick for a while and I'll get back to you."

There was no problem getting the chief's approval and Dan went back to Jimmy and told him to go and change into his day clothes.

He called Tish over and asked her to find out what she could about the country club and in five minutes was back with a Toughpad full of notes.

Sitting across from Dan, she smiled as she said, "Well, it's a bit poncey if you ask me; it's not far off the M11, they have a golf course and a spa, it's a busy wedding venue and Thursday night is called Flirty Thirty night, but looking at pictures on Facebook it attracts the Essex 'B' listers – more the Harlow crowd than Brentwood's *The Only Way Is Essex* lot, but you can bet lots of fake tits, trout lips and Botox. I've saved the interesting part until last… over the past six months a couple of girls have gone missing who were regulars at these Thursday nights, both reported to Missing People, which is the old National Missing Persons Helpline, but both had gone missing in the past, so it wasn't taken any further. It just makes you wonder if this guy is a pimp and is hanging around there; could that be a link?"

"Really, yes, it makes you wonder. Could you get on to the local nick there and see if you can find anything else about the place?"

"OK, I think the best idea is if I go there on Thursday, perhaps Jules can come as well and we can have a good look around, listen for accents, see if anyone stands out – what do you think?"

"You still need to check the place with the local nick first, but ask Julie and see what she says, I wouldn't want you to be there without backup just in case, but I can be outside. It might be the breakthrough we're looking for."

Trish spoke to the Harlow nick, to see what info she could glean on the place and, apart from a few drunks from time to time and some minor drug dealing, it all seemed above-board – the two missing girls were just thought to have run away from their council house homes in the town.

By late afternoon it was all sorted for Thursday, there was no point in getting there too early. Tish and Julie would arrive about 10 pm, but Dan and Jimmy Edmunds would be there from 9 pm and keep their eyes open for a black BMW 5 Series.

CHAPTER 12

Courtenay Avenue, Highgate, London, N6, in the London Borough of Harrow, is the second most expensive street in London after Kensington Palace Gardens, set between Highgate Golf Club on one side, Hampstead Golf Club the other, with the infamous Hampstead Heath to the south. The average house is priced at twenty million English pounds, although it's very unlikely many of the owners paid for their purchase in sterling; it would be far more likely to have been American dollars, United Arab Emirates dirham or, like the owner of one such house, Albanian lek although, with an exchange rate of 137 lek to £1, you wouldn't want to be paying for it in cash.

Possibly not as famous as the so-called Millionaires' Row of The Bishops Avenue, which is just a block away, with very similar houses; the big difference is that Courtenay Avenue is a private, dead end road, with guarded security barriers at the entrance and expertly protected with the latest security cameras.

This was the London home of Agron Sefiri, born over seventy years ago in Tirana, Albania, shortly after the country was put under Communist rule although, to look at him, you would think he was ten or fifteen years younger. He had always excelled at sports and still trained in his private gym five days a week. At a little under 6-feet tall, his hair now greyer than the jet-black of his youth but matching his distinguished moustache, he looked every bit the international multimillionaire businessman that he was.

His father had been a smuggler and taught his trade to Agron and his younger brother, Józef. The strict Communist rules meant nothing to them, in fact it only helped them become richer. They smuggled anything from cigarettes to booze and in the 1960s they even smuggled LPs by The Beatles. Agron recognised then that there was a growing market for marijuana, so they bought a remote farm and began to grow it. In a couple of years they owned four such farms and were smuggling it to Greece and Italy, resulting in their exploding wealth. His father had died some years before the Communist regime collapsed in 1990 and, while many chose to migrate to America, Canada, Australia or the UK, Agron stayed, taking over many of the former government businesses, some by force, others by bribes, in the same way many Russian oligarchs had when things first changed there. One of these was his first shipping line.

He was soon one of the richest men in the country with a business empire that included shipping, transport, manufacturing and hotels, but all backed up by smuggling and cannabis growing.

He had travelled to South America, Turkey and Afghanistan dealing with drug cartels and Taliban poppy farmers. With his years of smuggling experience and his shipping and transport companies, he became the main route for cocaine and heroin into Europe and, in return, shipping marijuana back to the Americas.

By this time many Albanians, claiming to be Kosovars, moved into the UK. He had spent some time setting up a base there but realised that London was one of the easiest cities in the world to launder huge amounts of money – why else would so many Russian oligarchs live there? And as the huge drugs market was ripe for the taking, he knew the time had come to make London his new home.

By upscaling the same chain of command he used elsewhere, in no time at all his Albanian mafia family or Fis controlled most of the drug, prostitution and people smuggling in the country.

Although much of the running of the different parts of his criminal enterprise was left to unit heads, he was still kept informed of any problems and dealt with them ruthlessly.

He was speaking on his EncroChat phone, which was well worth the three thousand pounds a year to be able to have secret, encrypted conversations anywhere in the world and most of his calls needed to be encrypted. It was the third similar call in the last few hours; this one from one of his lieutenants or Krye, who dealt with trafficking and prostitution.

Just answering 'po' or 'ja' for yes and no, he finished the call.

Agron Sefiri had learned many years ago that getting angry and losing one's temper rarely got the best results. Taking a deep breath, he calmly turned to his brother, Józef, who shared the house and was stood by the huge picture window.

"The day gets worse, Vellai Im (my brother); first the old man from Zandvoort's boat blows up, which may have just been an accident and, although we lost him and two men, at least they had delivered the cargo. Second, the police raided the warehouse in Suffolk and the Kutras boys have been arrested in Essex, which again is an annoyance, but I am sure they will get off – the CPS will be too sacred to press charges.

"But now I hear that last night, the farm off the A1 was attacked – buildings blown up – and our cousin Armend, killed, along with the two farmers and two of our soldiers. The merchandise has all been picked up by the police – what is happening?

"Our English traitor, the tradhtar, says there were anonymous phone calls about Suffolk and the farm; he thinks it must be a gang to do that much damage and it would need to be one with a strong background. But, who would be so stupid to do this to us? They all must know what we will do to them. This all feels wrong to me. I want the word out on the street; someone must know who is doing it. I want you to spend money, break bones, but find out! It is our family duty, our heritage, our kanun code and our right to take revenge for Armend. I want the person responsible for this found and brought to me. Now, get it done!"

CHAPTER 13

Tom spent the following morning downloading the images and videos he had taken the previous forty-eight hours and e-mailed them to Border Force via a VPN chain through a whole list of providers which bounce it all around the world, making it impossible to trace back to his IP address.

He continued searching the dark web for the next two days, looking for any more people smuggling leads and Missing People reports, using the hard drives he stole in Baghdad containing backdoor access to police and government files worldwide. There had been no more chatter on the link from Holland when another message appeared on it – 'Street of Stone Midnight'.

Referencing the east coast, he figured it would be a few miles south of their previous rendezvous point in a remote place called Shingle Street, north of Felixstowe, near the HM Prison Hollesley Bay.

After checking Google Maps and Google Earth, he realised there was much less cover than at Walberswick – just farm fields to the back and a long, he guessed, shingle beach at the front. The site also consisted of an old Martello tower, various Second World War gun emplacements, pillboxes and a very small car park at the end of a single file lane, so he realised he would have to park a long way away and yomp across farm fields.

He was soon packed and on the road; it all felt a bit like *déjà vu* taking the same A14 route, only this time he continued on past Ipswich and over the Orwell Bridge. Looking to his right he could see the dock cranes at Felixstowe and Harwich, ports where he knew that both people and drug smuggling was rife. Turning on and off the A12, he was soon on to B roads and, after passing through the village of Bawdsey, the road turned to just a single file track. He had recced a parking site on Google Street View and pulled off onto a tractor's track behind a long hedge between two fields. Carefully driving over the ruts and plough tracks, he parked in a tiny coppice, cutting some branches to give his car good cover. He sat waiting for the evening dusk to give way to night, anticipating in his head what lay ahead.

Dressed as usual for this kind of mission in all-black with night-vision goggles and his trusty backpack containing everything he required, he set off circling farm fields, using the cover of hedgerows and using the TopoActive map setting on his Garmin Tactix Delta watch on which he had pre-set way points. In just under half an hour he was approaching the beach. To the right, he could see the 19th century Martello tower and, in front, a small car park with, again, a pillbox, gun emplacements and a three-storey observation post.

Settling down in a dip of the dunes, surrounded by marram grass and reeds, he checked the time and saw that he had an hour to go before midnight.

At just after 11.30 he saw lights approaching from a far off distance; a van was bumping down the unmade road. It was another Mercedes Sprinter, which finally came to a stop in the car park. The doors opened and two men got out. Walking up onto the sea wall, one was texting on his phone and the other lit a cigarette. After a couple of minutes they both got back in the cab, so Tom set off silently, crawling through the grass and out onto the track to come up behind the van without being seen. Inch by inch he made his way forward until his head and shoulders were under the rear doors. Reaching into his backpack to get a tracker, he had half turned on one side when the back doors flew open and, with a yell, two men jumped down, both holding the latest Uzi Pro submachine-guns, firing shots into the ground near him. At the same time, the other two jumped from the cab and ran around to the back, both armed with Glock 17s.

The driver kicked at Tom's legs. "Come out or we shoot you. Don't fuck about unless you want to die."

He realised that it was a set-up, and he was stupid not to have realised it. There was no boat at midnight, just these thugs sent to get him. If Tom's mind wasn't completely focused before now, he was in total battle mode, weighing up the scenarios and wondering why they hadn't just shot him.

While the two with Uzis scanned the area, looking to see if he had backup, the other two grabbed Tom's legs and went to pull him out, but he held on with one hand to the underside of the van while he reached for his Glock from the backpack. He kicked their hands off once, they yelled, and the Uzis fired again into the ground. He knew that was a stupid tactic and a waste of ammunition. They began to pull again, and he struggled just enough to let him roll onto his front, with his gun underneath him.

"Come on, don't fuck with us. The next bullet goes into your leg. The boss may want you alive, but I don't give a shit if we almost kill you."

With that he kicked him twice in his side before they both returned their Glocks into their belts and grabbed a leg each with both hands. He held on still with one hand but had now made up his mind what he would do. Slowly, he let his grip slip and they began to pull him out. "Got you, you bastard!" and with one final tug he was clear.

They hadn't even let him go before Tom kicked out, turning at the same time and, raising his gun, he fired twice, taking down the two with Uzis who were standing with their backs to him, still scanning the darkness. In the blink of an eye they were both dead. The other two were frantically trying to retrieve their guns from their belts, so Tom rolled to the side, shooting the first one, with a bullet through the centre of his face. He was dead before he even hit the ground.

The second one was quicker and was already lifting his gun to fire, when Tom's first bullet hit him in his chest, but this one wasn't going to die easily and he fired as he fell back. The bullet hit Tom's left arm, stunning him for a second, as he rolled again further away to one side. This gave the injured man a second chance. With blood pouring from his chest he started to sit up, aiming his Glock and trying to focus on Tom. He fired but missed just as Tom fired again, this time hitting him through the top of his head, sending skull and brains flying everywhere.

Tom rolled onto his feet, gun at the ready in case they were still alive – he certainly wasn't going to take any chances and double-tapped the other three to make sure.

Checking the wound on his left arm, he was pleased to see it was a 'through and through', just on the top of his bicep. It was bleeding, but he had felt worse in the past and had time to do what needed to be done. Using his good arm, he searched each of the men, checking their wallets – all four had Albanian names. He took their weapons but left their spare ammunition and dragged them, one by one, into the back of the van. He then grabbed his backpack from under the van, taking out his IFAK (Individual First Aid Kit). After cutting though the arm of his jacket, he tore open a Celox Haemostatic gauze kit, wrapping the dressing on his wound and tied it in place with a bandage. He took three Ibuprofen and climbed into the van.

Driving nearby to where he had parked, he left the van at the side of the road, throwing their wallets just far enough away to be saved from the blast. He then jogged to get his car, driving it back to the road. Taking two timers and explosives from the boot, he placed one by the fuel tank and one in the cab at the front. Setting the timers for twelve minutes each, he climbed in his car and drove away, keeping within the speed limit, just in case he was seen by anyone. He was almost seven miles away by the time the van exploded. The next two hours of the drive were spent by him being furious at himself for falling for the ambush; he knew he needed to be much more careful going forward. One thing was for sure though, there would be no more missions until his arm healed.

CHAPTER 14

By late Thursday afternoon, Dan was frustrated at not getting any further ahead with the girl's murder and hoped the surveillance op tonight would help. At least Tish had some luck in court with Caden Smith, the jewellery thief who pleaded guilty. The duty solicitor, Mr McMichael, claimed extenuating circumstances, that Smith came from a broken home and was now homeless. But when Tish gave evidence, the court took the fact that he had held the knife to the shop assistant's neck and had tried to attack DS Makubuya with it, so gave a four-year custodial sentence.

Tidying his desk and bringing his policy book up-to-date, Dan told Tish to call it a day, to get ready for tonight and he made his way home.

Arriving home just after 4 pm, he was met at the door by Sue, who threw her arms around his neck and planted a big kiss on his lips. "Hello, my lovely, I've missed you today and it's made me feel really horny. Can we have an early night?"

"Missed me? You saw me at lunchtime; I'm starting to think you're sex mad, you gorgeous thing."

"Well, you're right on both counts, I *did* see you at lunchtime and I *am* sex mad for you, so how about it?"

When Dan reminded her what was planned for the night, she answered with a mock sulk. "So, Tish has only been working with you for two days and you're taking her out clubbing tonight, whatever next?"

Dan stuttered that he had explained it all to her two days

ago; she admitted she knew and was only winding him up. They laughed and hugged, but she did make him promise to wake her up, no matter what time he got back.

By 9 pm, Dan was parked in the far corner of the club's car park, with Jimmy sat next to him. He was aware of the CCTV in the car park but wasn't duly worried by it. It was slow to start, but soon taxis and minibuses were dropping parties of girls off, most fitting Tish's description of how they would look, Dan was shocked at just how skimpy the girls' outfits were. How things had changed since his youth!

Tish arrived in Julie's Mini just before 10 pm and glanced over to Dan's Freelander; they were certainly dressed the part and Dan had to admit that Tish was stunning in tight, black hot pants with a ruffled hem, bare midriff and a matching black, bra top with long sleeves. Julie was just as attractive in a short, black blazer dress, embellished with pearls.

They made their way in and up to the bar, both ordering fever-tree tonics, which at least looked like G and Ts while keeping sober. They sat on stools at the far end of the bar, knowing they could see whoever came in and they could also hear accents. By 11.00 they were on their second tonics and, although the place was busy and the music was getting louder, there was no sign of their target. Tish was keeping in touch with Dan on WhatsApp and, apart from two guys trying to chat them up (but being knocked back), there was nothing to report.

Sat in the Freelander, they passed the time with Jimmy asking about Dan's life in the Paras, which fascinated him.

In return, Jimmy told Dan about his great-grandfather who had been a copper in London and was part of the famous Battle of Stepney, the Siege of Sidney Street. Back in January 1911, following an attempted jewellery robbery by a gang of Latvian immigrants, three policemen were murdered. The police had finally tracked the gang to a house in Sidney Street and a firefight broke out. The police had inferior weaponry, so with the risk of more police deaths, the Home Secretary at the time, a thirty-seven year old Winston Churchill, called in the army. It was the first time the police had requested military assistance in London to deal with an armed stand-off. The siege lasted six hours, with the remainder of the gang being killed along with one fireman. Jimmy was proud that his great-granddad had been a station sergeant in Limehouse and was part of this historic event.

Another half-hour had passed, and Dan was starting to wonder if it was a waste of time. There had been two black 5 Series Beamers, but one was driven by a girl and the other was just dropping off. He was just thinking he would give it until at least midnight when the headlights of a car lit up the driveway. They ducked as a black BMW drove into the car park, pulling up about a dozen cars away from them. A man got out and Jimmy said, "He certainly matches the description the DJ gave us; it could be him."

Dan messaged Tish, 'I think we could be on, subject just arrived, black leather bomber jacket, white shirt.' Dan looked up from his phone just as Jimmy said, "Did you see that, Guv?"

"No, what?"

"He just stubbed out a cigarette on the floor; shall I get it?"

"Well spotted. Yes – put gloves on, take an evidence bag and while you're there, get the reg number."

Jimmy was out of the car and back in seconds, handing the bag to Dan. "I took a photo of it before I picked it up and the reg is Alpha, Lima, 7-8, Alpha, India, November."

Dan used his police radio to check the vehicle's details.

Tish turned to Julie and said, "I've clocked him, you stay here, hun," and she wandered up to the bar just far enough away to hear him order raki on the rocks. The accent was strong and the drink was a favourite in Balkan countries.

Purposely not looking at him, Tish took out her phone, pretending to make a call, but as she was opening the camera function and to ensure the flash was off, she turned sideways on and took a few quick pictures. She only managed his profile, but turning back to the bar she ordered two G and Ts this time. Still holding her phone, she lifted it to 'text' but got a good couple of front shots from the reflection in the mirror behind the bar. She put her phone away and took the drinks back to the table.

"I think that's him; defo Eastern European or Balkan. Oh and, by the way, these are G and Ts, I thought it would look sus just getting tonics." She messaged Dan, repeating what she had told Jules but missing out the drinks part.

Dan relayed the information to Jimmy as the car details came back. It was registered to Tirana Shipping, Fort Road, Tilbury, Essex. "Well, that certainly fits in with the Albanian connection and not far from where Tish said their big gangs are in Barking and Dagenham. This is good, but we could do with a picture, really."

"Do you want me to go in, sir?"

"No, Jimmy. No disrespect, but you will stand out – I'll message Tish," which he did, only to get the reply, 'Done it, can we go home?'

Knowing they would have a busy day tomorrow, he agreed.

The girls were finishing their drinks as the suspect left the bar to go to the toilets. Tish was straight up out of her seat, grabbing her bag. "Let's go quickly, babe. Hurry!"

Julie grabbed her stuff as Tish was approaching where he had been standing. Taking a couple of paper drinks coasters off the bar – without stopping – she picked up his glass, tipped the contents on the floor and in the same fluid movement, slipped it in her bag. With Jules now beside her, they linked arms and walked out to the car park.

Dan saw them leaving and started his Freelander. Following them out, Tish called on his hands-free, telling him about the glass and the rest of the evening. Dan told her about the cigarette butt and it was agreed that they would meet back in the office at 8 am the next day.

It was 1.30 before he had finally dropped Jimmy off and got back home. Pulling onto the drive he saw the downstairs' lights were still on and, as he opened the door and walked in, Sue was stood there in front of him in a see-through nightdress.

Walking towards him as seductively as she could with a huge grin on her face, she said, "And who is *this* coming into my house so late at night and catching me dressed like this? I wonder… are you here to take advantage of me, sir? Surely you don't intend to ravage me because that would be so very, very naughty of you," and with that she put her arms around Dan's neck, pushed herself tightly against him and planted a huge kiss on his lips.

They stood kissing in the hallway for a couple of minutes before Dan broke away. "Mrs Susan Hooper, you should be ashamed of yourself, taking advantage of a man who has just finished an 18-hour day and is totally exhausted."

They both laughed, but Dan did refuse the offer of a late-night coffee so he could get Sue into bed. It might have been a long day and he might be tired, but he was a man and couldn't refuse the woman that he loved so much.

Dan was in just before 8.00, but Tish and Jimmy were already there. "Morning, you two. You're bright and early."

Tish replied, "Yeah, I stayed at Jules' last night and she wanted to start on the glass and fag end as early as possible. She will be back here as soon as she knows something."

"OK, great. Jimmy, how are you on computers?"

"Fine, Sir, I've got an A level in computer science."

"Good, could you get on-line and find out anything you can about Tirana Shipping? I don't want to contact them yet as it may tip our hand."

"Tish, could you check on the photos you took to see if we can use any and try the facial recognition on the PNC?"

At that moment, DC Jones arrived. "My, what busy bees we are," and he started to sing, "Oh, what a wonderful thing to be, a healthy, grown-up busy-busy bee."

Tish turned and looked at him in amazement. "What the 'F' was that, Stan?"

Arthur Askey, my dear, many years before your time. He was like the Jimmy Carr of the 1940s and 50s, but without the bad language and with more songs."

They all laughed and Dan asked, "Can you get on to ANPR and get a marker put on a car? Jimmy has the reg number, to try and trace it from the North Essex Country Club from midnight last night. See if you can tell where it ended up."

"Right, Guv. Do I get the number from Jimmy Carr or young Jimmy?"

"Stan, get on with it!"

"Yes, Guv."

CHAPTER 15

Restaurant Emblema held a double-fronted position on Hornsey High Street, serving traditional Albanian food to a high standard. It was one of many businesses in close proximity, owned through a series of shell companies, by Agron Sefiri. Car sales, which were a good way to launder money and export stolen high end vehicles. Takeaway kebab shops, which were perfect outlets for drug distribution and nail bars and massage parlours, just the place for illegal immigrants, especially those forced to become sex workers.

There was much more to most of the premises than met the eye, with basements hidden behind secret doors and hidden panels, which were used for packaging drugs for distribution all around the UK. Also, were tables where bags and sacks of cash would be sorted into denominations and then counted in high-speed note counters, before being wrapped and packaged in boxes and transported to a main storage unit. Much would be recycled back through the drug buying system and the rest laundered or stashed away in illicit bank accounts.

The basement of the Restaurant Emblema was used as the kitchen, but the first floor contained a private bar and three offices, the largest of which was used by Aleksander Ajazi, a third cousin of Sefiri, from the Albanian port city of Durrës, a huge picture of which hung behind his desk. A former commando in the Albanian Army, he had come to London nearly twenty years ago claiming to be a Kosovan refugee, working on the door of clubs and bars before rising through the ranks of fellow countrymen, thanks to his sharp business brain and unflinching use of violence, where necessary. He was now third in line behind Sefiri and his brother.

Sat across from him and slouching in his chair, was thirty-eight-year-old Reni Kotri, looking unhappy after having been ordered here so early in the morning after his late night the previous evening, with Aleksander looking likewise. "What was wrong with you? You are *budalla*, stupid. What were you thinking? You were meant to get the slag, the *kurvë*, that tried to run away and do what we always do – take her to the farm, kill her there, let them cut her up and feed her to the pigs. It's the way we *always* do it; you even did it with the two local bitches you took and raped from that place you go to."

Reni Kotri looked up, sullen faced and angry at being bollocked. "You don't understand, she put up a fight, was off her head and was screaming like a wildcat. I didn't mean to kill her, I just wanted to knock her out, but with all the shit she had taken she kept coming forward – she could have killed *me*. I had to do it and would have taken her to the farm… I carried her downstairs, but as I got to the bottom I saw car lights, so I dumped her in the bins. I don't think anyone saw me, but I planned to go back later to get her, but I overslept. I did drive back there, but it was too late. I saw police cars and drove away. It's no big deal."

Aleksander stood up and walked around the desk. He grabbed him by his shirt and holding his face inches away, he yelled, "No big deal? You cunt – that's what you are, a useless *pidhi*. Our informer has checked on the police computer – someone *did* see you but it's only a very rough description of you and the car, which you need to get rid of – take it somewhere and burn it. No, better still –drive it to Hackney and leave it with the keys in; it will be gone in no time and if it is traced back to us, we can say it's been stolen. But, you better pull yourself together. Stop using the product and don't take any more girls and kill them. You need to lay low once you've sorted the car, so get back to your flat and stay there until I tell you different."

With spit dripping off his face, he finally pulled his hands off his shirt. Taking a step away he screamed, "You can't fucking talk to me like that, you work for my uncle; you think he will let you treat me like that? So, fuck you! One word from me, he would have you killed."

"You really think so? You open your mouth and shit comes out. Can't you see the fact that, as your uncle, if the police *do* trace you it's a direct link to him and he can't have that – *and* it will be you being fed to the pigs in Hertfordshire!"

"OK, OK, I will do what you say, I am sorry, but don't treat me like a fool."

Then don't act like one. Now fuck off and lose the car."

CHAPTER 16

By just after 10 am, Stan had traced the BMW, catching it on the automatic number-plate recognition (ANPR) at the bottom of the M11, before turning onto the A406, the North Circular Road where, again, it pinged cameras all the way around. The final one pinged being near the A11 Cambridge Road junction, but it didn't reach the A105 Green Lanes camera at Palmers Green.

Dan had been keeping an eye on PC Edmunds to see how he was doing on the computer and he was working hard, but he had a tangled web to unravel, so he made a call to William Clark, the station's high tech wizard, who fortunately wasn't busy and had time to come and help Jimmy unravel some of it.

Dan had just sat back at his desk when his phone rang. Answering it just as "Hooper," he heard a man's voice. "Ah yes, is that DCI Hooper?"

"Yes, can I help you?"

"Well, I certainly hope we can help each other, bud. I'm DCI Billy Davies, based at West End Central, but attached to the Specialist Operations Unit at the NCA, National Crime Agency. I've seen you've had a marker put on a Black BMW 5 Series. The point is, old chum, that that's part of an ongoing investigation that *I* am also dealing with, which I think will no doubt outrank yours so, if you don't mind, do us both a favour and just back off, will you?"

Dan instantly felt his hackles rise, pausing for a second

before he replied, "Well, without knowing what your investigation is, old chum, I wouldn't know which one outranks the other. I can tell you that mine is for a murder and I have a very good lead that the driver of that vehicle *is* the murderer, so at the moment I have no intention of backing off, Bud!"

"Alright, alright, don't get fucking arsey with me. You're the guy that got shoved off the Vigilante Case, which my old mate Henry Cornelius had to take over and it fucking killed him, so you don't impress me much – you just need to back off and leave it to the big boys."

"Yes, I *was* on the Vigilante Case and, without speaking bad of the dead, your old mate didn't get anywhere and the state his body was in, he could have died anywhere at any time. I have no idea who you are, but you won't get anywhere with me with that attitude, so if you want us to back off, get your boss to speak to *my* boss. In the meantime, if you have anything else to say, you know where I am. Why not come and say it to my face? Because, to be honest, you don't sound that brave to me."

"Hey, Danny boy, let's start again; I've had a bad day, I'm sorry. Let's try and work together – you tell me what you've got, I'll do the same and let's see where that takes us."

"Thanks for the offer, DCI Davies, but I'll have a chat with my Chief and if he thinks we need to involve you then I'll let you know. Now, if you'll forgive me I have a murderer to catch," and so he quickly put the phone down.

He sat there shaking his head, thinking what a strange conversation that was. He knew that often the Met Police thought themselves above other forces and he understood the reasons why, up to a point, with all the crime they dealt with, but the only other officer who had ever spoken to him like that was the late Superintendent Cornelius.

At that moment his office door opened and DS Makubuya

walked in.

"Are you alright, Guv? I heard you shouting."

"Yes, I'm fine, Tish. I just had some jumped-up idiot from West End Central on the phone telling me to back off the case as he has a more important investigation, but he didn't say what it was."

"West End Central? That's interesting, what's his name?"

"DCI Billy Davies, do you know him?"

"Know him? He's a total wanker, a bigmouth – thinks he's God's gift to women. He touched my arse once; I floored him in front of the entire office and they all laughed. He threatened to do me with disciplinary action until another DCI told him he had seen him grope me and to drop it, else he would grass him up. The man is an arsehole – no one likes him and I never trusted him."

"So, I take it the answer's 'yes' then! Ha-ha, I would have liked to have seen that. I'll go and run it by the Chief in a minute. How's it going?"

"Good… The picture's aren't that great, being side faced and reversed in the mirror, but I think it's this guy," she replied, showing Dan a printout of a passport picture. "He is Reni Kotri, aged thirty-two. I think he is Albanian because he came here claiming to be Kosovan. He hasn't got a record, but I am trying to get more details and will update you as soon as I do."

She was about to leave when Stan came in. "Guv, I think I've found it. ANPR got a hit on it in Mare Street, Hackney. Do you want me to contact the local nick?"

"Give it a minute, Stan, I need to talk to the Chief first, but that's good work."

Tish then commented, "I am surprised he is in Hackney. I know the Albanians are everywhere these days, but I gotta be honest, it *is* a strong black area. Mare Street is less than a mile from Upper Clapton Road and they don't call it Murder

Mile for nothing."

"OK, Tish, thanks. I'll mention that to the Chief."

Dan called him first to ensure his boss had time to see him. These days, with so much red tape and extra paperwork, the Chief Superintendent's work was never ending. "Come in, Dan, how's it going?"

Dan explained about the progress they had made and the phone call he had received.

"Don't worry about that, Dan, I will find out who he is working with and have a word. In the meantime, feel free to get Hackney to follow up on the car sighting; give them a call and inform the duty inspector first of all – it pays to be polite, unless dealing with prats like this one."

Dan thanked him, promising to keep him updated while Chief Superintendent Jackson said he would get back to him once he had spoken to West End Central.

Dan immediately got through to the duty inspector at Hackney, Geoff Howe, who was very helpful. Dan gave him a full description of their suspect and the details of the case, including the fact they thought he was Albanian. Geoff made a very similar comment to Tish about more blacks than Albanians in his patch, but they would do their best to find him. Dan knew all he could do was wait and trust they would do a good job to get the result.

He didn't have to wait long. Within the hour, Inspector Howe was back on the phone. "I have news, but perhaps not the news you wanted. We've got the car, it was parked on the Trelawny Estate, which for the uninitiated should be twinned with Damascus, but the Syrians would more than likely turn it down as the Trelawny is more dangerous. It had two occupants, neither fitting the description you gave by a long way though, both IC-3, both members of a local gang, which shouldn't surprise you as we have more gangs in Hackney than any other London borough. Neither of them have a link to the registered owners for they said they had just bought the car from 'A geezer in a pub car park for five hundred quid' even though the car's worth twenty grand. They've obviously nicked it and we have them in for questioning, but doubt we will get anywhere with them and CPS won't waste time on it. If you ask me, I think the car had been dumped with the keys in it, hoping it would get lost somewhere. As it's a murder case I'll get CSI to go over it and get back to you."

Dan thanked him and went to inform Stan of the news.

"OK, Guv, I'm searching CCTV along from where it was last seen on the North Circular up to the next ANPR where it didn't ping, but it's a very busy area; there are loads to check through."

"OK, Stan, stick with it."

Tish jumped up from the computer and announced, "I think I have something, Guv. I got hold of his bank records and, although there are no mortgage, rent or household bills on it, he has an Amazon Prime account that lists an address of 139 Apple Blossom Close, N13. It's a second floor flat on a small, newish estate, right next to the North Circular and the first left after the A10 Cambridge Road intersection."

"That's great, I'll check with the Chief again; we need to pay it a visit, but will need local support. Stan, could you leave the CCTV for now and help the others with the computer search?"

As soon as the Chief Super saw Dan he smiled. "I was just going to come for you. I have spoken with the Chief at West End Central who confirms that Davies is on secondment, but implied he was pleased to be rid of him. I then spoke to a deputy director at the NCA and they were very tight-lipped, but got back to me and said they could see no reason why we shouldn't follow up on leads from this suspect and, as long as it was all logged onto HOLMES with a link to them, they were happy for us to progress and move forward."

Dan supplied him with the latest news and the address and was given the go-ahead to contact the local police to arrange surveillance and backup, but to make sure the NCA were tagged onto HOLMES.

Dan contacted the Superintendent at Wood Green Police Station and provided him with all the details. He was obviously very busy, as his area had a high crime rate, but he was also very professional. It was agreed that he would arrange for officers, along with armed backup from the Territorial Support Group (TSG), to be available for an early morning raid at 6 am the next day, with Dan meeting up with them at Wood Green nick at 5.30 am, which was only a mile away from the suspect's house.

Dan called Tish into the room and informed her of the plans. "So, how are you for an early morning call?"

"Yeah, great, I'll be good to go. Are we meeting here or do you want to pick me up from Julie's? That's closer for you."

"Julie's it is, then. I can't see it taking more than half an hour but we need to be there for 5.30, so just to be on the safe side, I'll get you at 4.30."

"Great, so that's an early night for us both and no naughties for you tonight! Sue will be disappointed… Don't look so shocked, us girls talk, you know!" and with that she left his office while he sat there grinning and shaking his head.

CHAPTER 17

Dan was up at 4 am, he showered quietly and, giving Sue a gentle kiss on her head without waking her, he drove to Julie's. Tish was out of the door as soon as he pulled up; he wondered how anyone could look so good this time in the morning. Wearing jeans with a bomber jacket over a T-shirt and baseball cap, in all-black she could be modelling for the latest pop video. The good news was that she was carrying two coffee travel mugs and a paper bag.

"Morning, Guv, I guessed you'd skipped breakfast, so strong coffee and a bacon sarnie to set you up for the day and a few more Brownie points for me!"

"Tish, you are a treasure, thanks. Now, let's hit the road."

The early morning roads were empty and in no time at all they were flying down the M11 and onto the North Circular. They arrived at Wood Green Police station, an imposing three-storey brick building next to the modern Wood Green Custody Centre and drove into the back entrance and up into their car park at 5.15. Detective Chief Inspector Callum West greeted them, who took them through to one of the incident rooms. There were already a half-dozen coppers there, including three in full tactical gear from the Tactical Support Team of SCO19, the main specialist firearms command police unit in London. TST are the armed units, which usually partake in pre-planned operations.

As soon as they walked in the door, Tish yelled, "Robbo! I don't believe it, how are you?" and ran up to one of the TST men throwing her arms around his neck and they kissed on the cheeks. He asked her how she was and she explained what she was doing there.

She stopped, turned towards Dan and said, "Sorry, Guv, but me and Robbo were at Hendon together; we go way back but it's been a few years."

"No worries, Tish, and good to meet you all. Thanks for your help on this case."

DCI West walked to the large touchscreen fitted to the wall. Touching the side of the screen, he first brought up the pictures of Kotri and then various views of the block of flats from the front, back and above – all from Google Street View. Showing them where they would park, he explained that one member of the TST would gain entry using the enforcer, or big red key, as it's often called. As soon as the door was open the other two would go in, followed by West and two uniformed officers; Dan and Tish were to follow once the all clear was given. "I hope you don't mind," the DCI said to Dan, "but if either of you get hurt, as you're from out of town, the paperwork is a fucking nightmare."

They all laughed and Tish said, "Oh, thanks, guys. Don't worry about our safety, just paperwork."

Callum West ran over the plan one more time and led them out to the rear car park.

The three TSTs climbed into the BMW 5 Series, the three uniforms into a patrol car, while Dan and Tish joined West in an unmarked Vauxhall.

It was still dark as they pulled up out of view of the house, the armed officers took their Heckler & Koch MP5 submachine-guns and Glock 17 pistols, with Robbo carrying the enforcer and they quickly jogged around to the entrance of the flats. The main entrance had a basic number communal combination lock on it, which lasted about two seconds as Robbo, taking a large screwdriver out from his belt, forced it open. They followed up the stairs in the planned order with Dan and Tish holding back. As they reached the door, Robbo put the enforcer down, carefully felt around the door frame to where the hinges were. Turning to the other two, they all nodded, so he swung it back and hit the door directly on the lock. The frame split but it didn't give, but the second swing did. The first two were straight in, yelling, "Armed police – do not move!" time and time again. Robbo was straight behind them, followed by Callum West, followed by shouts of "Clear!" as they went from room to room.

Dan and Tish had been waiting at the top of the stairs when Callum and the three armed officers walked slowly out, all shaking their heads. The DCI was the first to speak. "No joy, I'm afraid. I think whoever was here has done a runner. Come and take a look."

The flat was nicely furnished with two bedrooms, a lounge kitchen and bathroom. The bed in the main bedroom was still made but the wardrobes were all empty. There were recent takeaway wrappings in the kitchen waste bin, a half-full bottle of Yeni Raki and fresh milk in the fridge. The bathroom still contained dirty towels, and the waste bin was empty, but there was nothing else to report.

Dan looked around at the others, all apart from Tish who was looking at him.

"What can I say? It looks like he was here very recently; in fact, I would guess that yesterday, if you ask me, he was tipped off."

Callum West obviously wasn't happy at that comment. "Hang on there, I hope you aren't looking my way for that. Only those here knew the full details, it must have come from your end."

Dan shook his head. "I can assure you it didn't; the three people who knew are myself, DS Makubuya and Chief Superintendent Jackson, so it's not from this end."

It was Tish's turn to speak. "But it's registered on HOLMES, isn't it? Anyone in the job could see it in there.".

They all agreed. Dan apologised to them all and they all understood. Sadly, it was just part of the job.

At that moment there was a knock on what had been the front door and a female voice called out, "Excuse me, hello?" They turned to see a thirty-something female in a dressing gown and slippers. "Sorry to interrupt; obviously all the noise woke me, but if you're looking for the man from here, I think he left in a hurry about eight last night. It's not that I'm nosey but he was chasing up and down the stairs carrying boxes and clothes and then a suitcase. He looked stressed and was in a real rush."

Dan walked over to her and said, "Hello, sorry that we woke you so early. I am DCI Hooper and you are..?"

"Oh, sorry, yes, I'm Gina Todd. I live over the passageway. I always thought he was a bit dodgy, to be honest. He comes home at all sorts of late hours and with some not very nice-looking men."

Dan continued, "Did you see what car he had?"

"Yes, and I thought that was strange as well, because he has had a BMW for a long time – a black one – but yesterday he turned up in a Mercedes. That was black as well."

You've been very helpful, Gina; we might need to get a statement from you at some time and if we do, I am sure DCI West will contact you."

As she turned to return to her flat, Tish said to the others, "Well, there is no doubt it was our man and if Ms 'It's not that I'm nosey' is right, he only got away by the skin of his teeth. He must have known to be in such a rush."

Shaking Dan's hand, Callum said, "I'll do all we can from this end. When we get back to the nick I'll put in a search with CCTV and ANPR – at least if we can get the car reg we can perhaps track him and if there is anything else I can do, just let me know. If there is a leak somewhere, I want to find it."

"Thanks, Callum, and all of you. It's not the result we wanted and it may have opened a can of worms, but we'll get him."

Together, they all moved down the stairs, walking out onto the street as dawn was breaking. Parked outside was a dark blue Volvo XC60, with a man leaning against it smoking. He began to walk towards them when Tish said, "That's all we fucking need – Billy Davies."

"Ah, it's Miss Karate Kid, the black ninja. So, you must be DCI Hooper and judging by the fact that you have no one in custody, I would say you've not only fucked up your case, but also tipped off a person of interest in my case. I told you to back off and leave it to me, but you just wouldn't listen, would you?"

Dan was a good three inches taller than Davies and he walked right up to him, almost standing on his toes.

"First of all, you ignorant fuck, you will apologise to DS Makubuya immediately. If you don't there are at least eight witnesses who I am sure will be happy to join me in reporting you to Internal Affairs, so apologise now, or perhaps you'd rather she put *you* on your arse like the last time you upset her."

"Oh, it's only a fucking joke, what's the matter with you all? Take a chill pill."

Dan just stood there looking straight in Davies' eyes, waiting.

"OK, OK, I am very sorry, DS Makubuya, it was a stupid comment."

Tish just nodded, but if looks could kill, he would be dead.

Davies climbed into his car and drove away while they stood and watched.

Callum was the first to speak. "What was that all about?" Dan filled him in briefly as they drove back to Wood Green nick.

After a quick chat with Callum West, promising to keep on top of things from that end, they both left and started the drive back. Traffic had picked up and it was now the morning rush hour. "I don't know about you, Guv, but I'm Starvin' Marvin. There's a good café at Walthamstow, just off the Circular and I think I owe you breakfast after you drilled Davies another arsehole."

Well, Tish certainly wasn't wrong; it was the best breakfast Dan had eaten in a long time. Soon, they were back on the M11 and they hadn't stopped talking about the morning and were both sure the suspect had to have been tipped off, but finding out wouldn't be easy.

CHAPTER 18

Józef Sefiri rarely visited the Restaurant Emblema and wouldn't have been there this morning if it hadn't been for his brother Agron on the insistence that he deal with their nephew, Reni.

Aleksander was sat behind the desk as usual, with Józef in a chair, leaving Reni standing. "Well, *Nip*, Nephew, have you any idea the trouble you have caused and how close you were to being arrested for murder?"

"Uncle *Ungji* Józef, I am sorry, but I have already explained to Aleks. It couldn't be helped, I have no idea how they traced me."

"They traced you because, somewhere, you have been stupid. I only have the brief details at the moment, but our contact should have all the details soon. If it weren't for the fact that we pay an informer a lot of money each month, we wouldn't have known they were going to raid the flat this morning. Agron wants you out of circulation; you are too close to the family for your own good."

It was now Aleksander's turn. "As it is, we have had a problem with bringing human cargo into the country; there have been some incidents – cousin Armend has been killed, a boat blown up and there has been the loss of two cargoes – we should know soon who was behind it as I had a team sorting it last night. But we can't afford for you to be arrested as well."

Reni began to shake with fear, tears forming in his eyes, "But *Ungji*, I will hide, I will do whatever you say; please, I beg you, don't kill me." He dropped to his knees, pleading.

Józef stood and reached down to drag him up from the floor. "Stand up, boy, what is wrong with you? We aren't going to kill you, at least, not if you do as you're told. We have another flat for you to use – not as nice as the last one but it is a very safe one. We will take you there and you will not leave until we tell you to. Food will be brought in and you can watch TV, but no contact on the Internet and no phone calls – it needs to be this way. Do as you are told and in a few weeks we can bring you back in, but for now, this is the only way."

He stood up, still visibly shaken. "Thank you, Ungji, thank you. I will do whatever you want."

Aleksander stood up from the desk and instructed him, "Right, give me the car keys. Someone will drive you to the flat and stay there with you today. They can get what food you want, just make sure you do as you've been told."

At that moment, Józef's EncroChat secure phone rang. Picking it up from the desk, he said, "Yes… what, are you sure? Well, at least it's not traceable to us… this is starting to really worry me… OK, I'll see you back at the house later." He then turned to the other two and said, "More bad news – we set up an ambush last night thinking we could get hold of whoever was doing this and to find out who they are working for – I had four good men on it, but the boss has just heard that the van blew up in Suffolk last night with all four inside. They had all been shot first with their wallets left at the side of the road for the police to find. This has to be stopped! Aleks, we need to call a meeting of the executive committee, I want everyone here for a *bajrak* at 6 pm tonight. Close the restaurant and ensure we have men all around the building, on foot and in cars. Reni, don't let me down; Ramush is waiting for you downstairs, he will take you to the new flat and stay with you for a while – now, go."

CHAPTER 19

DCI Callum West had been true to his word and by 9 am that morning, he had the results back from CCTV and ANPR, with the numbers of five black Mercedes in the area of Apple Blossom Close in the given time. Checking the registration details, two were Uber exec drivers, one a retired bank manager, one was the owner of a local clothing factory and one was registered with a marker on it for not paying parking tickets, but when the summons had been sent to the registered keeper in Bath, he said he had traded the car in as part exchange to his local Merc dealer, months ago.

This was the one Callum wanted to find and, in under an hour, it pinged a camera in Green Lanes, less than three miles away from the flat they had raided. He sent out a call to any cars in the area to keep an eye out for it and swiftly received a report back from a patrol car informing that it was spotted parked on double yellows outside an Albanian restaurant on Hornsey High Street. Upon asking the patrol car to do two discreet drive bys, he called Dan, telling him its location and asking what he wanted him to do.

"That's great work, thanks, Callum. If you can get it watched, if it *is* him, we need to get him before he disappears again – next time might not be so easy. I am walking out my office now and will be down there as quickly as I can – keep me updated." Dan finished the call and told Tish where he was going.

"Do you want me to come with you, Guv?"

"No, stay here," he replied, "but keep me informed if anything comes up."

Dan grabbed the keys to one of the faster, unmarked pool cars, an Audi A6, so he could use the blues and twos and, with the lights flashing and siren wailing, he was soon flying down the M11, touching one hundred and twenty mph.

The restaurant was just over a mile away from Callum's nick, but with the London traffic, that still took ten minutes. He found a parking space for his unmarked VW Golf along the road, in the car park of an education academy, which gave him a great view of the front door.

Callum checked in with Dan who, by now, was getting closer to the M25 junction and was wondering how long he would be waiting. Another five minutes later and the front door opened. A large man in a dark suit stepped out first, looking both ways along the High Street, before opening the door for another man to step out. Callum was sure this was their man. They walked quickly, turning left into a dead end side street that led to a Sainsbury's supermarket and large car park.

Callum pulled out rapidly onto the main road and stopped at the curb with the engine ticking over. A minute later, a silver Vauxhall Vivaro van pulled out, turned right and drove past him without a second glance. Callum let a double-decker bus pull past, before doing a U-turn and driving back along the High Street. Calling Dan, he said he would get Control to link them up on their on-board Airway communication system.

The van was about five vehicles in front of him, but moving very slowly in the heavy traffic. He and Dan agreed they needed to stop the van as soon and as safely as possible, so he requested for backup and, if available, an Armed Response Vehicle (ARV).

The van turned left, heading north on Green Lanes,

the A105. Dan was now at the bottom of the M11 heading towards Walthamstow at speed, although he couldn't help thinking that if more drivers looked in their rear-view mirrors and pulled over so he could overtake them faster, it would be even quicker. The support Callum had requested was getting closer, but there were no ARVs at the moment as they were on call at another incident back down Green Lanes at Manor House. All cars were now in touch on the same radio channel and the van was gradually closing in on the junction with the A406, the North Circular.

In the van, Reni Kotri was half-asleep. He was pissed off at being spoken to like that by his uncle, but knew better than to cross him. If it meant taking a week or two off, he could do that; he would get his hands on some gear somehow and just chill for a while. It was when Ramush's phone rang that he opened his eyes and sat up.

Ramush looked worried while he was saying, "Yes, I understand. No, I haven't seen anything, but yes, I'll change route now."

Turning to his passenger, he said, "That was Józef; he's had a tip-off. We are being followed by the police, so keep watching that side mirror and shout if you see anything."

Reni sat up, checking the mirror, as Ramush indicated to turn right onto the North Circular.

"Keep looking behind, I'm going to try and sort this." As the lights changed he was the first to pull away. The three cars behind him all indicated to turn but he floored it, going straight over, cutting up a car next to him and, in his side mirror, he saw the third and final car pull across and follow him straight ahead.

Callum was straight on the radio. "I think we've been sussed, but I don't know how. He appears to be making off, heading north still on Green Lanes, speed: five zero – fifty miles per hour."

A marked Ford Focus Incident Response Vehicle (IRV) joined the chase behind Callum's Golf, when Dan came on the radio and said, "I am getting close to the A10; what do you want me to do?"

Callum swiftly replied, "Hold fire there, I think; let's see where he goes. OK, he is going right, right, right, onto Oakthorpe Road. Traffic is light and road dry, speed six zero – sixty miles per hour. Can the car behind me pass and stick on the blues and twos, just in case he might stop."

The marked car passed Callum, who took over the commentary, but it made no difference – the van continued at high-speed, forcing oncoming cars to move out of the way, the police siren wail cutting through the air. The driver of the marked car said, "This road comes out back onto the North Circular; could we get a car to the Cambridge roundabout?"

"I'm almost there now; let me know what you want me to do," Dan replied.

Another car's driver already on the North Circular called in saying it would try to cut him off at the junction.

The van was bouncing everywhere as it turned left onto the three-lane carriageway, forcing through slowing traffic, narrowly missing a motorcyclist and a bus, but just in front of the approaching police car. Callum and the other marked car were twenty metres behind.

As Callum pulled out, the van sped up in the centre lane with the other three cars following behind. Callum kept up the commentary throughout, keeping all drivers informed.

At the last minute, the van swerved left in front of a bus to take the slip road up to a roundabout that led to the A10.

Still forcing its way through, braking off cars' wing mirrors and almost bulldozering cars out the way, it had no intention of stopping for the red lights at the roundabout either.

Dan had been parked on the roundabout, giving him the perfect view back down the road to see cars carrying on the North Circular into the underpass, or taking the slip road off. He had seen what the van was doing and waited until it was at the top of the slip road before shooting forward as the van jumped the lights. The Audi was broadside on, the van smashing into it and coming to a stop.

Reni Kotri jumped from the passenger door with a gun in his hand, half-sliding over the bonnet of a Mini on the inside lane in the process. He grabbed a motorcyclist next to the kerb, yelling, "Give me the fucking bike!" but the guy didn't move, so he shot him in the face, pushing him off the bike and climbing on.

Dan was already out of his car and running towards him. As he started the bike, Dan was almost there. Making a dive for him, Kotri fired at point-blank range, but Dan's momentum carried him half onto the back of the revving bike, grabbing him with one hand.

What happened next took place in the blink of an eye, but for those there it was like watching it unfold in slow motion.

As they struggled, the out of control bike shot forward in front of Dan's Audi along with a large container lorry which had stopped with a line of vehicles behind it, having all witnessed the crash. The bike careered straight into the path of a speeding delivery van in the next lane, which was oblivious to what had happened just the other side of the line of traffic.

The impact was horrendous. Dan's head smashed into the front of the van, the impact spinning him off sideways across the road, back towards the Audi.

Reni Kotri took the full force of the collision, throwing him off the bike and straight down onto the road with the van running him over and crushing him.

For a second, it was like the world had stopped; there was still the noise of heavy traffic on one of London's busiest intersections, but for one solitary moment the world was silent.

And then all hell broke loose. Callum was the first out of his car shouting orders to the other police; one was already calling for an ambulance and more backup, shouting, "Officer down! Officer down!" The others were told to arrest the driver and check on the motorbike rider and the body under the van. He ran straight to Dan who was lying in a tangled mess next to the Audi, not moving – Callum wasn't even sure he was still breathing.

He saw the pistol lying in the middle of the road and shouted an instruction to one of the PCs to bag it and seal it.

A woman came running up from the slip road and said, "I'm a trauma nurse, let me help; what's his name?" Reaching down to feel for a pulse in his neck and checking a large gash on his forehead, she then saw blood on the ground under his body.

"It's Dan, Dan Hooper – Chief Inspector Dan Hooper."

"His pulse is very weak and he's been shot. Hello Dan, I am Jilly; can you hear me?"

There was no response.

"I can't see the bullet wound and I'm worried he may have broken his neck or have spinal damage, so I would rather not chance moving him until the medics get here." They could hear a siren getting louder so they hoped it wouldn't be long. Jilly approached the motorbike rider, but after a couple of seconds she walked away, shaking her head. "I am afraid that's a fatal."

Within ten minutes there were ambulances, fire engines and many more police cars. Dan was still unconscious, but the medics had been able to secure his neck in a brace and get him onto a spinal board. The bullet wound was on his right-hand side, just below his ribs. They knew they had to get him to hospital as quickly as possible and, with the gridlock the incident had caused, trying to get him there by road was not the answer, so the air ambulance was called.

The fire brigade had used high-powered jacks to lift the delivery van enough to reach the body and police had put screens all around shielding it. They had done the same with the other body and were waiting for the pathologist to arrive before they could do anything further.

Police had slowly moved the traffic back around the roundabout, sending them onto the North Circular westbound and freed the A10 southbound traffic before closing the road.

The bright red helicopter landed with precision, right on the junction. The on board doctors examined him before agreeing to transport him. Once he was safely loaded, they took off for the ten-mile journey back to their base at the Royal London Hospital on Whitechapel Road in the heart of East London, which took less than four minutes, landing on the roof's helipad. Dan was now attached to various drips and a heart monitor was bleeping very slowly. The second it touched down, members of the trauma team were wheeling him inside on a trolley, but before they had reached the entrance Dan's heart monitor stopped!

CHAPTER 20

Tom arrived home as the ibuprofen had started to wear off and his arm was throbbing; every time he changed gear it had felt like a knife being driven into it. Although the adrenaline had subsided, he was still very much on edge. He stripped and showered, first washing the blood away from the wounds and feeling his bruised ribs where he had been kicked. As the hot water rushed over him, his mind went back over the events of the evening. Even though they had been sent to capture him, he had no doubt that, once they got whatever information they wanted, they wouldn't hesitate to kill him, so he felt no guilt in taking their lives.

Once out of the shower and dried off, he poured himself a very large glass of malt whiskey and downed it in two, before pouring another. He then got his home first aid kit and set about cleaning the wounds once again, before using Steri-Strips to close both wounds.

Once that was done and another glass of the malt finished, he turned in for the night, not knowing if he would sleep or if, after the night's combat, the dreams would return to haunt him again after such a long time.

He woke at 7 am and was surprised he had slept so well; his arm was very sore but at least there was no sign of infection. The bruises on his ribs were now a dark blue and breathing was painful, so there would be no running for a few days. Instead, he decided to take a walk, which would at least get him some fresh air and clear his head. It was a bright morning, the air was fresh and the birds were singing so he took to the footpaths through farm fields. It was a complete change from the previous night that brought him back down to earth, but he focused his mind on the trap that had been set for him and what he should do next.

An hour later he was sat at his desk with a large mug of strong, black coffee from his Sage Barista Express Machine and a doorstep sourdough sandwich consisting of grilled bacon covered in HP sauce – not his normal healthy choice, but a bit of comfort food that he felt he more than deserved after the previous night's adventures.

Turning on his MacBook Pro, he searched first to see if there was any news from the previous night. There was just one mention on the *East Anglian Daily Times*' website of police being called to an incident near Bawdsey after reports of an explosion, but so far, the police hadn't commented. There were a couple of texts about hearing an explosion, but no replies or other comments.

He finished the bacon sarnie and poured another cup of coffee, taking it up to his office to access the dark web. He realised that he needed to delve much deeper into the background of the human traffickers – he already knew it was linked to Albanian gangsters, but wanted to find out more about the hierarchy.

He knew he would need to rest the arm for at least a week, so he mentally prepared himself for some long days and nights trawling on-line through the murky channels of the dark web.

CHAPTER 21

Sue was coming to the end of a busy lunchtime session in the police canteen. Clearing a table, her mind was wandering back to her honeymoon, laying on the white sandy beach in Antigua, sipping a cocktail and laughing with Dan. Hearing footsteps behind her, she turned and saw Chief Superintendent Jackson with Tish. She beamed a huge smile, which instantly froze the second she realised it wasn't reciprocated. Dropping the cleaning cloth on the table, she enquired,

"What's wrong? It's Dan, isn't it? What's happened to him? Tell me, please!"

The Chief answered, "You need to sit down, Sue."

"I don't want to sit down, tell me what's wrong, he's not dead, is he? Oh my God, please don't let him be dead, just tell me!"

They sat at the table, Tish taking Sue's hand as the Chief continued.

"No, Sue, he isn't dead, but he has been involved in an incident and is in hospital in London."

"Incident, what incident? What's happened to him?"

"At the moment it's unclear, we don't know much other than while trying to detain a suspect, who was trying to escape on a motorbike, he was shot and they both collided with a van. The suspect died at the scene. Dan's been airlifted to the Royal London Hospital and we are going to take you there now."

Sue just sat there, mouth open, trying to take it all in. Tears began to run down her cheeks.

Tish moved closer and wrapped her arms around her. "He is in the best place, Sue; it's one of the world's finest trauma hospitals. Trust me, babe, I have had dealings with it before and they can work miracles there. Now, let's get you changed and get down there. Julie is going to meet Andy from school and stay with him, so you have nothing to worry about there. Come on, let's get you sorted," and with that she led Sue behind the counter to the staff changing-room.

They were driven to London in an unmarked BMW 7 Series, with a high-speed advance response driver at the wheel. They were touching nearly one hundred and twenty-five mph on the quieter parts of the M11 before keeping to a steady ninety past traffic, taking the left fork onto the bottom of the North Circular and onto the A13. The Chief Super sat in the front, letting Tish sit in the back to comfort Sue. Traffic was now very heavy and again, cars were frustratingly slow manoeuvring out the way, but they pushed on, taking the left slip road, passing the towering office blocks of Canary Wharf, before being flashed by speed cameras through the Limehouse Link tunnel. In no time they were back on the A13, Commercial Road, before turning right and finishing at the rear of the hospital.

They had called ahead and DCI West was there to greet them and introduce himself. He led them into a private side room.

On the journey down, a calmness had come over Sue as if she realised she had to be strong for herself and Dan. She waited to sit down before asking how he was.

Callum replied, "He's still unconscious; he took a really nasty bang to the head and is having a brain scan as we speak. The good news is the gunshot wound isn't too serious; it's in his right-side between his ribs and hip. They've removed the bullet and treated the wound; thanks to his well-muscled torso there is no major internal damage. He has a private room and as soon as he is back from the scan, we'll take you up."

Turning to the Chief Superintendent, he added, "There is a Post Incident Manager, a PIM, on the scene, and I have given my statement. The IOPC, the Independent Office for Police Conduct are also attending and I will speak with them later. The body of Kotri has been removed and the driver of the van has been arrested, but is saying that he is a self-employed driver and was forced to drive like that at gunpoint. He is in custody at Wood Green and I will interview him when I leave here. Because of the Albanian connection, I have arranged for a guard to be placed outside Dan's room 24/7."

At that moment a doctor came in and introduced himself as Stephen Lloyd, Dan's trauma surgeon. "Mrs Hooper," Sue stood up. "We have just completed an MRI scan on your husband who has suffered a TBI, which stands for traumatic brain injury. It is early to make a full diagnosis, but he has a cerebral microbleed, which is a small chronic brain haemorrhage. We would expect that in cases like this, it is just minor damage to the brain's small vessels. He has cerebral contusions, which are bruising of brain tissue. They are comparable to bruises of other areas of the body and consists of areas of swollen or injured brain mixed with blood leaked from capillaries. You will be pleased to know that I don't think his prognosis is life threatening, but the next forty-eight hours will be critical. I want him to regain consciousness naturally and if he worsens, we may have to put him into an induced coma. He should be back in his room now, so if you're ready, I will take you all up. But prepare yourself, he has been through the wars."

Walking next to Sue, the doctor told her about the hospital. "The new London hospital was opened in 2012, although the fourteenth and fifteenth floors have never been fitted out because the trust has been unable to afford to do so. We are on the site and linked to the old Royal London, which dates back to 1757. We have some of the best clinical results in the country and I am proud to say our trauma unit, which is taking care of your husband, is one of the best in the world."

Sue was hardly listening; all she wanted to do was see Dan and she didn't even notice what floor the lift stopped at, but was merely guided to his room, passing a policeman standing in the corridor.

Dan was unconscious, lying motionless, his face deathly pale with his head bandaged, with a breathing tube in his mouth and a cannula feeding pipes from various drip bags hanging from a stand. Above the bed, monitor screens bleeped away. There was a catheter bag attached to the side of the bed.

Just by seeing him, Sue began to shake and her legs began to give way. Tish reached out with one arm, holding her up while she regained her composure and sat her on the chair next to the bed. Sue's hands were still quivering as she reached out and placed them both on Dan's right hand. Speaking in a whisper, she managed, "Dan, my darling, I'm here now, we will get through this, you know we will. I love you so much."

The others just stood and watched. The doctor, who must witness scenes like this all the time was the only one without a tear in his eye. He turned as a nurse entered the room and said, "Ah, this is the ward sister, Angie Day; she is in charge here and will take care of everything you need. I must get on, but we will be monitoring Dan constantly. Rest assured he is in expert hands here."

With that he left and the ward sister walked further into the group, smiling at everyone and placing her hand comfortingly on Sue's shoulder. "Hello, Sue, I'm Angie. If there is anything you need or want to know, just ask; we are here to do all we can for you and Dan." Another nurse walked in and Angie continued, "This is Ayesha. She is my number one staff nurse and she will take personal care of Dan."

Ayesha said hello and offered to make teas for everyone. Sue just sat staring at Dan, oblivious to all around her, until the cup of tea broke her train of thought. Looking around she said, "Thank you, Chief, and you, Tish; it's such a shock."

Arthur Jackson smiled and said, "It's the least we could do, Sue. You know what respect I have for Dan and the fast car down here was a perk of being a chief superintendent, but I am really sorry I need to get back, but Tish, if it's OK with you I am happy to let you stay as long as needs be. There is a Holiday Inn just down the road; I will book rooms for you both there and we will obviously cover the bill. Anything you need urgently, just get it and claim it on expenses."

Tish smiled and replied, "Thank you, sir, that's great. I'll stay with Sue as long as she needs me; we will both need to get some clothes sent down, unless you'd rather I popped up west to get us both new wardrobes on expenses."

It was the first time Sue had smiled since she heard the news.

"I'll sort that when I get back; we could send Julie down with them and she could bring Andy if you want."

Sue replied, "Can I think on that? I don't know if I want him to see Dan like this."

"Of course, now keep me informed – Tish has my mobile number and keep positive – Dan will pull through this, I promise you." Turning to leave, he said, "DCI West, a word, please."

Callum followed him out into the corridor and the Chief spoke softly, "Keep me updated, Callum, and make sure that Dan is guarded. I know Albanians are vicious bastards."

CHAPTER 22

Agron Sefiri sat at his desk. For a man who believed that getting angry and losing one's temper never got results, he was doing a bad job at it. He was furious, shouting at his brother Józef. "What the fuck is going on? We lose four more men trying to find out who is fucking with our shipping and *still* have no fucking idea who is behind it and now this! Reni, our nephew, the son of our sister, Mirella – dead. I know he was a fool; he should never have killed that whore, but he shouldn't be dead. Mirella is heart-broken, for she is demanding to know who killed him and she will want our family to be avenged, it is the law of *kanun*. We must deal with this the Albanian way – whoever is responsible must die."

Józef agreed and said, "Yes, he must, but we must pick the right time; we don't know what other forces are at play here and I feel something is wrong. Our attempt at *kanun* for Armend failed – we lost four good men, we must take care."

Agron was furious and he yelled at his brother, "Take care? Listen to yourself, are you turning into a coward, a *frikacak*? I will *not* take care – that isn't how we have ever worked. I want whoever is responsible for Reni's death killed and I want it done soon. Get on to the *tradhtar* – our man on the inside – we pay him enough. If he knew Reni was being followed he must know who was doing it. I want to know who it is – this needs to be done now!"

Józef looked directly at his brother, unflinching, and nodded his head. "As you wish, my brother but, first, Ramush is here, he was released on bail. I had him brought here in the back of a delivery van so he can't be traced to us."

Agron nodded, "Bring him in."

Ramush looked frightened, he had never been to the boss' house before. Sure, he had heard the stories of the wealth and opulence, but for a lowly soldier, an *ushtar*, it was a very rare thing. He had met the boss on many occasions and had always got on well with him, but this was different.

He stood in front of the desk, but realising his hands were shaking, he put them behind his back.

Agron just sat and looked at him for a few seconds before speaking.

"So, Ramush, how are you and your family, your lovely wife and three boys back in Blloku, the loveliest part of Tirana; are they all well?"

He nodded, "Yes, *Shefi*, they are well, thank you."

"Good, I am pleased to hear it. Now, tell me what happened today. You were given a simple job, to drive my nephew to a safe house in Waltham Abbey. Did you speed? Did you not see police following you? I need to know the truth of what happened."

Talking swiftly, Ramush replied.

"I never speeded, *Shefi*, and I didn't jump lights; I drove normally. I didn't see any police cars until the end and neither did I see any cars following us. The first I knew was when your brother called me. I was indicating right on to the North Circular, but didn't turn, I carried on… that's when I saw a car pull out from about five cars back and follow me. That's when Reni screamed at me to pull away – he kept yelling to go faster, but I was flat out. He had a gun and at one time I thought he might try and shoot the car behind. Other police cars joined, but I drove as quick as the van would go… I took backstreets and got back onto the North Circular, then I forced my way through traffic and was getting close to a roundabout when a car, from nowhere, skidded across the front of us. I'd never seen this car; it wasn't the one chasing us. I couldn't miss it. Reni was out of the car, he shot a man on a motorbike so he could get on it, then the guy from the car that we crashed into dived at him. I think Reni shot him as well, but he held on and as Reni tried to drive away, they crashed into a van coming around the inside of the roundabout. Reni was thrown under it and was crushed and the other guy was thrown off – I don't know how he wasn't killed. I was arrested but told them I had been forced to drive like that and didn't know who Reni was. The air ambulance landed and they took the guy away. I am so sorry, if there had been anything I could have done to save him, I would have done it."

"Thank you, Ramush, you did what you could and I have something for you." Reaching into his desk, he took out a 9mm Beretta pistol fitted with a silencer and fired two shots into the man's chest.

Looking at him lying there dead on the floor, he turned to his brother and said, "He failed us, Józef, he had to die and I promise there will be more deaths to avenge Reni."

Józef didn't look happy about it and he looked down at the body. "I'll get this taken care of; they can take him to the farm. If the copper was taken by air ambulance he will be in the Royal London at Whitechapel, but they may have him guarded, it won't be easy to get near him."

"It's OK, Józef, I know how to get to him."

CHAPTER 23

Tom had spent the past six hours on the dark web making notes of everything he found, building a picture of some of those behind this evil trade.

He had taken a break to rest his eyes, grab another coffee and take some more painkillers when a news alert he had set up months ago, pinged on his phone.

Clicking onto it he was shocked to see the report of a policeman seriously injured, a bystander shot and killed and the suspect killed after a chase in London the previous day. He went cold when he saw the policeman was Dan Hooper.

From one of his hard drives, he accessed the police HOLMES computer programme and quickly found the details of what had happened. Unfortunately, it didn't show where Dan was or, indeed, how he was.

He did, however, have Dan's mobile number – should he call it? Would it cause more problems than answers though? He didn't know what to do for the best.

He sat drinking his coffee slowly and thinking, weighing up the pros and cons. He guessed a police colleague would be looking after his phone so that might not be the best idea, but if he could find Sue's phone number, then that might be a better option to find out more.

By searching her name and address on the database of all the main mobile suppliers, it didn't take long to access the number.

Using a burner phone for safety reasons, he dialled the

number. It rang four times before a female voice answered, "Hello?"

Tom replied, "Sue, is that you?"

"No, Sue isn't taking calls at the moment. Who is this?"

"It's an old friend of Dan's. Who am I speaking to?"

"I am DS Makubuya, I work with DCI Hooper. Would you please tell me who you are?"

"Of course, I'm sorry, my name is Tom Greensted, but Sue may remember me as Poacher, my service nickname. We met briefly at her wedding. I was in the services with Dan."

"OK, Mr Greensted, I'm sure you can understand. Sue is in a state of shock at the moment and, without going into case details, we need to be very careful who we are talking to and what information we give, but if you give me a second, I'll ask if she will talk to you."

Tom waited for a few seconds before a shaky voice came on the line, "Hello?"

"Hello, Sue, I don't know if you remember me but we met briefly at your wedding. It's Poacher, Dan's old services mate."

Speaking quietly she replied, "Yes, of course I remember you, Dan has spoken of you a few times."

"I just saw a news report and wanted to know how he was."

Sue explained briefly what had happened and what Dan's condition was.

Tom replied, "Well, your husband is a tough man and I know he will get through this. You have my number now and if there is anything, and I do mean, *anything*, I can do to help, be it money, support, private health care – anything at all, please don't hesitate to call me."

"Thank you, that's very kind of you. I just want him to wake up so I know he is alright, it's horrible seeing him lying there in this mess."

"It must be awful for you, Sue, but he is in the best hands. Now, don't forget what I've said and could you pass me back to DI Makubuya?"

Tish took the phone from Sue once she'd said goodbye. "Hi again, what can I do for you?"

"I have just told Sue that if there is anything I can do, if he needs private care, etc, I'll pay for it, anything he needs at all, could you please let me know, DS Makubuya?"

"Please call me Tish and yes, of course I will."

"Thanks. I don't suppose you can tell me anything about the case, can you?"

"Hmm, not really, but you're obviously a friend and the press are bound to get more details soon. It was a murder enquiry, of an Albanian prostitute." And she went on to explain to Tom the brief details.

Tom thanked her and said he would call back in a day or so to check on Dan's condition if he hadn't heard anything.

His attention was then returned to the web to search the names and places that Tish had given him. He wanted as much information on these as possible.

It occurred to him right then that, even though he had only ever spent very few hours in Dan's company from their time in the services and their more recent encounter, he was now perhaps the only friend that Tom had. There was no one else.

CHAPTER 24

For Sue and Tish, the next twelve hours felt more like twelve days. Sue still refused to leave Dan's side for anything more than a toilet break, or doctors' inspections and had barely slept for more than ten minutes at a time in the chair, not even taking her eyes off her husband for a minute, until they shut with tiredness, only to jump open again a few minutes later.

Tish had grabbed a few hours' sleep at the hotel and was pleased when Julie Burton arrived just before 7 am, having left early to miss the traffic and bring changes of clothes, messages from Andy and the nick.

Under different circumstances they may have been happy to have the use of a nice hotel room for an hour or so, but not in this situation and by 7.15 they were back at Sue's side.

They had only been there for five minutes when Dr Lloyd arrived with the ward sister, Angie Day, to examine Dan. The three ladies decided to leave them to it and Sue thought it would do her good to shower and change and was directed to the shower room by one of the nurses. By the time she was out again the doctor was waiting for her. "I hope you feel better after that, Sue, you certainly look it," he said, with a smile. "Well, I have some good news. As I said, it's very early days but we can see from the feedback that his brain is starting to respond, so we will give him another MRI scan shortly and that will show us what improvement there is. Trust me; it's a step in the right direction."

Once the porter came to take Dan, they decided to go and get breakfast in the hospital's café and, although Sue kept saying she wasn't hungry, in the end she did manage an omelette and toast.

After a while, when there was still no news of Dan's return, they took a short walk outside on Whitechapel Road to get some air. They looked across to the busy market and turned right, passing shops selling sarees and Asian food. Tish pointed out The Blind Beggar pub further down on the corner was infamous for the 1966 murder of a crook called George Cornell, by underworld legend, Ronnie Kray, thus claiming to be the most famous pub in the country. At that moment, Sue's phone buzzed with a text that Dan was back in his room and so quickly made their return.

Dr Lloyd was present and speaking to staff nurse, Ayesha. They both turned towards Sue, smiling, and then looked at Dan. Sue looked confused for a second and then realised that the breathing tube had been removed from Dan's mouth.

Ayesha spoke first realizing Sue had noticed "Yes, we have removed the breathing tube from Dan's throat and replaced it with the nasal cannula. He is breathing well and, hopefully, when he comes round, he will be able to speak with you."

The doctor added, "The MRI has shown improvement from yesterday; one can never be certain with head injuries, but I would say your husband is in good physical shape and I would expect his progress to continue."

Sue had tears in her eyes as she listened to the doctor. "So, he isn't going to die, is he, doctor?"

He took a second or two before replying, "I don't believe his injuries are life threatening now, but I have to be honest, one never knows until consciousness is regained what brain damage or memory loss there may be. But I can assure you, slowly but surely, he is on the mend."

With that he left and Sue sat down, took Dan's hand and kissed it gently. Tish and Julie looked at each other and smiled one of those *'wasn't that lovely'* smiles.

Julie had to leave at midday, passing DCI Callum West who stopped for half an hour, checking they had all that they needed.

The hours were starting to drag again; the rhythmic bleeps from the monitors and the regular flashing from the patient monitor above the bed was almost hypnotising. That, mixed with the lack of sleep, but relief that Dan may be on the mend, had left Sue totally drained. They had drunk numerous cups of tea and coffee, but had barely eaten any food brought in at meal times.

By just after 8.00 that evening, Sue decided to go and freshen up in the toilet, leaving Tish to watch over Dan. Sue hadn't even been gone a minute when the door opened and, much to Tish's surprise, in walked DCI Billy Davies.

Tish stood up and demanded, "What on earth are you doing here?"

He gave a strained grin. "Sweetheart, there ain't no need to be like that, I'm here to check on a colleague, darling – after all, we were both looking for the same man, it's just that your boss got there first. Now, do me a favour, luv, and pop off and get me a coffee, will ya? I've not stopped all day and I'm parched."

"Piss off, I ain't your skivvy! Get it yourself."

"Oi, just remember who you're talking to, Detective Sargent, and do as you're fucking told – now, get it!" Tish glared and shoulder barged him out of the way as she left the room.

The instant she had left, Davies scanned the room for cameras and, seeing none, walked to Dan's bedside. He really wasn't happy doing this, but he was in far too deep now with the Albanians to not do what they ordered. Pulling on surgical gloves, he removed the nasal cannula from Dan's face, placed one hand over Dan's mouth and the fingers from his other hand were pinching his nose, cutting off any air flow to Dan's lungs.

At that moment the door opened and Tish walked back in, saying, "I've left my purse– what the fuck are you doing?"

Davies kept pushing down on Dan's face and as Tish grabbed him, he hit her with the back of his elbow, knocking her back towards the door.

"Are you fucking mad? Leave him!" she yelled and went for him again, this time more cautiously. He tried to back-elbow her again, but she was waiting for it… Leaning back, she let his arm fly past her, before grabbing it and turning him away from Dan, applying a Kimura armlock. He was forced to let go of Dan and swung a left hook that hit Tish on her jaw, stunning her and knocking her against the wall. This gave Davies a chance to get his arm free and he lunged at her. With both hands grabbing her throat, he gripped her tight, realising now that he would have to deal with her *and* Dan.

"You stupid bitch, you don't know who you're dealing with," he snarled while he tightened his grip even more. Tish had been dazed and stunned before during many mixed martial arts contests, but that was always when her fighting instinct really kicked in. She brought her knee up viciously into Davies' groin, making him yell and at the same time he loosened his grip on her throat. Reaching up, she grabbed a gloved thumb in each hand, ripped them away and, using all her strength, she kept twisting them until both thumbs snapped. Davies screamed again but Tish wasn't about to stop. Pushing him back a pace she kicked him in his stomach before kicking again, this time to the side of his jaw, knocking him onto the floor. She dived onto him, giving him a rear chokehold and he tried to get up, but she forced him down. Feeling him weaken, she held on until he passed out.

She slowly stood up, opened the door and called for help. Angie Day was at the far end of the corridor and ran towards her as Sue emerged from the toilet and followed quickly behind her. Everyone was shouting and, spotting Davies lying unconscious on the floor, the ward sister knelt down next to him, looking up at Tish in credulity. "What on earth is going on here?"

"He's a policeman – DCI Davies – he came in and ordered me to get him a coffee, but I'd left my purse, so I came back for it and he was leant over Dan, trying to kill him. I tried to stop him, we had a fight and I've choked him out. He will come round in a bit, but where's the PC meant to be guarding here?"

Angie, who was now checking Dan was unscathed and popping his nasal cannula back, answered, "He said he had been told to take a break. He was going to the canteen; I'll send for him."

Sue began to cry, so Tish put her arm around her while calling DCI West on her mobile. She told him what had happened and he said he would get a unit there immediately.

The PC returned after running down the corridor and said, "I am sorry, the DCI told me to take a break. I said I wasn't to leave here but he insisted I go; I really am sorry."

Tish replied, "It's not your fault, he did the same to me. I need him handcuffed now. Could we take him into another room, Angie?"

"Yes, of course, there's an empty one just down the corridor."

As they lifted and dragged him to the other room he began to come round, moaning and said, "What's going on? Why am I handcuffed? Let me go!" and he began to struggle. Tish pushed him down into a chair and said, "Just shut up and stay there, else I will knock you out properly next time."

Hearing heavy boots thumping down the hall, she looked out to see three armed officers of the TST. The first one stopped and laughed. "Tish, *not* you again! We can't keep meeting like this."

"Robbo, how did you get here so quickly?"

"We've just been on a call out in Stepney – the call came through as we were almost outside the front door here. I'd heard about Dan, but I didn't realise you were here. What's happened?"

Tish was explaining about Davis as another unit arrived, but Robbo said his team would stay until DCI West arrived. She then called the Chief Super to bring him up to speed. He was both shocked and angry at the news and said he would get on to the Met immediately to make sure there was proper protection.

No sooner had Callum arrived when another group of police officers appeared in the corridor. Recognising the person in charge, Callum introduced Tish to Chief Superintendent Norman Fox from West End Central, who listened carefully to all that was being said, before leaving with Tish and Callum into the room holding Davies.

As soon as he saw CS Fox, Davies looked up. "Ah, thank God, Guv, this is all a stupid mistake. The silly cow attacked me for no reason, the stupid bitch – she needs sectioning, she's fucking crazy!"

"Not so fast, Davies… In that case, why are you wearing gloves? Why did you send the PC and DS Makubuya away? I reckon you had no reason to be here, but first things first," he said, now facing towards Tish, "has he been searched yet?"

"No, sir," Tish replied.

"Will you do the honours, DS Makubuya?"

Tish went through his pockets, taking out two mobile phones, a wallet with ten fifty-pound notes, along with credit cards in two names.

After inspecting the wallet's contents and then placing each phone against the broken thumb of Davies' right hand to unlock them, CS Fox continued.

"It shouldn't surprise you to know that I have had someone looking into you this week. The call I got from CS Jackson got me thinking and suddenly it all started to fall into place – seeing what's in your wallet confirms some of it. Why would you have bank cards in the name of Edward Davies who I now know was your younger brother who died when he was six-years-old, over twenty years ago? These cards link to the NatWest Bank Bournemouth branch, which we had already traced; it has over two hundred thousand pounds in it and pays the mortgage on a five-bedroomed house in the town, which is also in your late brother's name. The account receives a regular monthly payment from International Trans Logistics, a company that we can trace back to having links with human trafficking from Albania. To add to that, we also found that a passport was issued five years ago, also in your brother's name, to the Bournemouth address. And to top it all off, here is a text message giving you the details of the hospital, followed by 'Just Do It'. I can assure you, had this not have happened today, your days on the force were already numbered. It gives me great pleasure to say something I haven't had the chance to say for some years, 'You're nicked!' and as soon as you are charged, I shall ask for you to be remanded to Belmarsh; they would love a bent copper in there."

The Chief Super thanked Tish and informed Callum that he wanted some armed officers guarding Dan 24/7, before leaving.

Tish and Callum returned to Dan's room to check on Sue who remained holding Dan's hand while Ayesha was busy updating his notes.

Sue looked up from her seat and said, "That was an awful attack – why would anyone want to kill Dan?"

Callum answered, "It is more than likely for revenge – the Albanians are big on that. Obviously, Davies was in their pay, which I guess is how they kept getting tipped off, but I am amazed they ordered him to do that – he will be going away for a long time."

Sue was about to comment but the words stuck in her throat. Dan began to cough, it was as if he had a tickle in his throat and then his eyes opened. Ayesha walked to the side of the bed, putting her hand on Sue's shoulder and said, "This is good; speak to him."

"Dan, can you hear me? It's Sue." His eyes flickered and he turned his head slowly towards her.

In a whisper he spoke just one word, "Who?" and then closed his eyes and went back to sleep.

Sue began to cry again and said, "He doesn't know who I am; why can't he remember me? We only got married a month ago," and she sat down, sobbing.

Ayesha took her hand. "Sue, this is quite normal in cases like this – it can take time for memory to come back and there is no reason why it won't, so try not to worry."

Tish walked over and gave her a hug, saying, "I have to make a phone call, I won't be a minute," and she walked towards the corridor.

CHAPTER 25

Tom was still sat at his desk wading through the dark web, when the burner phone he had used to call Sue, rang. "Hello, Sue?"

"No, it's Tish – DS Makubuya; is that Poacher?"

He confirmed it was and listened intently as she told him of the day's events, asking her to repeat the details of Davies' bank account and where they said the money came from. It was a name he had recalled noticing at the warehouse in Suffolk.

"OK, thanks, Tish, I have been trying to find out what I can about Kotri and who he has links to. I know the logistics company are linked to human trafficking, but I can only get so far in tracing things further up the line before I keep hitting dead ends. Someone has spent a lot of money making sure they are surrounded by extremely sophisticated firewalls and proxy servers, but I won't give up; in fact, after what's happened I promise you I will find out who is responsible."

"Just a minute, Poacher, I am confused – I thought you were just an old friend but now you are sounding like something else."

Using the cover story he used many times in the past, he continued with, "Tish, I need you to trust me on this, I am on your side. Even if I were allowed to tell you which department I work for, which I am most certainly not, you wouldn't have heard of it, be able to find any details of it, or anyone who would admit to its existence. Just believe me when I say I will find who is behind this. I'm happy to keep you up-to-date, but I must ask you to keep my name and presence out of this as far as anyone else is concerned."

Tish didn't know what to say, she was still shocked, but thought about her answer before saying, "You sound like fucking James Bond, this is crazy. But I have only known Dan for a short time and I know he is a good copper and I trust him, so if he trusts you then so do I."

They agreed to keep each other in the loop and Tom finished the call. He sat thinking about it for a while, planning what to do next. If he couldn't get any further in tracing who was behind this, he knew of someone who could and logged into a clandestine forum deep in the dark web.

Sunjay Bhatt was born twenty-two years ago in the Lalbagh slum of North Delhi. Abandoned by his parents when he was just a four-year-old, he survived on the streets, sleeping anywhere he could find safety, eating scraps from bins and avoiding the sexual predators who frequented the area.

His saviour was the Asha charity, which, for over twenty-five years helped people living in the city's slums and encouraged them to realise their full potential. From his very first day at school it was obvious that he wanted to learn and was soon reading long before his friends, some of whom were years older. By the time he was sixteen, with help from the charity, he studied at the University of Delhi and gained a Bachelor of Science honours degree in computer science.

West Delhi had become one of the world's most active areas for HaaS (Hacker as a Service), where unscrupulous companies will hack anything from your wife's phone to your university grades, for a fee. So, upon graduating it was no surprise that Sunjay was employed by one of the smallest but most prolific of these companies, BellTrox, operating from a small room above a shuttered tea stall, in a West

Delhi retail complex.

His talent was soon recognised and he was quickly moved to the upper echelons of the company, spying on high profile public figures and celebrities, international criminal cases, banks and financial institutions, along with senior politicians, government prosecutors, CEOs and journalists. In fact, there was virtually nothing Sunjay couldn't hack.

But he wasn't happy; the company's boss kept demanding more, asking for more risks to be taken and Sunjay felt that the time had come to move on, fearing that the company would soon become exposed. It was time to get out before the shit hit the fan but he was scared his boss would become violent if he knew he was quitting.

Leaving work one Friday evening with just his laptop and hard drives, he took a taxi to the Indira Gandhi International Airport and flew the two hours to Mumbai. From there he built a new life, joining the notorious Dark Basin group, becoming a hacker for hire, known as Mongoose, but seen online as his alias, M0^6005£.

Tom had never used him before but knew how to contact him, by leaving an encrypted message in the forum. He only waited a few minutes before contact was made, asking him to use WhatsApp and providing a phone number. He understood that the reason for this was because all messages sent via WhatsApp have end-to-end encryption, meaning they are unreadable if intercepted by anyone, including law enforcement and WhatsApp themselves.

Tom was beginning to wonder if he should buy shares in a phone company with all the burners he was using. Unwrapping another unused one, he sent his first message.

Tom began by providing Sunjay with a brief outline of what information he required and they messaged back and forth for about fifteen minutes. Sunjay quoted the price of two thousand dollars to be paid in bitcoin or other cryptocurrencies via 'user 2 funds'. Tom then forwarded the rest of the details, including the names of the logistics company and the restaurant, along with Kotri's and Davies' names.

As it was the first time they had dealt with each other, it was agreed Tom would pay half upfront and then the balance after viewing a synopsis of the details found; however, Tom knew that Mongoose had a good reputation and was happy to agree on the price after being told he should hear back within twenty-four hours.

CHAPTER 26

Meanwhile, in Courtenay Avenue, Agron Sefiri was sat behind his desk. Both his brother Józef and Aleksander Ajazi stood watching him and both looking worried.

Sefiri was angry and began, "What a fool Davies is; he not only failed to kill the copper, but he got himself arrested and I don't trust him to keep quiet."

Józef replied, "Surely he would be too scared to inform on us for he knows what would happen to him."

"We can't take that chance as too many things are going wrong as it is. He's being held at West End Central. If we can't get to him there, I want him taken care of as soon as he is remanded. I don't care where it is and make sure that whoever is doing it gets it done for we can't afford any more mistakes. Aleks, I'm leaving that to you – don't let me down."

"I won't, boss," he replied.

Sefiri continued with, "But that still leaves us with two problems; one, we have lost our best link in the police and God knows we spent enough money and time cultivating it; and two, the copper who is responsible for Reni's death is still alive."

Józef replied, "Fortunately, he's not the only copper that we pay, but he is the most senior. We have a sergeant at Scotland Yard who is very helpful, thanks to the pictures we have of him fucking a fourteen-year-old. He says they have armed guards all over the hospital now, it will be hard to get to him."

Sefiri replied, "In that case, we find another way to hurt him – he has to suffer."

"He will, my brother, he will. *Shqiptarët vdesin dhe besen nuk e shkelin.*" (I would rather die than break honour).

CHAPTER 27

Tish had stayed with Sue in Dan's room overnight, even though there was an armed guard outside and two more further down the corridor; she knew that Sue was not only terrified, but totally exhausted and she wanted to be there for her. Neither of them did much more than doze in their chairs all night and by six am as ward sister Angie arrived with some breakfast for them, they were both already awake but very tired. Sue could only face some toast and jam, but Tish managed a couple of bacon rolls.

They had just finished eating when a familiar face rushed into the room.

Sue smiled before standing up to hug him.

"Bronco, you're meant to be on holiday, what are you doing here?"

Still holding her, he replied, "The Chief called me and as soon as I heard what had happened, I had to get back, so I got a taxi from Ypres to Lille and then Eurostar to London; it was easy. How are you? How is Dan?"

"Bless you, Dave, it's really good of you. Dan has shown some improvement, in fact, he spoke one word yesterday and then fell asle… Oh, I'm sorry, I need to introduce you two to each other." Tish stood up, smiling, and held out her hand.

"DS Makubuya, meet the lovely DS Dave 'Bronco' Laine. Dave, meet Tish."

They shook hands, both saying "Pleased to meet you at

the same time," which made them giggle.

Bronco turned back to Sue. "So, under the circumstances, how are you really? And what's been going on while I've been away?"

Sue played down how rough she felt and Tish then set about bringing DS Laine up-to-date. He was stunned with all the revelations. Turning to Dan, he lent over the bed and said, "Morning, Guv, how are you? Now, there's work to be done, so time to get your backside out of that bed – come on, now."

Both Sue and Tish were watching when Dan's eyes flickered open and he spoke slowly. "Bronco, what's happening?"

Sue jumped up, grabbing Dan's hand. "Oh, Dan, my darling, I love you."

Dan's eyes tried to focused on her face, but then they closed without him saying anything else.

Ayesha was standing outside next to the armed guard, had seen what had happened and explained again that it was very early days and that Sue shouldn't worry, but that didn't stop the tears.

The morning passed very slowly and it was clear that Sue was exhausted. Bronco took both of her hands. "Sue, you need to listen to me. First of all, Dan is on the mend and I am sure, in no time at all, his memory will return and he will be getting back to normal and you have to be ready to help him. In the nicest way though, you can't do that if you are ill with exhaustion and so when he comes around you want to be looking your best. So, why don't you take a trip back to the hotel, have a proper rest, a nice hot bath and a change of clothes and even something to eat? We will be here and if there is any change, I promise you we will text you and you could be back here in a couple of minutes. It's the right thing to do and, what's more, it's what Dan would want you to do."

She looked at him but he could sense the uncertainty in her face.

Tish spoke next. “Sue, hun, what he says is right. If you make yourself ill you won’t be helping Dan and he will need your help. I’ll come back with you to show you to your room and we will text as soon as there is any change. Come on, let’s do it.”

Without saying a word, Sue leant over and kissed Dan gently on his lips before letting Tish lead her out the room.

CHAPTER 28

The Holiday Inn London – Whitechapel is a modern, 133-bedroomed hotel standing on the corner of Cavell Street and Commercial Road, one of East London's main thoroughfares. Sue's room was on the fifth floor with views across to the towering skyscrapers of Canary Warf. Tish opened the door first carrying Sue's suitcase and Sue walked in. Looking slowly around, the first things her eyes set on were two complimentary Kit Kat Chunky bars. Taking one for herself and passing one to Tish, she smiled. "Thank you, Tish, I bet you didn't expect all of this to happen in your first week working with Dan; I expect you're having second thoughts about getting transferred to us."

Tish shook her head and replied, "No, babes, nothing could be further from the truth. This is what you sign up for – not Dan getting injured but doing proper jobs and going after proper villains, plus I get to spend more time with Jules and lovely people like you and Dan. Now, I am going to run you a hot bath and leave you to rest. Try to eat something you can call down for room service, and we're not even paying for it. So, like I said – make the most of it." It was less than a five-minute walk back to the hospital, for Tish so she grabbed a magazine and a couple of bottles of Diet Coke on the way and decided to keep the Kit Kat Chunky for later.

Once back it was good to have time to chat with Bronco as he told her of his time in the Met and the work he had done with Dan. She was amazed how quickly time had flown while they were talking and he excused himself to go to the café to get a snack. Tish was happy reading her magazine, getting all the latest showbiz gossip and had just finished when Dave Laine returned. He stood outside the room chatting with one of the armed guards for a few moments before walking back in. He thought he would try talking to Dan again and stood next to his bed. "Come on, Guv, I need to tell you all about my trip to Ypres, it was very emotional, the things you see and the stories of such young Tommies being killed in their thousands was heart breaking, but I'm so pleased I…" He stopped mid-sentence as Dan stirred, his eyes slowly opening.

Bronco continued with, "There you are, Guv; have a look around."

Dan's eyes remained open and started to focus on the room. "Bronco, what's happened? Where am I?"

"You've had a bit of an accident, Guv, and you're in hospital."

While this was going on, Tish was texting Sue while she walked to the door to call the nurse at the same time.

Dan laid very still, his face looking strained as he tried to puzzle out what was happening.

Bronco continued, "What do you remember?"

At that point, ward sister Angie Day came in and stood next to Dan. "Hello, Dan, I'm Angie, I've been taking care of you. How are you feeling?"

His eyes were more focused now, but he was having problems keeping them open. In a whisper, he replied, "How long have I been here?" Glancing across he spotted Tish. "I know you, you're… Hmm, you're… you're Tish, aren't you?"

"Yes, I am, Guv; it's great you are beginning to come round. Sue… you know Sue's your wife?"

"Yes, I know Sue's my wife."

"Well, she has been here, she's just popped out but will

be back soon. She hasn't left your side for the past two days; she will be angry she wasn't here just now." But just as Tish finished speaking she realised Dan had fallen back to sleep.

Angie checked Dan over and began writing on his notes. "Well, that's a step in the right direction, but Sue will be disappointed."

Tish looked at her phone. I did text her but she's not read it – perhaps she's asleep or in the bath, I think I'll call her; she'll want to know, especially that he remembers her."

Holding the phone to her ear it rang about eight times before going to voice mail. She left a brief message and turned to Bronco. "That's strange, I hope she's OK. Do you think I should go and check?"

Sue had been unsure about leaving Dan but knew deep inside it was the right thing to do. Tish had been so helpful and, as she lay in the bath overflowing with bubbles, she slowly felt the tension ease from her; her eyes slowly closed and she drifted off to sleep. She woke with a start, at first, not knowing where she was and then realising the bath had gone cold and she was shivering. Wrapping herself in the complimentary bathrobe and patting herself dry, she got dressed and laid on the bed while reading the room service menu. The bath and rest must have done her some good because for the first time in days she felt hungry and she phoned to order a burger and chips. She had only been lying there a few minutes when the doorbell rang and a voice called "Room service!" *That's quick* she thought and began to open the door but it was forcibly pushed back, making her stagger. As the door fully opened, two masked men rushed in, one swiftly putting a cloth-holding hand over her mouth while the other hand held the back of her head. In less than a second, she was unconscious.

CHAPTER 29

Bronco had agreed that Tish should go back and check on Sue at the hotel; for an unknown reason she had started to run back down Cavell Street. Entering the hotel, she took the lift to the fifth floor. Running down the corridor, she reached Sue's door as a waiter was just walking away. Knocking frantically on the door, she called, "Sue, are you OK?"

The waiter turned and called to her, "There isn't anyone in there, madam. I just brought the food she ordered and when there was no answer I opened the door with my pass key, but there's no one there. I'm taking the food back to the kitchen."

Tish shouted, "I need you to open the door for me now!" Showing her warrant card, he obediently placed the tray down and opened the door. Tish ran in; looking in the bathroom she saw the wet towelling robe. Her suitcase was open on the stand with dirty clothes laid over it, but her heart almost stopped when she spotted Sue's mobile on the bedside cabinet. She knew she wouldn't go anywhere without it, especially now.

Turning to the waiter, she demanded, "Get me the duty manager up here now, I think someone has been kidnapped!" She called Bronco, followed by Callum, who said he would get officers there right away and that he would be there himself in ten minutes.

The duty manager, Anna Kaminski, a thirty-five-year-old from Gdańsk, like many Poles, spoke perfect English. Tish explained what had happened and asked what CCTV they had.

"All of our corridors, plus lifts and public rooms, are covered. We also have coverage of the front, the car park too and fire exit on Nelson Street at the back".

Tish was impressed. "Right, I need to see it now. There will be a lot of police here very soon. Someone needs to guard this room and not touch anything. Could you find out what time she ordered her food?"

Anna took Tish to an office in the basement, calling for someone to come and join them and then introduced her colleague when they arrived. "This is Jan, he is the best at working the cameras. The food was ordered at 2.46 and taken to the room at 3.12."

Tish thanked her. OK, Jan, I need to see the corridor footage on floor five from 2.30 pm."

With a few clicks of the mouse his computer screen showed an empty corridor. Jan sped the recording through, stopped at 2.58 and then ran it back a few seconds as they could see that two men walked from the fire exit to Sue's room. They were both wearing beanie hats pulled over their faces, making them look like balaclavas, with eye and mouth holes. They all watched as they rang the bell and, as the door slowly opened they forced their way in. It was less than a minute before the men came out again, one on each side, holding Sue up, as they made their way back to the stairs and the fire exit.

Seeing her friend manhandled like this, Tish was shaking. "Right, can you now show me the fire exit at the back?"

Jan made a couple more clicks and the street came into view, showing the shuttered entrance of the car park and, just beyond, the fire exit doorway. "Run it back to the same time in case we can see them arrive."

He sped through again and at 2.50 he stopped as they saw the backs of the two men walk in to view, from further down Nelson Street and nearing the fire exit.

"Can they just get in from that door?" Tish asked.

Jan answered, "No, they shouldn't be able to, but I know they can be forced with a tire lever, or something similar."

At that moment, two PCs entered the office, so Tish introduced herself and told them briefly what had happened.

They kept watching the screen as a black van backed up towards the doorway, stopping half in and half out of view, so they couldn't see its number plate. One of the PCs spoke and stated, "That's a long-wheelbase Mercedes Sprinter and a fairly new model at that."

Still watching, they saw Sue almost being dragged out by the two masked men. The driver must have opened the back door, out of view from the camera and one man must have climbed in the back with her, while the other walked around the side looking directly at the camera, letting it be known he was aware of it. He climbed in and the van drove away.

Trish turned to the PCs, "Could you two see if any more backup has arrived? We must get as many men out the back looking for other CCTV cameras and checking if anyone has seen anything. If you hear anything at all, let me know – we have to get a number for that van or at least where it went."

A PC replied, "I'm sure there are a couple of cameras in Nelson Street, so we should be in luck."

Tish was walking back up to the reception area when Callum arrived at the same time as Bronco, who was on the phone to Chief Superintendent Jackson. He began relaying what Tish was telling him at the same time that she was explaining to him what they had seen.

Callum was the first to speak, "I need to tell Serious Crimes at the Yard that this is getting too big for us to handle. I'll get a call out for the van but it won't be easy, I bet there is a half-dozen within a half-mile of us. Let me see how they are getting on in Nelson Street."

Bronco finished the call and said, "The Chief is really angry about this. He's going to get on to Scotland Yard as well – there must be someone big time behind this to try and get Dan first and now this."

Tish was still upset. "I should have stayed with her – if only I had this wouldn't have happened."

But Bronco wouldn't accept any of it. "You can't blame yourself, we need to block those thoughts out and find her."

They both looked at Callum in anticipation as he ran back in the room and reported, "We've got a partial number plate. No luck yet from any cameras, but someone saw a masked man in the van and remembered part of the number. There's still a chance we will find a camera that has all of it. All departments have been informed so both ANPR and CCTV should soon find it; also, every police car from here to the M25 will have the details – they can't get far, surely."

Tish agreed and asked for the part of the number they had. She then excused herself to the toilet. Checking no one else was present she called Tom, explaining what had happened. He listened intently, but was furious. He said, "They won't get away with this – if they even harm a hair on that woman's head, we will find her, Tish, and I promise they will pay for it." He told her that he should soon have all the details of who was behind it and asked how Dan was, which was at least one bit of good news. They agreed to keep each other up-to-date with any progress.

As she made her way back to the others she was torn as to whether she should tell them about Poacher. She wasn't sure his back story added up, but then Sue definitely seemed to know him and he was certainly determined to find her, so for now she would do as he had asked as she daren't do anything to hinder Sue's safety. Callum was finishing a call on his phone as she walked back to him.

"Right, we have received hits on ANPR, but from just after they left here, in Whitechapel Road and the Mile End Road, but nothing since. I reckon they are either taking back roads or they've changed vehicles, but at least we have the full reg number, so if it does show up we will find it."

CHAPTER 30

Sue opened her eyes and for the second time today had no idea where she was, only that it was dark, she couldn't see anything and she was lying on her side being bounced around in a vehicle. It all then all came back to her – the hotel room, the masked men... She realised she had a hood over her head, her hands and feet were bound and that she was terrified. She knew she was in a vehicle and it then felt like it had come to a stop and she heard doors being opened. She thought to herself, *What Dan would do?* but she knew she should be listening and trying to take everything in after remembering Dan lying unconscious in hospital.

She was dragged out of the doors and dropped on the floor, before being lifted and rolled into another van, this time a white Ford Transit. The doors slammed shut and they pulled away. Sue realised there was lots of stopping and starting as if they were in heavy traffic. It was impossible to judge the time and after a while they speeded up a bit, but she could still hear other traffic until eventually they reached a steady speed, *Perhaps a motorway*, she thought. She could sense someone near her and thought she could detect movement.

In as calm a voice as she could muster, she called, "Is there anyone there?" No reply. "I know you're there, why won't you answer?"

This time, a voice with a strong accent replied, "Shut the fuck up, or else I will hurt you."

So, she thought it best to do as she was told, at least for now.

In the front of the van was Aleksander; Sefiri had insisted he take charge of it and had sent two of their top men to help. Roan, sat with him in the front and Roel Tanush, sat in the back, were twenty-five-year-old twins, very distant cousins of Agron and Józef's family from the city of Shkodër in the north of Albania. In the three years they had been in London they had proved themselves to be both intelligent but violent when required – the perfect make-up for Albanian gangsters. Alexander and Roan had commented on how well the kidnap had gone and that changing vans was the right thing to do. Once they were in the new van, they carefully drove along the A12, past the Queen Elizabeth Olympic Park at Stratford and onto the M11. Careful to keep to under sixty along the motorway, lest they attract attention to themselves, they turned left at the Birchanger Green services onto the A120, before turning right onto a B road, laughing about the strange English village names like Stansted Mountfitchet, Ugley and their final destination, a remote pig farm, close to the aptly named Maggots End, which they found hilarious as it was the site of their body dump.

Birch Farm was an old-fashioned pig farm, accessible down a long secluded driveway where the pigs lived outdoors in sties and domed pig huts. It was small by modern standards, only holding about fifteen breeding sows and up to seventy-five boars at any one time. But it wasn't there to make money, rather to launder it and, as an added bonus, devour anyone who fell foul of the Sefiri empire.

Aleksander drove to the back of the farmhouse and parked next to an old concrete air raid shelter, probably left over from the Second World War, with the weed and moss covered dome rising out of the ground. The entrance was down six steps and through an old reinforced iron door.

Sue was roughly dragged from the van and yelled at to 'move, bitch; move,' but she purposely made herself as heavy as she could. Her ankles were still tied together so she couldn't walk anyway, let alone move them, so she thought, *Let them drag me.*

The twins dragged her down the steps and through the door, which opened out into another set of steps, taking them down to a much larger area that had obviously been an addition much more recently. At the bottom was a large area with various chairs and benches, while on the wall were a variety of saws and other dangerous-looking instruments. To the left were two brick cells, both with solid metal doors, a spyhole and food flap at the bottom. They wouldn't have looked out of place in Belmarsh, or indeed Abu Ghraib prison in Baghdad. She felt the ties on her wrists and ankles being cut and she was pushed into the cell. Unable to see where she was, she fell painfully onto the floor as the door slammed shut behind her.

A voice called out, "You can remove the hood now; hope you like your new hotel room," which made the three men laugh.

Sue slowly pulled the hood off, her eyes squinting with the light shining from a heavy-duty recessed fitting in the ceiling. Looking around, she could see an old dirty mattress on the floor and an empty bucket in the corner with a toilet roll next to it. The concrete floor had a small, covered drain in the centre. Taking all of this in she suddenly went weak at the knees. With her legs beginning to give way, she slowly sank to the floor, rolling herself into a ball and crying. She was thinking over and over again, 'What will happen to me? How is Dan? Will he know what's happened to me?' She hoped, by now, Tish would realise she was missing from the hotel room.

CHAPTER 31

The moment Tom finished the call with Tish, he changed phones to WhatsApp Mongoose for he needed to get the information now if he were to find Sue before, in the worst-case scenario, they killed her:

SITUATION NOW URGENT IMPERATIVE
I GET INFO ASAP WILL PAY DOUBLE
NEED UPDATE NOW

He received a reply almost immediately:
DRAFT FOLDER
P0&(|-|3£@xn----88sbbdP1a8ck.com
PASS. C^:zI>0oT
MORE IN 12H
NO NEED 2 PAY MORE

Logging on as always, using various VPNs to hide his IP address, the draft folder was being used as a 'dead drop', something that terrorists had used for some time, with no e-mails being sent or received – it was merely a Dropbox for messages or documents. It contained just one PDF file that he quickly downloaded, before scanning for any viruses or malware. Opening it, the first thing he saw was a long list of business names and addresses, telephone numbers, bank account details and balances in both the UK, Albania and the traditional money laundering countries. That was followed by a list of people's names, some with addresses and phone numbers, some without, but some with bank details. The next list contained properties linked to any of the bank accounts or companies. Finally, there was a note reporting how far he had got. He knew that to get right to the top of this organisation would take more time because of their sophisticated firewalls, but it was only a matter of time before he got through them. Tom was aware there would be more information available shortly, so he would continually check back to the same place.

Tom copied the file over to each of his devices so he would have on-the-move access to it and then printed it off, knowing he could study it better that way.

Scanning through the addresses, the first one that jumped out was Cringle Farm, Colsterworth – the scene of his encounter with the human traffickers. Further down the list he spotted the warehouse in Suffolk. The link between Dan's case and the people he, himself, had had been tracking was undeniable, but where would they have taken Sue?

He set about drawing up a list of the most likely places; warehouses were his first choice. Entering each address into Google Maps, although some were dismissed immediately, the rest were added to a list. It took almost an hour for Tom to go through them all and it left him with a possible twelve, so, to cut the choices down he began to go through them again, this time thinking where *he* would take someone in similar circumstances. One by one he crossed several off, either too near houses, overlooked by other buildings, or easily seen from a busy road. That brought it down to six. Checking each one again on Google Street View and Google Earth, he found what he thought was the place to have taken her – a small, closed down market garden between Waltham Abbey and Nazeing, just off the M25 in Essex not far from Epping Forest. He saved various pictures of the buildings, along with aerial shots and he set about drawing up another list, this time of what he would need to get in in order to find Sue and deal with the kidnappers. It would take a few hours to do that and he planned to be there before first light, armed and ready.

CHAPTER 32

It was early evening by the time Tish and Bronco made their way back from the hotel to the hospital, leaving Callum there reporting back to New Scotland Yard. The first piece of news after the ANPR sightings had been that the van was likely to be on cloned plates, meaning that the gang had copied the vehicle registration number from another similar van, in a different part of the country. The main consensus was that they had either changed vehicles or gone back on to the original reg number. So, the call went out to stop and search any newish, black, long-wheelbase Mercedes Sprinter vans and, at this particular moment, vans were being pulled over and checked, causing traffic hold-ups all across the capital.

With the Restaurant Emblema being the only concrete link the police had to Kotri and this case, Callum ordered for a TST unit to raid it, but the restaurant was closed with no one there. However, search teams were systematically going through the offices and would be reporting back shortly with their findings.

As they got to the door of Dan's room, one of the armed guards said, "We've heard what's happened to his wife and that's terrible; we are bringing in extra plain clothes armed officers as backup, to be on the safe side. He's been awake for a little while, the doctor and ward sister have been in with him."

Before they could go in, Angie Day called them to come to her office and, sitting down at her desk she looked very serious. "We have been told what has happened to Sue. Dan is improving , but has a long way to go. He is understandably still very tired while his brain and body are recovering, but is waking up more frequently and is more responsive, but it's down to you to decide if you tell him about Sue or not. I don't think it will affect his recovery, but I can't be certain."

Tish turned to Bronco and asked, "What are your thoughts?"

"It's a tricky one, but knowing Dan, I *do* think he would want to know."

Tish replied, "OK, let's see how he is and play it by ear."

They both walked in and Dan was awake. Seeing them together he said in a weak voice, "So, you've met each other then?"

They both replied at the same time, "Yes."

"Good, she's a bit special, Dave. Where's Sue?"

They both looked at each other and Dan sensed something was wrong.

"Where is she? She was here before, wasn't she?"

Bronco sat on the chair next to the bed and said, "Dan, this isn't easy. I don't know how much you remember of the past couple of days, but did you know that Billy Davies tried to kill you? If it wasn't for Tish, you'd be dead." Dan looked shocked and confused, as Bronco continued, "Then I doubt you know that Kotri died in the crash that put you in here and it would seem that they want revenge. They tried to get to you and failed and there are now armed guards everywhere here, so when they couldn't get to you they tried for Sue and, I'm really sorry, Guv, but they've kidnapped her."

A lesser man may have panicked but Dan's training kicked in, along with a huge dose of adrenaline to quickly clear his head. "Kidnapped – how, where and when? I need to know everything."

So, the two detective sergeants spent the next five minutes

informing him of every little detail, often stopping for him to question them. By the time they had brought him up-to-date, his heart monitor was bleeping much quicker and his blood pressure was rising, setting off an alarm.

He started to sit up, saying, "I have to get out of here to find her."

But Angie Day entered the room and realising what was happening she swiftly put her hand firmly on Dan's chest and said, "Dan, you aren't going anywhere, you're still very ill and I doubt you'd make it to the lift before passing out. That won't help Sue at all and all it will do is make it easier for whoever wants you dead, to finish the job."

Both Tish and Bronco agreed and spoke at the same time telling Dan that Angie was right and that he would be more of a hindrance if he left hospital.

Dan closed his eyes, trying to take it all in, before asking where his things were.

Tish replied, "They're here, but you aren't going anywhere."

"No, I just want my phone and then I need to be left alone for a while."

Tish gave it to him, reiterating that he wasn't to go anywhere. Dan repeated that he needed to be left alone, asking them all to go and close the door behind them. Bronco informed Tish he would go and check in at the hotel and was going to bring them all a treat back.

Meanwhile, Dan scrolled through the names on his phone, stopping on one and thinking of the words that Tom Windsor said to him only a few weeks previous at his wedding. *"Take this card; that's my own private number. If there is ever anything you need, or anything I can do to help you any time, just call me."*

He would never have dreamt then that he would need to make that call, but if anyone *could* help him in this, his darkest hour, he knew it was Poacher.

It was answered on the second ring. "Dan, is that you?"

"Yes, I'm sorry to call you but I need–"

"Dan, stop, I know what's happened. I know about Sue, I called her yesterday to see how you were and I spoke to Tish. I've fed her a story that I work for a clandestine government department and she mustn't tell anyone about me.

"Trust me, I am on it – I have a world-class hacker in Mumbai tracking the people involved and I think I know where they may have taken her, but it's better I deal with it – if the police go charging in anything could happen. You have my word, Dan, I will find her and those responsible will pay dearly – just trust me."

"Thanks, Poacher, keep me up-to-date and if I can't call you, I'll get Tish to; she's very good and I am sure we can trust her." Intrigued about what Tom said earlier, Dan asked, "What exactly have you told her about us?"

Tom explained what he had said to her and told Dan he would be in touch.

As the call ended, Dan called for Tish to come back in and told her about his phone call and how he trusted her to keep the knowledge of Poacher to herself. He was certain that was their best chance of finding Sue.

Bronco had checked in at the Holiday Inn and took a slight detour on his way back to remind him of his days in the Met. Walking to Brick Lane, a London street world famous for its curry houses, he bought three meals from The Famous Curry Bazaar. He walked back quickly, hoping the food would help lift their spirits.

CHAPTER 33

He had parked his car on Turner Street, just a couple of minutes from the rear of the hospital. He stood at just over six feet tall in a pair of old Timberland Pro work boots, black jeans and a black, leather bomber jacket – concealing something large in the inside pocket – over a dark blue Fred Perry polo shirt, his shaved head even more tanned than his rugged face, which looked like it had received its fair share of beatings in its fifty or so years. Walking to the hospital, he checked CCTV cameras en route, as a force of habit. He turned right under the modern adjoining parts of the hospital on Stepney Way, before a left turn took him onto Milward Street and into the main entrance with its futuristic glass ceilings. He wandered around the reception area and, without even realising it, took note of his surroundings. He casually strolled into the café area of the hospital, constantly looking around. He picked up a discarded newspaper and pretended to read it while casually surveying his surroundings. He knew what he needed to be able to get to Hooper and knew he must be patient if he were to find him. It wasn't as if he could just ask at reception that wouldn't help. He tried to earwig what the nurses and doctors said, but although he heard snippets, he was still none the wiser. But then, he saw what he needed.

Making his way to the lifts, he queued next to three nurses who were chattering away and an Asian doctor, plus a man carrying a bag of takeaway food who pressed the fifth floor button. While the nurses were alighting at the third floor, the doctor hadn't pressed a single button, but didn't exit when the nurses did.

As the doors opened at the fifth, he followed the man with the curry out into the corridor. They had walked about ten steps when the 'doctor' yelled from behind him, "Armed police! Get down on the floor now, let me see your hands!" At the same time, two armed Tactical Support officers appeared, shouting the same thing at him while pointing their Heckler & Koch MP5 carbines. He swiftly fell flat on the floor with his arms out, yelling, "Don't shoot! I am unarmed, repeat – I am unarmed. I am a friend of Captain Hooper."

The doctor, who was in fact a sergeant in the TST, placed his Glock back in its holster under the white coat he was wearing, pulled the man's hands behind his back and handcuffed him, while the other two kept their guns aimed.

Bronco had dropped the curries on the floor and reached down to search him, removing a cardboard tube from inside the bomber jacket.

"I've told you, I am a friend; I was Captain Hooper's staff sergeant in No 1 Para. Tell him it's Smudger Smith and he will vouch for me. Look in that tube, it's a regimental picture of us both."

DS Laine turned and walked to Dan's room. Tish had come to the door from hearing the shouting and Dan was still awake.

"Guv, there's a man outside, says he was your staff sergeant, Smudger Smith. He just nearly got himself shot; reckons he's come to help you."

"Smudger? You must be joking," Dan replied. "He's a good man, let him come in."

Tish was still by the door, so she waved for them to bring him in, which they did, with an armed policeman on either side.

"Captain Hoop, how are you, sir? I saw on the news what had happened and came to see if you needed any help."

Dan smiled. "Smudger, only *you* could do something like this. Please remove his handcuffs for this man has saved my life in the past – he's on our side."

"Well, if I remember right, sir, you saved mine as well, so I owe you one and that's why I'm here. I knew you were here in the Royal London, but had no idea what floor, so I hung around downstairs until I saw this geezer carrying a bag of curries. One look at him, he had to be a copper, so I figured I would follow him to see if I could find you and then this lot jumped me. If I'd have known you were this well guarded, I might not have bothered," he laughed.

Dan looked at the armed officers first and said, "Thank you so much and this man is far from harmless, in fact, he can be deadly, but you don't need to worry about him." Looking at Smith, he continued, "Bless you, Smudger, it really is appreciated."

Dan introduced him to Tish and Bronco, who had gone to collect the takeaway bag and with a smile on his face he announced, "A treat for you all and I'm sure there's enough for all of us. It's the best curry in London, if not the whole country, all the way from Brick Lane."

With everyone's minds on Sue, the meal was no celebration or happy reunion. Dan hardly ate and dozed a couple of times. But when he was awake he was completely honest with Smudger who, in turn, listened carefully, taking it all in and then asking all the right questions.

With the meal out of the way, Dan gave Tish a look that she rightly took as a signal. Standing up and stretching, she said, "Well, if it's OK with you, Guv, I think it would make sense for us to turn in for an early night; what do you think, Dave?"

He coughed and looked a bit worried.

Dan grinned and Tish laughed before she said, "Obviously you've not told him, Guv. You're more than safe with me, Dave, I bat for the other side, mate."

Bronco saw the funny side and chuckled. "No worries – I didn't really think you meant a night of passion with me, coz, to be honest, I think it would just about finish me off."

To which, Smudger said, "Yeah, but what a way to go, mate!" After the laughter the two of them left, promising to be back early in the morning and giving Dan a chance for a serious chat with Smith.

CHAPTER 34

Once Dan knew they had left the building, he began to speak.

"Do you remember Operation Barras back in 2000?"

"Yes, of course, that's where we both saved each other. Fuck, what a dog fight that was! Why do you ask?"

"Well, there was an SAS trooper called Poacher with us."

"Yes, I think I can remember him."

"Well, without going into too many details, he helped me out big time on the QT last year. He's been out of the Regiment for a few years, done all the PMC stuff and is now on a bit of a one-man crusade to do some good. Well, he knows what's happened and is going after them to rescue Sue and, in his words, deal with the culprits in a way that will prevent them from ever doing so again."

"He sounds like a man after my own heart, Captain. I've done my fair share of PMC work, mainly abroad. The money was good, but I hated it – not enough discipline. That was when the wife finally left me; I can't blame her, I was never at home, but I do alright for a fifty-five-year-old. Don't ask me why, but I have no problems pulling the birds; the last one was only thirty-six. You should have seen her huge tits – nipples like organ stops. I've got a nice flat and enough in the bank to see me out, so if he needs help, I am up for it."

"Thanks, Smudger. I have to say, it goes against a lot of what I have always stood for, but to do this to Sue is just too much – they deserve all they get. It's killing me because *I* should be the one helping get her, but common sense tells me I would be no use and would slow him down, but if you are really sure you want to, I'll call him. But I will warn you, he has been through a lot over the past few years and there will a load of things he won't want to talk about, so it's best you don't question him about his past."

"Captain, let me tell you, he ain't the only one – there's many a thing that *I've* done that I wouldn't even be able to tell *YOU* about, so that's no problem for me. I'm here for you and to help you get your wife back, unharmed, and the sooner we do it the better, so call this geezer and let's get things moving."

"OK, give me a couple of minutes; I need to talk to him on my own first."

"Yes, Captain. I'll be in the corridor and just hope I'm not jumped on again," and he left with a smile.

Dan explained at length to Tom, who at first was uncertain, but having listened to all that Dan said, he reluctantly agreed, knowing that a second pair of eyes and hands might be useful against such a remorseless foe. He took Smith's mobile number and gave Dan some details to pass on and finished by telling Dan he would be back in touch by noon tomorrow at the latest.

Dan called Smudger back in and told him it was on. He needed to meet Poacher at the Marriott Hotel at Waltham Abbey just off the M25. Once he had sorted all the equipment required and the dark blue VW Transporter on a '14' plate, he would be on his way and would be there in just under two hours.

"The Marriott, I know that – it's where Gazza lived for a while when he was playing for Spurs. I'm living in Leytonstone, so I can stop for a change of clothes and some bits that I might need and still be there in good time."

They shook hands and Dan said, "I can't thank you

enough for doing this, but do take care and bring Sue and yourself back safely."

"No thanks needed; the time spent in No 1 Para was the best time of my life and a lot of that was down to you –we will all get back safely." With that he left and Dan fell back to sleep, exhausted.

CHAPTER 35

Sue was shivering with both cold and fear. It would have helped if she had put her watch back on, back at the hotel, but she hadn't and had subsequently lost all track of time. She heard footsteps outside and then the flap on the bottom of the door lifted from the outside and a tray was pushed through. It had two packs of sandwiches and a litre bottle of water. A voice called out, "You had best eat up, bitch; I want you strong when I fuck you," and he laughed as he let the flap close and then bolted it.

Sue was terrified, but her time working at the police station had taught her to have faith in the police. Although she had worked in the canteen, with her overall knowledge of working at a station she knew there would be lots of people doing everything they could to find her.

She realised that she had hardly eaten anything for two days, so she unwrapped the nearest cheese and tomato sandwich, which would do and she was surprised how good it tasted. Not knowing when they would feed her again, she saved the second one, but took a good swig of the water, drinking almost half of it, before she felt drowsy and her head started to spin. Her eyes began to close, but as she was fighting to keep them open, she mumbled, "They've fucking drugged me," and rolled over on the floor, unconscious.

CHAPTER 36

Tom was busy packing enough equipment for two and, in the circumstances, thought it better to take his van than the Audi, knowing he would always rather have too much equipment than too little. He double-checked all he had, including his new piece of kit, a DJI Mavic 2 Pro drone quadcopter, capable of flying for forty minutes at up to six thousand metres – with an HD camera, it would be able to see places Tom couldn't.

With the van loaded he set off, making his way across country to the M1, which, for a pleasant change, was clear all the way onto the M25 clockwise, then he turned off at junction 26, where he saw the hotel in front of him on the far side of the roundabout. Pulling into a quiet part of the car park, a black Range Rover Sport pulled up next to him. Both looked across and nodded to each other, before Smudger climbed out and walked around to Poacher's door.

Getting out, Tom smiled and said, "I'm told we've met before; you were on Operation Barras?"

"I certainly was; I don't think anyone there will ever forget it. We may have bumped into each other at Brize Norton before we flew out. Once we were there it was crazy and I know afterwards they flew us to a Royal Fleet Auxiliary ship, I think it was RAF Angus, so we didn't see any of the Regiment when it was over. It would be good to reminisce over a beer or three when this is over, but for now, what can I do to help get Sue?"

Tom was opening the back doors of the van while looking around to ensure that there was no one nearby and no CCTV. He knelt down and slid a small, hidden panel on the left wheel arch to one side, revealing a keypad. Tapping in a number, a section of the floor sprang up. Tom lifted it and Smith whistled as he looked at an arsenal of weapons.

"I think I've packed all that we will need; there are two M4 carbines, or if you prefer, there's a Heckler & Koch MP5, two Glock 19s, flashbang stun grenades and some C-4 plastic explosive. I've also got night-vision goggles, oh, and a brand new drone."

"Fucking hell, Poacher, thats awesome, but I won't need the Glock 19, I've brought this with me," he advised, removing a Beretta M9 from his jacket pocket.

Tom smiled and said, "OK, nice one. Let's shut this down for now and check in; I've got all the details we need on my iPad. I want to do this at 04.30 hours so we have a bit of time. We could get room service as I don't know about you, but I'm starving."

At 3.30 am they were ready to leave. Keeping to back roads, they made the six-mile journey and in no time were parked behind a derelict barn about six hundred metres from their target. They kitted up with night-vision on and made their way alongside hedges and around the edge of a farm field before finally carefully manoeuvring through a thicket of bramble bushes to come out next to a half-dozen old commercial greenhouses, all dilapidated, most with their glass smashed – they couldn't have been used in years. Stealthily, they made their way onto a muddy driveway, with fresh tyre tracks, leading to an old cement block barn with boarded up windows, next to a bungalow built with the same blocks.

This is where Tom suspected Sue was being held hostage. They both drew their pistols and silently approached the barn. Tom signalled to Smith that they should go around the back first. As they moved closer, they could see that the windows had all what looked like black bin bags taped over them, giving them no idea of what was inside. Having circled the building once, Tom whispered they would enter by the back door. Smith put his pistol away and held his M4 carbine at the ready, while Tom removed a stun grenade from his pack and took a few steps back in readiness. Launching himself sideways, shoulder checking the door, it gave little resistance and crashed open, pulling down plastic sheeting that was draped behind it. He was about to throw the grenade when he abruptly stopped.

Lifting his right hand to stop Smith further, it was clear that Sue wasn't here – he had picked the wrong place. They both stood looking at what was obviously a cannabis farm. Stepping in, they could see that every room was filled with plants in various stages of growth, with all the equipment needed to get a good and quick harvest.

Tom shook his head and said in exasperation, "I've fucked up! I've picked the wrong fucking place!"

Smudger patted him on his back and said, "You weren't to know, mate; it was always going to be a chance. Let's get back to the hotel to re-group and we can both go through the list of other places."

"You're right, but I'm still pissed off about it. We'll need to check that barn before we go and I'm not going without leaving them a calling card."

They made their way to the barn and, although the windows were all boarded up, there was a door on the side that Smudger managed to kick open. Unsurprisingly, it was also filled with cannabis plants and growth equipment.

Tom reached into his backpack, taking out some of the C-4 plastic explosive and detonators, handing some to Smith.

"Let's set these off and take this place out – at least it will hit them in their pocket." They spent the next fifteen minutes placing the charges where they would make the maximum damage. Setting the timers to fifteen minutes, they swiftly made their way back to the van and were already halfway back to the hotel when they exploded.

CHAPTER 37

Packing the weapons away in the van's hidden compartment, they made their way to their room and promptly downed a couple of cups of coffee whilst looking at the properties list on the iPad. Tom had scrolled up and down a few times when Smudger halted him.

"Hang on a minute, that place sticks out like a pork chop in a synagogue. I'm guessing that most Albanians are Muslims, so why on earth would they own a pig farm in a remote part of the Hertfordshire countryside?"

"I should have noticed that. Well done, let's have a look at it."

Putting the details of Birch Farm, Maggots End, Bishop's Stortford, into Google Maps, he was able to zoom in and study the farmhouse in detail: pigsties, barns, outbuildings and what looked like an old air raid shelter.

"It looks promising to me, mate; what do you think?"

"I think you're right, Smudger. If you can continue without getting any kip we could travel there now and check it out."

Smith agreed and, after looking at the map, it was decided they would take both vehicles and rendezvous at the Birchanger Green services on the M11 near Stansted Airport, where they would leave Smith's Range Rover and recce the farm in the van.

It was just after 10 am when they met at the services. Smith climbed in the van and they set off looking for Birch

Farm. They were soon on single file roads with not much cover, which Tom thought could be a problem. The satnav took them past the entrance, which gave them a view of the long drive, with the pigsties on either side and with the house and buildings in the distance. Tom continued driving for another mile before seeing an opening onto a field with a concrete hard stand, behind a hedge. Pulling in, he parked and they opened the back doors to retrieve his new toy, the drone.

Checking the batteries were fully charged, he placed the drone on the concrete, opened out the rotors and turned on the remote smart control unit. It started up with almost no noise and hovered for a second, before lifting vertically and flying back towards the farm. They both watched the monitor on the control unit as the HD camera fed back images of open fields before it reached its destination.

"Won't they be able to spot it?" Smith asked.

"No; I'll take it up high and zoom in when we are overhead, but I need to be careful because we aren't far from Stansted." After a half-minute, he said, "There you go – that's the farmhouse and the outbuildings. Look, there's someone taking food to the pigs. He looks like a farm worker."

"Can you see the van? Could we get the reg number?"

Tom replied, "Let's try." He manoeuvred the drone to a better angle, zoomed in and took a few pictures.

As they continued monitoring the screen, two men emerged from the house. Tom zoomed in again and took pictures of them; one carried a tray with food, walked down the steps and into the old air raid shelter.

"That has to be where they are holding her, but we need to be certain. I'm bringing it back now and need to call Tish."

Once the drone was down, he called Tish, gave her the van's number and asked her to check it on ANPR cameras from when and where they lost the Mercedes. He instructed her to do it urgently and she promised to get straight back to him.

He put the drone on charge via a USB cable in the van and turned to Smith.

"So, how do you think we should approach this?"

Rubbing his chin, Smudger thought for a while and said, "Well, seeing them take food in, if it *is* her, we at least know she is still alive. If we had more time, I think we would both rather go in at night and take them out one by one, but we can't chance leaving her there that long. Have you any ideas?"

Tom smiled, "Oh yes, I have, but we will need a few more bits first. Could you drive in to Bishop's Stortford? I'll give you a list. While you're gone, I'll fly the drone again; it would be good to see exactly how many men we have to deal with."

Smudger was soon on his way and Tom had the drone in the air again, circling the farmhouse and outbuildings. He dropped it down to about 10-feet to see into the barn and then hovered over some of the pigsties. Taking it back up again, he let it hover, knowing he only had about twenty minutes of battery charge left. He saw the door open again and an older man walked out. He was talking on the phone and waving his arms about as if he was having an argument. Tom took photos of him, but thought if his plan worked, he wouldn't need them.

He had just landed the drone, when Tish called back, "Yes, we have hits on the van on the A12 at Stratford, Leytonstone and Redbridge, and then again on the M11, near Harlow, and then nothing."

"OK, Tish, thanks; that's what I had hoped to hear. Hopefully, I'll have some good news for you soon. I may just need your help once this is over – I'll let you know."

CHAPTER 38

Once Smudger returned, Tom stopped what he was doing to talk to him. "I have seen one more man there and he didn't look like a farmer, so that makes four, as far as we know. But I want you to know before we go any further that when I go in there, I won't be taking prisoners and I don't intend to leave any witnesses behind. As far as I am concerned, they've tried to kill Dan – God knows what they have done to Sue, so they deserve to die. But if you aren't comfortable with that, I understand. I could drop you back at the services and you can go on your way, no hard feelings, but if you stay we do this my way and the only ones to walk away from that farm are you, me and Sue."

"Poacher, mate, we are both on the same page – fuck them, they deserve to die. Let's do it!" He held out his hand for Tom to shake.

They began to put their plan into action and an hour later they were set to go. First, Tom flew the drone again, this time with a small sling hanging under it containing a package. With the extra weight he kept it low, skimming across the fields and around to the back of the barn. He landed it then and just bumped it up and down and moved it backwards and forwards to deposit the package on the barn floor, before bringing the drone back. Packing it away, Tom climbed into the back and laid out two burner phones, both with colour coded tape on them.

Smith placed a parcel on the bench seat and a piece of

white card on top of the dashboard with 'Hermes' written on it. He then walked around to the driver's side, checked his gun on the floor next to him and set off. He turned into the farm driveway and drove right up to the house then reversing around, so that the van was facing back down the drive.

Picking up the parcel, he got out and started walking to the front door when it opened, two men stood there and one called out, "What do you want?"

Smiling his best smile and in a cheerful tone he said, "Parcel for Birch Farm, mate. Nothing to sign for – cheers," and handed it to him, walked back to the van and started it up. They drove only for about twenty metres, noticing in the rear-view mirror that the men were still looking at their van, and then abruptly stopped, which was the signal for Tom to press 'call' on the first mobile. The two men were still watching them and holding the parcel when it exploded in their faces, blowing them both back through the door, blasting a hole in the chest of the man who was holding it, while the other lost his arm and half his face.

Smudger was quickly out of the van. As the back doors opened and Tom jumped down, they were both armed with their M4 carbines. At that moment, the older man fired at them through the front window of the house. Bullets whizzed past either side of them as they both dived to the floor for cover. They returned fire instantly, blasting the windows and Tom crawled closer before he hurled a stun grenade through the smashed window.

With no return fire, they ran quickly to the front door, jumping over the two bodies just as the farm worker appeared at the top of the stairs brandishing a shotgun. Yelling in a foreign language that neither of them understood, he was just lifting the shotgun to his shoulder when a volley of bullets slammed into him, sending him tumbling down the stairs.

This time, Smith threw a stun grenade into the front room and they quickly entered it, strafing the front room entrance with 5.56 mm calibre rounds. The gunman was lying on the floor with wounds to his chest but was still breathing. Tom walked over to him, drew his Glock 19 and, without a second thought, shot him twice in the forehead. *The perfect double tap.*

They ran to the air raid shelter, but the door was locked and they knew they couldn't chance using explosives, so Smudger ran back to the house and found a bunch of keys on the floor in the hallway where they had been thrown from the blast. Unlocking the door revealed more steps and a second door, which they promptly unlocked. They both called for Sue but received no reply. Looking around, they saw two cells, one of which was open, so Tom looked through the spyhole in the other door and saw her lying on the floor.

"She's in there – open it up!"

As soon as the door was open, Tom was in and kneeling at her side. Feeling for her pulse, he cried, "She's alive, thank God! But she's very weak." Gently stroking her face, he spoke softly to her. "Sue, it's Poacher, you're safe now. Come on, my lovely, wake up for me; we're taking you back to see Dan. Come on now, time to wake up."

Cautiously, she began to stir. She coughed a dry cough, her eyes began to open and she started to shake with fear. Looking confused and dazed, she instinctively pulled away from Tom, before he spoke soothingly again.

"Sue, it's me, Poacher; you remember me, don't you? We met at your wedding and we talked on the phone. It's over, you're safe." Turning to Smith, he said, "This is another of Dan's old service pals, Smudger."

"Hello Sue, shall we get you back to Dan?"

Sue started to cry; they figured it was all too much for

her. The cries turned into sobs and her body shook as the tears flowed.

Carefully, they helped her up and it was obvious she had been drugged as her legs were very weak. They made sure she didn't see the bodies on her way to the van and when they reached it they sat her on the bench seat.

"Smudger, will you stay here with Sue? I have some unfinished business to deal with," and he jogged back to the house. He searched the rooms for any clue of whom he was dealing with before searching the bodies. Finding their phones, he was surprised they were all in one piece after the blast and gunfire. He pocketed them before dragging the bodies out of the house, each to a different pigsty. Lifting them up, he dropped them in with the pigs that were instantly rooting away on them, attracted by the fresh meat. He then ran into the barn, making safe the plastic explosive attached to a burner phone, saving it perhaps for another day.

They gave Sue some water and an energy bar which seemed to give her a lift, although she was still drowsy and confused. Tom took his time explaining what had happened and the cover plan they were using. It was agreed that she would be more comfortable in the Range Rover, so Smudger would drive her back to London and drop her as close to the hospital as he could, but in a street with no CCTV. Tom then told her what to say when she got there, but to use being drugged as a reason for being unsure of things. He told her that he would let Dan and Tish know and they would help cover for her.

Tom said his goodbyes to both of them and Sue was in tears again. He agreed he would keep in touch with Smudger. As they left, he called Dan's phone, which he answered on the second ring. "Poacher, what's happened?"

"It's done, she's safe and on her way back to you, but don't let on, she should be there in a couple of hours and the culprits have been dealt with. She'll need your help with her cover story and I'll let Tish know. Rest well. I will be in touch again soon or call if you need anything." He then called Tish and, without going into any details, he let her know Sue was safe and to help with her story, as no one could know what had happened. She said she was so pleased that Sue was safe and alive and that the plan would be no problem. He said it would be best for her to be near the front entrance of the hospital in a couple of hours' time, just in case the Albanians had anyone watching the place.

After that, Tom set off back to Northamptonshire, relieved that Sue was safe and well, knowing the human traffickers he was tracking were the same gang as this one. He knew that he wouldn't rest until they were all brought to justice – Tom's Justice.

CHAPTER 39

Sue began to feel better on the journey back down the M11, helped by a large coffee and a Burger King Whopper. Smudger relayed to her some stories of Dan in No 1 Para and she was excited about seeing him again. He dropped her off on the corner of Newark Street and gave her directions, but once she turned the corner, she could see the two blue-clad buildings of The Royal London Hospital. Going over and over in her head what she was meant to say, she slowly walked to the main entrance and was pleased to see Tish stood by the front doors.

They both hugged and Tish told her that Poacher had called and that she was here to help. Taking her arm, Tish carefully walked her over to the lift and nodded at one of the plain clothes armed guards, who then followed behind. When they got out of the lift Sue tried to run, but it was more like a quick limp as she hobbled to the door of Dan's room. Bronco was in the room and turned towards her first. "Sue, thank God you're OK! How did you get here?" But she ignored him and, for a second, just stood looking at Dan, who was sat up in bed with a huge grin on his face.

He held out his arms and said, "Darling, come here, let me hold you. I have been so worried. As Dave just said, thank God you're safe! What happened? How did you get away?"

Sue explained about the knock on the hotel room door, masked men bursting in and something put over her mouth. That was all she really remembered apart from a vague recollection of being on the floor in a room, eating a sandwich, drinking water and falling asleep again. She didn't know where she had been and she only came around when she was thrown from the van; she didn't know where it was but had seen a street sign saying E1 so thought it must be close to the hospital and just walked until she saw it in the distance.

"It really is all like a dream; they must have drugged me because I'm sure as soon as I drank the water I felt strange. More might come back to me in time, but Dan, look at you, darling, you're looking so much better!"

"I'm feeling better, darling, hopefully they are going to move me, well, both of us now, to a safe house. We can have Andy there as well if you want."

"Yes, I do want to see him, if you're sure he will be safe with us."

Bronco answered, "I think he will be much safer with you both, Sue, and don't worry, we have a guard with him now anyway." Dan agreed.

Just then, ward sister Angie walked into the room. She was thrilled Sue was back safely and told her that the room next to Dan's would be made available for her to use that night, meaning she too would have armed guards protecting her. Sue beamed her biggest smile of the week, saying, "Well, it's a good job there are armed guards, Angie, because I might have been tempted to creep in and take advantage of him."

Everybody roared with laughter and Dan said, "It's a sure sign you're feeling better, Mrs Hooper!"

That's when the door opened and Callum West came in, smiling as he saw Sue. "I had a call you were back. When you're up to it, I need to interview you to find out what you can remember from your ordeal."

Tish replied, "To be honest, I don't think she remembers

anything. We've talked it over and she was drugged for most of the time, isn't that so, Sue?"

"Yes, it is, but if anything comes back to me, you'll be the first to know, well, after Dan and Tish, of course."

"No worries, I am just pleased you're safe. By the way, there is some other news… Billy Davies was found hanged in his cell at Belmarsh just over an hour ago. It's being investigated by major crimes and because a copper is always a target in jail, it may not have been suicide. I'm sure at one time he was a good officer, but obviously greed got to him and it's not a happy ending."

CHAPTER 40

On the return drive Tom's thoughts were consumed with the previous few hours, along with the thought that, no matter what had just happened, it may well not stop these people continuing to try and harm Dan or Sue. He knew they would both be well guarded now, so perhaps his best option would be to try and give these people something to distract them.

He was back in his house in just over an hour. He unloaded all the equipment and made sure the weapons and ammo were safely locked away. After taking a shower and a change of clothes, he was back in his office logging onto his computer and checking the phone he had used to correspond with Mongoose. There was a new message advising him to check the same e-mail address as there was some new information for him, but that he was still searching for more and would be in touch.

Tom had soon downloaded and printed out the documents; they listed more names and addresses, not only in the UK and Albania but The Netherlands, Belgium, Dubai, Greece, Turkey, USA, Chile and Columbia. This really was a worldwide set-up and much bigger than he had anticipated. No matter how big, he was determined to get to the top of the chain and cut the head off the serpent.

His next job was to check through the phones he'd collected. They were all currently locked, but he had a programme on one of the hard drives that would open them. In a few minutes, he had downloaded all the text messages and calls, along with names and numbers in the address books and printed them off.

Taking all these lists and the phones, he went down to the kitchen. It would take a few cups of coffee and some food inside him before he could concentrate on all of this. It was back to comfort food again – another sourdough grilled bacon sandwich, with lashings of HP sauce – this was becoming a habit that couldn't go on or his waistline would start to expand.

Once the food was out the way, he set about trying to connect phone numbers to names and names to addresses and text messages. It was a long and tiresome task, but he knew it was the best way to fully know and understand just whom he was dealing with.

Two of the phones were burners and he hadn't expected anything different, but one was a BQ Aquaris EncroChat encrypted phone and it was easy to see it belonged to the oldest man. The text messages were a mixture of English and what he guessed to be Albanian. The most recent calls were to a Józef, although he couldn't find that name on any of the lists, but checking all the times, one call would have been when he was watching this man from the drone, apparently arguing. He was tempted to call the number, but after inputting the number into one of his own burners, he thought he would save calling it for another time.

Moving on to the addresses, there were various warehouses in names of different shipping companies, all around the UK. Ideally, he would like any that were remote and, after searching through, he found three side by side, about half an hour from Hull docks, just off the M62 and under two hours' drive from his house. He soon checked them out on his usual sources and thought they fitted the bill perfectly. Checking the time, he loaded the car with everything he needed and, when that was done, he thought he should get some shuteye, so went to bed setting the alarm for 10 pm, which would give him ample time to get to the target site just before 2 am.

Like most servicemen, Tom could fall asleep anywhere and at any time; his only trouble in recent years being the nightmares waking him night after night, replaying the revulsion and horror of the events in Baghdad almost two years ago. Thankfully, they had faded and tonight, he was refreshed from just a few hours' sleep.

Setting off just after 10 pm, the route took him north on the M1 before turning east onto the M62, driving though the flat countryside as far as Goole and then onto the A63, crossing the River Ouse and finally stopping about eight hundred metres away from his target. This was a dead-end layby shielded from the road by trees and with the sight of the six, huge cooling towers of the Drax Power Station belching plumes of white steam into the clear, moonlit sky.

Crossing the road, he made his way down onto the banks of the River Derwent, taking cover in some bramble bushes, which gave him an undistracted view of the buildings. Removing his Accolade thermal imaging binoculars from his backpack, he zoomed in on the buildings. He saw there were no cars in the car park and no lights on anywhere, so he carefully made his way towards the entrance. Spotting an alarm box high on the side wall, he thought it best not to force a door, but as he was walking around to the back of the first building, a door opened.

Tom, fortunately, was stood by a stack of wooden pallets and swiftly dropped behind them. He heard the footsteps walking towards him and heard the man light a cigarette. Hidden in the darkness and motionless, he held his breath as the man casually walked past him. He was only a pace away when Tom leapt up, with one hand over the man's mouth, knocking the cigarette to the floor, the other around his neck, shutting off the carotid artery. In a few seconds, his legs gave way and Tom lowered him onto the ground. Using gaffer tape and cable ties he trussed and gagged him, before making his way to the unlocked door.

Once inside, shinning his torch through the darkness, he was surprised to see two container lorries that appeared to have been partially dismantled. The cabs, which were separated from the trailers, had their doors taken off and the inside door panels removed, as were the roof linings, dashboards and seats. The trailers looked like they had secret compartments underneath, which had been lowered to the floor containing large packages wrapped in black plastic. There were similar packages on benches against the wall; in total, he counted over forty of them. Some had been opened to reveal smaller parcels inside of what Tom knew to be drugs. This was a much better result than he had hoped for; there must be at least a couple of million pounds' worth. But, just as he was thinking that he heard movement behind him, he spun round and there was a large man in the darkness, holding what appeared to be a shotgun.

CHAPTER 41

"Don't move and lift your hands, or I shoot you – understand?"

Thinking quickly and remembering what he had learnt from the phones, Tom replied, "Yes, I understand and you can lower the gun. Józef sent me to test the security; well done, that's very good. Now, how about a drink?"

The man looked confused and unsure what to do.

So, Tom continued with, "Where's the other one? There's meant to be two of you here?"

"He just go out for smoke, he back in minute."

"Well, lower the fucking gun, then; if you aren't sure about me, call Józef."

He began to do as he was told but still looked unsure.

"You don't have his number, do you? That's OK, I thought you might not; you can use my phone, it's an Encro." Without waiting for approval, Tom casually began to reach into his jacket.

"Stop! You think I am stupid, reach with your left hand."

Tom thought, 'Well, that *will* make it easier,' and smiled. "No worries, whatever you say," and used his left hand to get the phone.

"Throw it to me."

"Are you fucking joking? These things cost over three grand if you break it; they will take it out on you and your family back home. Don't be such a pussy, just take it." Offering it in his left hand, he lowered it slightly, causing the man to let go of the shotgun with his left hand and look down to the phone, which left him completely open for a quick and solid right hook to his jaw. He was unconscious before he hit the ground. Tom swiftly pulled out his Glock 19, firing instantly – the first shot to the centre of the man's head, the second hitting his chest.

Tom turned away without a second thought. These people had tried to kill Dan and God knows what they might have done to Sue, so they deserved no sympathy.

Finding the switches, he turned on the lights and was able to see clearly what was here. After checking what must be the staff room and office, he found two further rooms converted into bedrooms, which must be where the men stayed.

He went outside and dragged the unconscious man back inside. He searched both men, taking phones and IDs and in the office he took pictures of documents and found a large set of keys. On the wall was a sheet of paper with the pass codes for each warehouse.

Taking the keys, he made his way out and around to the next warehouse. From the outside it was identical to the other and, after a couple of attempts, he found the correct key and went in, entering the code into the bleeping alarm. Turning on the lights, there was a freezer trailer with its back doors open containing orange net sacks of onions. Next was a tautliner truck with plastic curtain sides that were pulled back to reveal pallets with drums of cooking oil. Just looking around, it was plain to see that both were concealing drugs. There were bins filled with the brown outer skin of the onions next to a bench stacked with ball-shaped packages of white powder wrapped in clingfilm. On the other side were lines of the cooking oil drums, some with the tops cut off them and in the oil were wrapped bags of drugs. Again, Tom was amazed at how much it must all be worth.

He couldn't wait to check the third warehouse, but once he was in he was taken aback by the awful smell. There were ten empty containers spaced around the room; most had their doors open, the insides littered with old clothes and reeking of stale urine and human excrement. But one had its doors closed. Carefully pulling them open, he was forced back for a second when the putrid smell really hit him, making his eyes water. Inside were five naked bodies, some curled up in foetal positions and a couple just in a tangled mess where they had been dumped. From the smell and their putrefied green and purple colour, they had all been dead for a few days.

Tom turned away and retched. He had lost count many years ago of the number of deaths and corpses he had seen, but this was something else – these weren't soldiers, terrorists or gang members. With the bodies decomposing it was hard to age them. There were two males, neither older than teenagers and three females, one who looked pubescent and the other two not much more than teens. Once again, he was enraged at the callous and cold-blooded nature of this evil gang. There was nothing he could do for these poor souls but would do all in his power to bring justice for them.

Once he had made his way back to the first warehouse, he grabbed the first man and slapped him around his face to bring him round. Ripping the tape from his mouth, he showed him his workmate dead on the floor.

Holding the Glock to the man's head, he said, "See him? Well, unless you tell me what I want to know, you'll be next, do you understand? Who is your boss?"

The man just looked at him.

"You only get one chance to live, so tell me now – who do you report to? Who is your boss?"

The man continued to stare, then spat in Tom's face and said quietly, "If I tell you, they will kill me. I have no fear of death and am proud to be Albanian, a Shqiptare and will happily die for the oath of Besa," and he spat again. This time, Tom fired the pistol against the man's temple and blood and brains flew everywhere as Tom let him fall to the floor.

Picking up his backpack, knowing that his supply of C-4 was getting low and that he would soon need to get more from his dark web contact, he made four smaller than normal charges and added slow burning fuses to them. He taped one against each of the trucks' fuel tanks. He then ran to the second warehouse and set charges in the rear of the truck with the oil drums, the other against the fuel tank of the refrigerated truck. He would leave the third warehouse intact for the authorities to find. He then opened the huge roller doors; he wanted the fire and explosion to be seen and lit the fuses. Speeding back to the first one, he lit those fuses, grabbed his backpack and ran back to his car. He drove back fast along the A63, passing a sign for the village of Howden. He pulled to the side of the road and turned to see the flames shoot into the air across the flat countryside. Using a burner, he called the emergency services to inform them of the explosion he had seen just off the main road. He ended the call when asked for his details and removed the SIM card, which he broke in two. Pulling out on the road again, he threw the pieces out of the window, one at a time, over a mile apart and by the time he was back on the M62 he saw two police cars and two fire engines racing in the opposite direction.

It was just after 4 am when he returned to his house. The effects of the previous forty-eight hours were starting to take effect; his mind wanted him to check for further news from Mongoose, but his body said to take a good hot shower and get some sleep. Which is what he did.

CHAPTER 42

It hadn't been a good day for Agron and Józef Sefiri and it seemed things were getting worse. Following their conversation that afternoon, where Aleksander had argued that he didn't want to be at the farm and should be back in London, Józef had called him time and time again on his Encro phone with no reply; he also tried both the Tanush twins, with the same result. He sensed that something had gone wrong and dispatched men to get to the farm to see what had happened.

It was dark by the time the two men arrived. Driving slowly down the drive with headlights on full beam, they could see the smashed windows at the front of the house. They pulled up next to the Transit. Both carrying powerful flashlights on them, they climbed out of the car and drew their pistols. Scanning the beam towards the front porch, they lit up a group of rats gnawing on something by the front door. As they approached, the rats scattered and, looking closer, they could see the chewed remains of a man's arm. They slowly walked into the house with the flashlights moving in sync with their guns, scanning first the stairs and then the front room. There were bloodstains everywhere and the walls were riddled with bullet holes.

After checking the rest of the house – the barn and the air raid shelter – they called Józef and told him the situation and that there was no sign of anyone apart from the half-eaten arm. He told them to check in the sties for bodies. It didn't take them long to find what was left of the four bodies.

It was after 10 pm by the time they called back with the news of the bodies. Józef was upset – Aleksander was not only family but had been a good friend for most of his life.

Agron was sat at his desk, looking concerned. Józef informed him of what had happened and asked if they should bring the remains of the bodies back, but he said it was too late for that. He asked for them to come back as they would need to send someone from one of their other farms to run the place; it was too useful to give up.

Józef ended the call and walked to the drinks cabinet taking out a bottle of Raki, two long glasses and a bottle of mineral water. Pouring large measures, he handed a glass to Agron who stood. They looked at each other and raised their glasses to Aleksander. *Shoku im Zoti ju bekofte brohritje* – 'Goodbye my friend, God bless you'. They finished their drinks and Józef sat down opposite his brother.

Agron slammed his fist down onto the desk, sending the empty glass tumbling onto the floor and smashing. "We can't let this go on. Aleks was like a brother to us. As important as it was to make them pay for Reni and Armend, this takes it to another level. I want them all to pay and pay dearly."

Walking to the drinks cabinet he grabbed a new glass, filled it and took a large gulp of it. Sitting down again he continued talking.

"None of it makes sense. Yes, the police were after Reni, for the girl's murder, but there is no way the police would have done this at the farm, to get the copper's wife. Then there was the cannabis factory near Harlow getting blown up – how can this be linked? But perhaps it is, I just can't get my head round it. At least Davies has been taken care of in Belmarsh, so he can't grass on us."

Shaking his head in bewilderment, he continued, "The police have been all over the restaurant. I don't think there was anything there to link back to us, especially with Aleks gone, but we can't use it again."

Józef nodded and said, "I agree. It can't be another gang for they wouldn't care about the copper's wife. I seriously think we need to bring in more men. We can get men in from Amsterdam by tomorrow night, but I am tempted to bring in a team from Tirana; we need to take revenge and we need to stop this once and for all."

Agron agreed. "And we will make the calls to bring in more men – someone wants war and they will get it!"

CHAPTER 43

Agron and Józef finally got to bed sometime after 2 am, but Józef was woken up by his phone ringing at 6.30 am. He listened carefully, telling the caller he would get back to him. Climbing out of bed and pulling on his dressing gown, he walked to his brother's bedroom, knocked on the door and entered, calling his name. Agron woke instantly and sitting up, he asked what was wrong.

"Dardan, who runs the Hull warehouses has just called. He has a local cop on the payroll who has told him that they were broken into last night. The two holding consignments of heroin were destroyed by explosions and fire. The heroin was worth over three million and losing it will cause big problems in the supply chain, which is going to upset a lot of people. The third wasn't damaged, but the police found five bodies that should have been taken to the farm to be dumped over a week ago and dirty containers where we had been holding the last consignment of bodies – at least they had all been distributed. We had two men living there and they have both been shot, in what looks like a professional hit."

"For fuck's sake, this is never ending; why didn't Dardan get the bodies dumped? Tell him to cut all ties with the place; get away from there and come back to London. While you're doing that, I am going to call Luan – he needs to get on his computer and make sure there is no way to trace anything back to us from Harlow or Hull. They won't know about the pig farm so we can at least still use that."

They spent the next hour making plans to try and cover the supply chain. Fortunately, they had two larger warehouses filled with drugs, one in Essex not far from the Lakeside Shopping Centre and one in Rotterdam, but they could quickly get supplies into the country. With all of this to deal with, Agron called his personal assistant at his shipping company, telling her he had picked up a stomach bug and to cancel all of his meetings for the day.

He had just finished the call when his Encro phone bleeped. The caller ID showed it was Mehmet Ligor, someone he would rather not talk to, but it was best that he did.

Answering the call, he said, "Mehmet Sabah şerifleriniz hayrolsun – 'May your blessed morning be full of goodness'. What do I owe such an early call to my friend?"

Mehmet was a few years younger than Agron, but to see the two of them you would have thought he was ten years older. He was the owner of over one hundred takeaway food shops throughout London and the Home Counties, which were the centre of his drug selling empire. Although he was a multimillionaire, he still chose to live in a small, detached house in a side street in Southend and, unlike the Sefiri brothers, never showed any sign of his wealth.

In a deep growl of a voice, the result of years of smoking, he replied, "I am hearing much bad news. I am worried that you may be letting things slip, my friend, and that you may not be able to deliver on time. You have to know that if that's the case, then we have a big problem."

"Mehmet, in all the many years you have known me, have I ever let you down? No, I haven't and I won't now. Yes, there have been some problems, but they are being dealt with, as are those causing these problems. I don't like to say this, my friend, but you seem to know a lot about my business. If you know anything about who is behind these problems, it would be to your benefit to tell me."

"I know that someone stupidly tried to get a policeman killed in hospital and failed, so they kidnapped the man's wife and then had a bent policeman killed in Belmarsh. What I *do* know is that all of this ridiculous gangster activity will bring the eyes of the police on us all and that is no good for any of us. Take my advice – concentrate on business and it is an old but true saying – revenge is best served cold."

"Well, thank you for the advice, Mehmet, but I really don't need to be told how to run my business. I am totally isolated from the illegal side of my business and could buy you and your poxy shops out with the change in my office safe. I have always supplied you the best merchandise at the best price, which is why you deal with me, but listen carefully, my friend… don't cross me because you will live to regret it or will die before you have time to."

There was a long pause before he replied, "Yes, I have known you for a long time and I have never heard you act this way. You have always been a calm and reassuring man, which makes this outburst and these threats from you even more worrying. I was trying to help you and you should recognise that; if I hear anything that will help you, I will tell you, but please, for all our sakes, think carefully before you make any other plans for revenge."

With that the call ended, but Agron was far from happy. "Józef, you should have heard how that filthy Turkish kebab seller spoke to me. Who the fuck does he think he is telling me to concentrate on business and get revenge later? Fuck him! When I have dealt with this I will bring him down as well."

Józef walked over to place his hand on his brother's shoulder. "Agron, my brother, you know I would give my life for you, but this isn't the Agron Sefiri that built an empire; this is more like a backstreet mobster and that isn't you. If we knew who was behind this it would be different, but I think with the extra men we are bringing in, we need to put more guards on all of our businesses, make sure supplies aren't interrupted and then we can find who is doing this. It might even be the Turk for all we know and it will be easier to kill the copper in a month than it will in a week."

But Agron wasn't satisfied. "I understand what you are saying, I will compromise; the supplies shouldn't be a problem and I agree about the guards, but I *do* want the copper dealt with. We have to make a show of force to let everyone know we are in control or it won't just be the Turks, but the Russians, Jamaicans, the Somali Mali Boys and on and on – they will all try to grab a part of the business. We must show strength."

Agron concluded with, "I need to find out what is happening at the hospital. This is what I need you to do."

CHAPTER 44

The next two days had passed slowly at the hospital. Sue had been able to sleep there and be with Dan for most of the time. He was slowly improving, but had tried to get out of bed and became very giddy, almost passing out. The doctor said it was to be expected and would get better with time. Sue had a FaceTime call with her son, Andy, and was very happy that he was being well looked after by Julie Burton and a police guard, which he found exciting.

DS Laine had left that morning as his holiday was now over and he was needed back at the nick; DS Makubuya had travelled with him and they would both be covering for Dan for a while. Chief Superintendent Arthur Jackson had arrived in the afternoon, having brought some clothes for Dan. He would be staying at the hotel that night and travelling with them in the morning when Dan was discharged from the hospital to a safehouse.

Dan was upbeat about getting out of hospital, but naturally worried for Sue's safety after what had happened to her. She was very pleased about it all and was offering Dan bed baths at least twice a day.

DCI Callum West was co-ordinating the transfer from the hospital to the safehouse with CS Jackson and explained that they had special dispensation to be flown from the hospital at 5.30 am in a police helicopter, India 99, to the new Met Police Air Support Unit (ASU) HQ at the new North Weald site, which wasn't due to be open for a few more months, but had better access than the old Lippitts Hill base in Essex. From there, Dan and Sue would travel in a Range Rover with a driver and an armed guard, in convoy with two BMW X5 armed response vehicles, one in front, one behind. Their destination was to be a remote six-bedroomed farmhouse, a few miles south of Great Dunmow in Essex. It had been selected because it was secluded enough for security, but near enough for close colleagues to visit.

Both Arthur Jackson and Callum West left for the evening, both arranging to be back at 5 am in the morning. Dan was very tired, so Sue agreed they should turn in for the night with the early start the next day and, after packing her case, she got into bed and drifted off to sleep quickly.

CHAPTER 45

By the time Callum and Arthur had arrived just before five, Dan and Sue were dressed and ward sister Angie Day had given Dan his discharge documents and a course of painkillers. At 5.15 they started to make their way to the helipad. Dan wanted to walk, but Angie insisted he sit in a wheelchair, which Sue pushed. They all took the lift to the seventeenth floor, before having to walk up two steep ramps onto the actual helipad. It was a dark and cold morning and they were pleased they had winter coats on, but the view was amazing – looking across London they could see the lights of the Shard and even Big Ben on one side, with views of sparkling Canary Wharf on the other. Angie said that on a clear day you could see as far as the Queen Elizabeth II Bridge at Dartford. The yellow and black Eurocopter EC145 with Metropolitan Police emblazoned on the side, was waiting for them.

Callum and Angie said their goodbyes, with the DCI telling Dan that he would keep him informed of any updates. They were introduced to the civilian pilot and the two tactical flight officers, or TFOs. They were seated on board, with their seat belts and headphones on, as the pilot ran through his pre-flight safety checks, before lifting off into the dark, wintery sky. Soon, they turned ninety degrees and began the 15-minute journey to North Weald. Hearing it was Sue's first helicopter trip, the pilot helpfully pointed out some of the lit landmarks such as the Olympic Park and a host of new skyscrapers around Stratford, on their right-hand side. They followed the line of the A12, passing Leyton and Leytonstone, which made Sue think of Smudger, and how grateful she was to him and Poacher. They were soon flying above the M11, over open fields with only darkness surrounding them until, and in no time, they were crossing above the M25. A couple of minutes later they descended onto an airfield next to the Essex & Herts Air Ambulance base. As their landing progressed, they could see the convoy of police cars waiting for them, watching the landing.

As Dan climbed down from the helicopter, thanking the crew, he was met by an old friend, Inspector Simon Nunney, an authorised firearms officer and former Operation Desert Storm veteran.

The inspector smiled and greeted him with, "So, I hear I need to nursemaid you; what's the world coming to?" and with that he gave Dan a gentle hug.

Dan replied, "I just wanted to keep you busy, mate, thought you might be slowing down at your age!"

They both laughed and Simon said, "Seriously, Dan, really sorry for what's happened to you and Sue and I wanted to make sure I was here to keep an eye on you both. I've got my best men here for you, so let's get this show on the road."

After that they loaded up, CS Jackson travelling in the front ARV. Dan and Sue were in the back of the Range Rover with Simon in the front, followed by the other X5 ARV.

It was still a couple of hours before dawn as Inspector Nunney confirmed all his men were linked on their Airways coms units and signalled for them to move out. The first few hundred yards off of the airfield, were down a narrow, private driveway past a care home, with the blue flashing lights of the ARVs lighting up all around them.

Simon explained they had mapped the route carefully; the journey should only take about twenty minutes and not all would be taken on main roads. Turning right onto the A414 Chelmsford to Harlow road, traffic was very light as the convoy kept at a steady 60 mph, in close formation, preventing any car getting between them.

After five miles they turned left onto a smaller B road and then slowed down through the village of Fyfield. After speeding up again, they came up behind a farm tractor towing a wide seed drill, which slowed them back to under 30 mph. Simon told the lead driver not to overtake as they may get split up; the tractor driver seemed oblivious to the flashing lights and now there was a motorbike and a truck slowly catching up from behind. So, everyone was relieved when he finally indicated to turn right at the next junction.

What happened next took less than ninety seconds but would feel like hours to those involved.

CHAPTER 46

The tractor slowly started to turn but appeared to have misjudged it and was stuck, blocking the road, with the convoy having no choice but to come to an abrupt stop right behind it.

Simon began to order everyone to remain alert but hadn't finished speaking when an HGV container lorry sped out from the road on the right-hand side, smashing into the first ARV, crushing the side and pushing it off the road.

At the same time, the passenger in the HGV opened up with automatic fire on the Range Rover, shattering the windscreen, with bullets ripping into Simon and the driver.

Dan screamed at Sue to get down and pushed her into the back footwell. He reached across the driver's already dead body to grab his Heckler & Koch submachine-gun to return fire through the broken windscreen, hitting the HGV passenger.

At the same time, the approaching truck slammed into the rear ARV, sending it into the back of the Range Rover.

The motorbike pulled up next to the ARV and the rider pulled out a pistol, firing a volley of shots into the driver and passenger, before moving forward to the Range Rover.

Dan, seeing the man at his door, fired a burst of bullets through the side window, hitting him in his chest and smashing through the visor on his helmet. Bullets exploded on the back window above Dan's head, from the truck driver who was now out in the road.

Dan told Sue again to keep down and not move as she lay there shaking with fear and realised he had no alternative but to try and take the initiative.

Opening the back nearside passenger door, he slid over Sue and rolled out onto the road.

Looking under the vehicle, he could see the truck driver walking towards them and Dan sprayed bullets across his pathway, hitting him in his shins. He collapsed, screaming, to the floor.

Crawling to the back of the Range Rover, Dan could see the man lying in the road and fired another burst into his body just in case, but then realised he had used up all the thirty rounds in the magazine.

By now, both the tractor and HGV drivers were out of their cabs, firing round after round into the first ARV, as one of the officers was trying to climb out of it.

Dan told Sue not to worry as he reached in to grab Simon's H&K and the Glock, which he put in his trouser pocket. Keeping low, he scrambled around the back of the Range Rover and, again, looking under it, could see the feet of one of the gunmen. He opened fire, hitting him, then leaning around his vehicle he fired again as the man was already falling to the floor.

Realising he was the only one left, the tractor driver climbed up into the cab of the HGV as Dan walked forward and emptied the thirty rounds of this magazine into the cab, blasting holes in the passenger door and hitting the man, but not killing him. Dan dropped the H&K, pulled out the Glock and, climbing up onto the cab step, fired a double tap into the man's head.

Suddenly, everything was eerily quiet, but the smell of cordite filled the air. Dan checked all the assailants were dead and ran to check on Sue who was sobbing as he sat her back up in her seat.

"It's over, darling, you're safe, but we can't stay here, there must have been a tip-off – we can't trust anyone." Holding her tight, he helped her out of the car and sat her on the grass verge. "I have to check on the others, so stay here." And he went first to check on the Chief Super in the first ARV. He was still held in by his seatbelt, behind the driver – the impact of the collision had crushed the right-hand side of his body and the side of his head, which hung down at an unnatural angle. He had also suffered numerous bullet wounds. It sickened Dan to see his boss and good friend's life end this way – after all, he was only there to make sure Sue and Dan were safe. After checking that the other officers were dead, he went back to Simon Nunney who had been hit in the head and chest; at least he would have died instantly, as had the driver. He finally checked the other officers and, sadly, none of them had lived.

He took Simon's radio and called for help. "This is DCI Dan Hooper. I was being escorted from North Weald Airfield to a safehouse and we have come under attack – seven officers killed, including CS Jackson and five assailants dead. We are just north of the village of Fyfield." He ended the call and reached into the rear ARV, taking another H&K that he slung over his shoulder and took both of the dead officers' Glocks. Dragging the dead motorbike rider out from under the bike and standing it up on its rest, he went to Sue, gently helping her up. "Listen, darling, we have to get away from here now; they are bound to have backup nearby. Trust me, I will get us away but we have to use the motorbike. I need you to be brave and hold on tight to me." Sue nodded, looking terrified.

They climbed onto the bike and Dan slowly threaded it between the HGV and the tractor. Turning to Sue, he called out, "Here we go, hold tight, darling." Dan didn't know where to go but knew they had to get away quickly. His first mission was to get some miles between him and the ambush, while watching carefully for any other vehicles, in case they were the gangs' backup or police, because he knew there must be a mole somewhere and he couldn't trust anyone, apart from a few very special people. Fortunately, they didn't pass anyone. After five minutes, the cold winter's morning air was eating into him and he guessed the same for Sue as well and was scared of her going into shock. Looking for somewhere to stop, hide and take stock of the situation as calmly as he could, he was pleased when he arrived at a T junction with a main road. Turning right, he soon found a single-track sheltered drive leading into some trees.

Pulling in, he parked the bike and helped Sue off. Standing there, they hugged and Sue didn't want to let go. Still trembling, she said, "I can't believe all those people died and we are still alive. Poor Arthur and Simon; who are these evil bastards?"

Dan just held her and said, "You have to listen to me, Sue. As hard as it is, our only thought must be to keep safe and get away from here as soon as we can safely do so. I promise you we will get out of this." He cleared an area on the ground under a tree, laid his coat down and told Sue to sit there to try to keep warm, he had some things to do. Jogging painfully back to the start of the drive, he pulled a small branch off a tree and swept the tyre marks away. Checking his watch, it amazed him that it was only just over a half-hour since the helicopter landed. Taking out his phone, he rang the only person he knew could help, Tom Windsor, who answered on the second ring. He may have been asleep but in an instant was wide awake. "Dan, what's wrong?" Dan quickly explained the situation and his rough location. Tom asked him to send a pin drop of his exact location. Tom continued, "Knowing you, I'm sure it's a good location but it will take me almost two hours to get there. I'm going to call Smudger from Leytonstone, he could be there in forty minutes. Will you be OK until then?"

"Yes, we will be fine; I'm armed but I don't think anyone will find us here. Just get here as soon as you can." Finishing the call he then called Bronco and again explained the latest developments. Bronco was shocked but listened carefully as Dan asked him to call Callum West and explain that he and Sue were safe but were going into hiding on their own until the mole was found. He wasn't prepared to let anyone else put their life on the line to protect them, they would do it for themselves. But he also wanted Bronco to get Andy and keep him safe somewhere. Dan promised he would be in touch shortly with a plan.

Dan then lay down next to Sue who was still cold but had stopped shaking. "It's OK, help is on the way – hopefully Smudger and then Tom. Just try to keep calm, the worst is over now. Bronco is getting Andy and we will arrange to meet up with him later. Just try to rest until they get here." They cuddled together and as Dan turned onto his side his head started to spin like it had in the hospital. He sat up slowly, holding his head and he suddenly felt very tired as the adrenaline drained from his body. He gradually lay down again and instantly fell asleep.

CHAPTER 47

He must have been asleep for about twenty minutes when Sue woke him.

"Dan, quickly – someone's coming."

Opening his eyes, his vision a bit blurred, he replied, "It will be Smudger – that was quick." But looking up, he was shocked to see a man walking out from the trees pointing a machine-gun at them.

In a thick Albanian accent, he shouted, "Let me see your hands now, else I shoot you both. Quick, hands up and then stand up slow, or you dead."

Once again, Dan could see how scared Sue was. He smiled, trying to reassure her and they both stood up.

The man with the gun laughed and said, "So, you are the copper who thinks he's clever and likes to kill Albanians. Well, Mr Policeman, you not so clever. You wonder how I find you? It's easy, we have your phone number and track you here, like tracking deer in the forest, but they wouldn't be asleep on the floor waiting to be killed like you are. We were told to bring you alive because the boss wants you to pay for killing many of his family. He pay ten thousand pounds for you alive, or five thousand dead. At first I thought alive, but I have seen what you have done today, so think the five thousand will do. Maybe I get a bonus for killing your wife first, then I fuck her dead body after I kill you." While he was speaking, Dan was assessing the situation when a shot suddenly rang out and the man's head exploded, as Smudger appeared from behind the trees holding his Barrett M95, still pointing it at the body. Looking up at Dan, he said, "Fucking good job I didn't stop for breakfast on the way," and laughed. "You need to take your SIM card out and destroy it and we need to move away from here." He then walked over to hug Sue after what she had just witnessed, as Dan dealt with his phone.

"Right, let's get you two away from here sharpish, just in case. You can call Poacher on my phone once we're moving." Smudger kept his pistol in his hand while Dan picked up his coat and took out a Glock as they walked out to the black Range Rover Sport, leaving the dead body on the ground with the machine gun. Dan would let Bronco know about it later.

Wanting to keep out of the way as best he could, Smudger drove through the country lanes to Great Dunmow and parked at the rear of The Saracens Head hotel off the High Street. He called Poacher and told him where they were and that the hotel was open for breakfast, so he was going to take them in and at least get some coffee in them. Poacher informed him his ETA should be about thirty minutes.

Dan then called Bronco, who had passed on all the information about the attack and was now with Andy. "Listen, mate, these guys are very dangerous and appear to know too much of what's going on, so could you take Andy to Braintree? We will look for a place to meet and let you know – just be very careful you're not being followed."

Walking through from the car park into the back door of the hotel, Smudger was on high alert, but was relieved the place was empty. They just ordered coffees to start but after the first cup, all felt a bit more relaxed so Smudger ordered the full English, Dan the scrambled eggs on sourdough, while Sue could only face toast. They had just started eating when Poacher arrived. Giving Dan and Sue a hug, he ordered the full English as well and they quietly went over the morning's events, before making their plans for the rest of the day.

Between bites of his breakfast, Poacher laid out his plan. "The sooner I can get you two away from here, the better – your pictures could soon be on every TV channel and newspaper, so we can't check you into a hotel – the safest place is back at mine as there is no way they can trace you to there. I think it's best if Smudger gets Andy and then brings him to mine. At least once we are there, we can assess the situation again, but this isn't going to go away until these people are dealt with properly."

Checking the maps on his phone, he turned to Dan and advised him, "Tell Bronco to meet at the Holiday Inn Express, it's at the junction of the A120 and A131. But it's important that we don't tell him yet where you are going. I know you can trust him, but we need to be so careful."

They finished eating and made their way out to the car park. Tom opened the boot of his Audi and took out two burner phones, giving one to each man, saying, "Smudger, we need to lose your SIM card, so take this for now and I'm sorry, Sue, but we need to lose yours as well. I will give you another phone back at the house, but for now it's not safe to keep it."

Dan made the call to Bronco who advised he could be there in thirty minutes, not asking any questions about where they were going, but he did let Dan know that there was a shitstorm going on with the police and even anti-terrorist officers at the site of the ambush – the press were all over it. He had been in touch with DCI West who in turn had contacted Chief Superintendent Fox, who was liaising with the National Crime Agency. Questions were being asked about Dan's whereabouts, but it was agreed for him to keep as low-key as possible and that they keep his name away from the press until they could find the mole.

Poacher gave his address to Smith and warned him to

be very careful and to watch out for any tails. His reply was, "I've got eyes in the back of my head; you don't need to worry about me."

CHAPTER 48

Both cars set off onto the A120, one travelling eastbound to Braintree and the other westbound to join the M11 for the return journey to Northampton. By the time they were passing Cambridge, Sue had drifted off to sleep, while Dan could feel his energy fading away again and became drowsy, his mind filling with thoughts of Arthur Jackson and Simon Nunney.

By 10 am they were pulling into Tom's driveway. Opening the front door and turning off the alarm, he helped Dan and Sue out of the car and gave them a brief guided tour of the house. He bought a five-bedroomed house for the extra room, not because he was anticipating entertaining house guests; in fact, no one else had ever set foot in the place since he owned it.

He was pouring them all a large mug of coffee when they heard Smudger's Range Rover Sport pull up outside. Sue ran to the front door as Andy climbed down from the car, laughing. She threw her arms around her son and said, "Andy, it's so good to see you, but what are you laughing at?"

Andy grinned and looked at Smudger. "It's OK, Sue, I may have been telling him a few army tales to pass the time, haven't I, Tommo?" he replied while roughing the boy's hair.

The boy replied, "Yes, Smudger."

Sue looked puzzled. "What's this 'Tommo' nonsense?"

"It's my army nickname, Mum. Smudger said I am in his unit so needed one."

Still looking puzzled she said, "So, what's Dan's nickname then?"

"Oh, he's Hoops, Mum. It's Poacher, Hoops, Smudger and Tommo in this unit."

She smiled back and said, "Don't you start misleading my son, Smudger Smith, or you'll have me to answer to." And with that she wrapped her arms around her son and walked him into the house as everybody laughed.

Sue and Andy sat chatting, while the men went up to the office. Tom turned to Smudger and said, "You're most welcome to stay here if you want, but if you need to get back to London, that's fine."

"No, I'll stay – if the Captain is still in danger, then I'm here to help."

Dan patted him on his back. "Thanks, Staff."

"The thing you both need to understand is that it's going to get even nastier from now on. I was hunting whoever is behind all of this before they attacked Dan as I was following leads on human trafficking. I intend to find them and deal with them." He then went on to tell them about the hacker in Mumbai and what he had found out about the size of the operation, from people smuggling and sex workers, to drug smuggling, money laundering and protection racketeering.

Smith was the first to speak. "Well, I think we made a good team in finding Sue, so you can count me in. I'm game for whatever you've got in mind."

"So am I," agreed Dan, but the other two both spoke at the same time, "No, you're not!"

Tom continued, "You need to get yourself healed and fit first, Dan, there is loads of stuff you can do here and it would be wrong to leave Sue and Andy alone for the time being. Let me see if any more info has come in from Mumbai." Switching over to the burner phone he used for Mongoose, he saw he had a WhatsApp message. "Yes, he has been in touch, so I have to log into somewhere a bit delicate and afterwards we can brainstorm some ideas. But first, let's check the news, we need to know what's being said but we don't want Andy seeing any of it."

So, Tom logged onto Google News and the main headlines were, *'Shootout in Essex, Seven Police and Six Gunmen Dead.'* The press obviously didn't know any more and were even questioning if it was terrorist-related.

Tom was then left to log into the dark web and the secret website he used to correspond via the draft folder, while the other two made their way back downstairs.

There were two more files with more names and addresses and some transcripts of EncroChat calls, including the one between Agron and Mehmet. There was a message with it, which stated, "I have traced one of the parties, he is Mehmet Ligor. I have sent you all his business details; he is a big player in narcotics. I cannot find out who the other party is but will keep searching. I think you are on a crusade and am happy to help as much as I can. Fight The Good Fight, My Friend."

Tom began to scan through the pages but thought it best to print them all off in triplicate so the others could also study them. There were a lot of details to go through and he knew they had to be extra careful the further they went with this but, no matter what, he had no intention of stopping.

He took the printouts down to the others, saying, "I think you will find these very interesting. Have a good read, I am going to shoot out; I don't have much food here and don't want any of you going out. Sainsbury's is only fifteen minutes away, but I'll stock right up. Tommo, what are your favourites? Anyone want anything special?" They all called out their choices and, once that was sorted, he left them to it. With both men reading carefully through the printouts and making notes as they went through, they hardly spoke to each other, they were so engrossed with what they were reading.

Tom was back within the hour and had at least ten bags of shopping, which Andy and Sue came to help him unpack. Smiling at Sue, he said, "I am told you are an incredibly good cook, Sue, and have tons of catering experience. Could I leave you in charge of the food? If it were left to me all we would get would be bacon sandwiches."

"Flattery will get you a long way, Poacher. Of course I will and it will give me something to focus on; just leave it with me."

While Andy helped Sue sort out in the kitchen, the men went up to the office.

"So, what evil plans have you thought up while I've been to Sainsbury's?"

Dan replied, "Well, Poacher, first of all, this info is brilliant. I don't want to know how much it's cost you, but it's dynamite. After talking it over and us realising it's such a large organisation, it's going to be almost impossible to take it all down on our own. But with the details of this Mehmet guy and how he is upset with the other person who, it appears, is one of the top guys, it might be easy to turn them against each other."

"That's a great idea. What do you think, Smudger?"

"I like it; let them start taking each other out. If this other bloke is the top man he won't just be supplying the Turks. Let's stir them all up; if he has a war on his hands it will stop them worrying about Dan. We have the addresses of all the Turks' takeaways; there must be about a hundred, so he must have storage somewhere to supply them all. If we can find the storage and take it out, along with as many of his shops as we can, all in one night, it will really fuck him up and start a shitstorm."

"Right, let me get back on to the hacker and see if he can

find that out for us. I am going to need to get some more ordnance supplies; I am almost out of C-4 and I think we will need a fair bit. I may be able to pick that up tonight."

Dan was shocked and asked, "It really is that easy to get?"

"Dan, you would be amazed. There almost isn't anything you can't get these days, the country is full of it, but don't ask me where I get it from. I think I am going to be using it a lot over the next few weeks, so if you guys can leave me to it, I'll see what I can do."

Dan replied, "Yes, no worries. I really need to call Bronco and see what's happened."

While Dan was talking to Bronco, Tom was busy purchasing all the armaments he needed and was pleased that he could collect them later that day. He then left a message in the e-mail draft folder for Mongoose and asked for a quick reply.

Dan was waiting for him once he had finished on-line. "Bronco says that they have had a phone call from the Yard and I am to contact Assistant Commissioner Laura Harris, if possible, by video call or FaceTime so they can confirm that it's me. Obviously, they need a statement of exactly what happened. I have a phone number for FaceTime and an e-mail link for video call; what do you think?"

"A video call is safest with the VPNs I have set up here as no one can trace the IP address. When do they want to do it?"

"ASAP, if we can."

"OK, leave it with me. I'll just move a few things around, so nothing is on show that could link you to here. I will sort a link and you can text it to Laine, who can pass it on to them."

CHAPTER 49

AC Laura Harris had only recently been appointed to the post, having spent over twenty-five years in the force, starting off in West Midlands where she became its Head of CID, working with Counter-Terrorism and Organised Crime Units. Many thought that with her background she would end up in either MI5 or MI6.

Tom had re-arranged part of the office for the video call, with a black sheet hung across the room, blocking out all of the office. After showing Dan what to do, he left him to it.

Dan was nervous as he clicked on the link, which took a couple of seconds to connect, before AC Harris appeared on the screen.

She smiled before speaking, "Detective Chief Inspector Hooper, it's good to see you are in one piece after today's tragedy. I must first of all send you mine and the forces' sincere condolences at the loss of CS Jackson, I know you were both very close."

"Thank you, ma'am; yes, we were, he was a dear friend and a first-class policeman. Inspector Nunney was also a good friend, but the loss of all those men is, as you say, a tragedy and one that I take personal responsibility for as they were there to protect me and my wife."

"I understand completely, but you mustn't blame yourself. How is your wife handling it, especially after the kidnapping?"

"Surprisingly well, but there is still time for the shock to come out; she's a very special lady and we will get through this."

"That's good to hear. Now, obviously, we have ongoing investigations into what happened and, under normal circumstances you would be *here* providing a statement. Are you sure you don't want to come in and let us protect you?"

"With respect, ma'am, I don't. I can take care of myself and Sue and will come in as soon as I think it's safe to do so, but there has to be a mole somewhere in the force who leaked our plans for this morning."

"As much as it goes against the grain, I have to agree with you. In my mind, bent coppers are the lowest of the low. Just so you know, I have brought in a team from my old manor at West Midlands and given them carte blanche to find out who it is. Now, in place of a statement I would like to record this conversation and bring in Chief Superintendent Norman Fox and DCI West, both of whom you know, and would like you to talk us through all the events of the morning, right from the start. We will stop you if there is anything we need you to expand on. Is that OK?"

Dan replied that it was and spent the next twenty minutes recounting all the morning's events up to and including taking the motorbike and the last death.

DCI West was the first to speak. "Dan, first of all, thank God you and Sue are safe and, of course, my condolences for the losses as well. Now, I am assuming that from this point on you don't intend to give us any more details of where you went, etc, and I understand that. Could you think of anyone who may have been at the hospital paying attention to what was happening this morning, or hanging around last night?"

"I have racked my brains and I can't, but it would only take something said in a lift or canteen for plans to get out, but they wouldn't know things like routes – that has to have come from *inside* the job–"

AC Harris interrupted him. "OK, Dan, there is just one more thing that this has thrown up. We are assuming that we are dealing with a ruthless Albanian gang and we all know just how much of the country they have their filthy claws into, but HOLMES has thrown up a series of events recently, all appearing to be attacks on Albanian targets – human trafficking in Suffolk and Lincolnshire, drugs and more trafficking in Yorkshire and even buildings, vehicles and a boat being blown up. I am not sure of the body count but it's big and appears to be getting bigger almost daily. Do you, DCI Hooper, have any connection with any of these events or know anything about them or who is behind them?"

Dan's heart pounded, but he knew he had to keep calm. "No ma'am, not at all. Why would I?"

"OK, it's just that after all that has happened to you and your wife over the past few days, it's a hell of a lot of action and effort just because you were involved in a murderer getting killed in an RTA – road traffic accident. It just doesn't make sense to me…"

At that second, a thought flashed into Dan's head as the AC continued speaking. "So, again, if you can think of anything else at all, please let me know. In the meantime, take care of yourself and your wife. Feel free to keep in touch with DS Laine and let's hope we get to the bottom of this soon."

The connection was then broken and Dan quickly called to the other two. He told them all that had been said and then relayed the thought that he had.

"I can't believe I hadn't thought of it before – sometimes you're just too close, but something Laura Harris said sparked it. Just *why* would they go to all this trouble to get Sue and I if it were just one of their men that died in that crash? They wouldn't, would they? It must be someone close to whoever is at the top of this organisation. We need to find out more on Kotri's background; I bet he is a close relation to whoever *is* the boss, or why else would they cause all this trouble?"

The others both agreed and Tom said, "I will get my man onto it, but I have to go out later to get the much needed ordinance."

Dan and Smudger took the hint to leave him to it and then Dan went to see Sue, who jumped up off the sofa at the sight of her husband. "Well, Mr Hooper, I guess we will be sharing a bed again tonight, it could be like a second honeymoon."

Andy made a sound like being sick. "Mum, that's gross."

She replied, "Sorry, son, I forgot you were there. Who fancies a cuppa then?" she asked, trying to change the subject and they all laughed.

They were all sat around the table chatting and Sue was getting upset talking about Arthur Jackson. "He was such a lovely man, we will all miss him." Dan was about to answer when Tom came bounding down the stairs and called the guys over. "Sorry, Sue, but it's best we keep this away from you." Turning to Smudger, he said, "This guy can find anything – it would seem that Mehmet owns a small self-storage building in Southend; it only contains a few units, but there are no company records anywhere for it, so it would appear to have no customers – this may well be his main storage depot. He also has a bakery in Manor Park, Ilford, which has been closed to the public for four years, but he still pays business rates on it. I think that could be a distribution centre."

Smudger chuckled and said, "That's brilliant."

Tom continued. "So, while I'm out, could you two draw up a plan of attack, mapping in the self-storage and the bakery to include any of his shops we can safely get to in an hour; we don't want to look suspicious driving around

London in the early hours, but the more info we can get the better, to avoid ANPR and CCTV." Both Dan and Smudger agreed and disappeared into the office to start work while Tom prepared to collect his order.

CHAPTER 50

He took the VW Transporter as he felt much safer having everything hidden in its secret compartments. His journey wasn't going to be a long one, in fact, just a half-hour up the M1 to junction 21, a few miles south of Leicester and then circling around to cross the M1, heading out into open countryside before joining a maze of side roads and a dirt track. This led him to the entrance of a smallholding that was certainly not big enough to be called a farm, with signs at the closed gate – 'Cooney's Breakers' and 'Beware of the dogs'. He stopped at the gate and hit his horn five times. He waited for one minute before repeating the action, but this time just twice. At that point, an old army jeep bounced down the driveway with two men. One got out while the driver stayed in the cab. It was plain to see he was holding a submachine-gun. Unlocking the gate's padlock, he nodded at Tom and said, "You know where to go. Wait in your van at the compound." Tom drove up the drive as instructed while the gate was locked behind him and watched in his mirrors as the jeep turned around and followed him. The compound was filled with wrecked cars, many flattened and piled on top of each other up to five or six high. There was a Portakabin office that had seen better days and what looked like a workshop. The jeep stopped behind him and both men got out, holding guns. Tom had dealt with these guys in the past, so he wasn't worried; he knew this was their normal routine. An older guy, perhaps in his late sixties, who Tom knew as the boss, emerged from the office and waved Tom over to the far corner of the compound. Tom slowly drove over and was signalled to stop. The older man walked up to the van, opened the driver's door and, in a broad Irish accent spoke, "Good day to you, my friend. I have your order waiting here. Your payment has been received. You know, I do miss the days of getting a nice roll of fifties in my hand for every order, but this Bitcoin thing is very good and safe, don't you think?"

"Yes, it is, and it's safer for everyone. I'll open the back doors so we can put it straight in," and he tapped the hidden touchpad and the secret compartment opened.

While the two from the Jeep stood watching at a distance, the older man went to the boot of a flattened Bentley lookalike, a Chrysler 300. Taking keys from his overalls pocket, he opened the boot and lifted out two square, metal boxes that he handed to Tom, before retrieving two similar ones, followed by a longer box, all of which Tom took and placed in his van.

"Feel free to check the merchandise, my friend."

"No, that's fine; you won't let me down because you know I'll be back for more."

Closing the boot, he smiled to himself. As the man reached into the front of the car and took out a long, thin, brown paper parcel, which he handed to Tom, he replied, "That's the truth; you'll be back as long as you stay safe. That's not Play-Doh in them boxes but, to be sure – you know that anyway."

Tom finished loading, satisfied he had everything and climbed back into the van. The Jeep followed him to the gate where the same guy as before opened it to let him out.

CHAPTER 51

He was back at his house in half an hour, promptly loaded the boxes into his garage, before grabbing the parcel and going in to find out how the plans were coming on. As he walked into the house, the smell of cooking made his mouth water. "Something smells good, Sue."

She called back from the kitchen, "Chicken biryani; I hope you're hungry."

As he went up to the office, he replied, "Starving; it's been a long day, hasn't it?"

Dan and Smudger had Google Maps open on the computer and had drawn a rough map with addresses next to it on a pad. They both looked up and Dan asked how it had gone.

"Yes, fine; no problems. I've got more than enough for this mission. How are you doing?"

Smudger replied, "All good; so far we have pinpointed both places, the self-storage and the bakers. They are about 30 miles apart, but both the A127 and A13 are good roads so, either way, about forty-five minutes maximum travelling time at night. We have also picked five of his bigger takeaways in-between; there are a lot more smaller, but these look the best," and with that he handed Tom the list and map.

Tom was pleased. "That's good work and to make things easier, I have got these." Ripping the brown paper, he took out four pairs of number plates. "They are cloned from matching Transporters or Range Rover Sports, just in case we are caught on CCTV. We can sort the C-4 tomorrow, then we can hit them tomorrow night." Tom continued to look at the plans until Sue called them down for dinner.

After dinner, Dan had arranged with Bronco to have a video call with his team back at the nick the next morning. So, at just after 9 am with the black sheet set up again, he clicked on the link and the screen opened to show the office with Bronco, Tish and Brenda sat on chairs, with Stan and Jimmy seated at the desk behind them.

There was a happy but sad look about them all. They all agreed how pleased they were that Dan and Sue were alive and well, but understandably they were still mourning the death of their boss, Chief Superintendent Jackson. Even Stan Jones was in a serious mood and that was a first for him. It was actually Brenda who mentioned him first and, as she did, it hit Dan that with all the excitement and adrenaline of the previous day, he had pushed the deaths of his boss and good friend to the back of his mind and instantly felt huge floods of guilt and grief wash over him. Fighting to keep his emotions under control, he asked what they were working on and Tish explained that with the death of Kotri, Operation Silverfern was being closed; the NCA were dealing with the attack and were just catching up on paperwork. She continued, "If there is anything you need, or anything we can do, Guv, just let us know."

Dan forced a smile as he replied, "Thanks, Tish, and thanks to all of you. We will be fine; I am resting and healing and Sue is taking good care of me. I hope you all understand the reason for such secrecy and it certainly isn't because I think I can't trust any of you. Hopefully, I will be back soon." After that, they all said their goodbyes. Dan sat for a while thinking of Arthur Jackson, Simon Nunney and all the other officers who had lost their lives trying to protect him and

Sue. Tom joined him in the office and could see something wasn't right, so they sat talking and Dan explained his feelings.

Tom listened to all that Dan had to say and replied, "I understand completely and that's the reason why we have to attack the ones at the top – they can't be allowed to get away with this. I have been having a go at them but, after tonight, it won't just be us after them."

The men spent the morning going over the routes and plans for that night and it was agreed that they would take their own vehicles fitted with the cloned plates, but hit the self-storage together, then split up to hit various shops before rendezvousing to deal with the bakers in Manor Park.

All three men had been trained in setting explosives, but Tom had the most recent experience, so he took charge with the other two assisting. He made a few larger charges, along with some smaller ones, so as not to cause collateral damage. By 5 pm, they had everything they needed for the night ahead.

Sue had, again, cooked a delicious dinner and afterwards, both Tom and Smudger retired to their rooms for a few hours' sleep, agreeing to wake at midnight and be on the road by half past, giving them an ETA of about 2 am, which should be perfect for their mission.

CHAPTER 52

Sue and Andy had gone to bed, but Dan had no intention of sleeping until the night's mission was done. Tom and Smudger were both dressed in all-black, but Tom had provided hi-viz vests for them both to wear for the journey, making them look more like delivery drivers or couriers. They set off at 12.20 am, driving south on the M1, turning onto the M25 clockwise and, once in Essex, they took a left onto the A127, all the way into Southend.

The self-store was situated at an old 1950s industrial site not far from London Southend Airport. There were eight single storey buildings of various sizes housing car repairs, a double-glazing company, a physio and a second-hand tyre dealer, all looking in poor repair. The largest building was A1 Self-Store, situated at the far side of the site.

They were in contact via burner phones and Tom said he would do a drive-through to check if there was anyone about. After ensuring it was clear, they drove up to the side of the store. A quick recce showed an alarm box on the wall. Smudger smiled and said, "I'll deal with that," and Tom passed him the collapsible portable ladder that would extend from a metre to almost fifteen metres, along with a can of builders' expanding foam, which he sprayed into the alarm box. They put the ladder away and waited for the foam to set.

Laying out the explosives, they each took two packs already linked with fuses. Choosing to avoid the front door,

Tom took a large crowbar and broke the padlock on the side door, then jemmied it open. They agreed they needed to be in and out in under five minutes, so they both entered the building swiftly and in military fashion, their high-powered torches lighting the corridor showing storage units down the far side. After checking throughout the building, Tom started to break open the unit doors, but as he opened the first one, they could see that most of the dividing walls had been removed, making one long room. With tables fixed to the far wall, it was obvious it was used for breaking down packages of drugs into various smaller sized parcels. There was at least fifty kilograms of cocaine, worth in the region of five million pounds. Tom began to place larger charges by the load-bearing walls, while Smudger forced open the final remaining unit. Inside were two long tables with banknote counting machines, piles of the bank currency strips that banks put around notes and rolls of clingfilm. Stacked in the corner were four, large, sealed cardboard boxes. Taking a penknife from his pocket, Smudger cut open the top of the box to discover it was filled with clingfilm-wrapped bundles of fifty-pound notes. He called Tom over and opened the second box that contained the same. Sneaking a quick look, Tom said, "There could be a couple of mill there. We'll take that, it can fund the next mission."

As Tom finished laying the charges, Smudger took the boxes to the van and as he was loading the second box, Tom came out and said, "All done. We have ten minutes to get as far away as possible – job well done, on to the next ones." Just as he finished speaking, a van with its full headlights on came speeding into the area, skidding to a stop. A man jumped out attempting to fire a pistol at them, but his bullets went wide, hitting the side of the building, but in a split second both of them returned fire, their bullets hitting the man in his chest and head.

Realising the clock was ticking, they quickly dragged his body into the building, got into their vehicles and drove away. By the time the building exploded, sending a small fortune of cocaine into the Southend night air, Tom was turning off the A127 into Basildon where, just past the station, he pulled in behind a row of shops. After he forced the back door of the takeaway open, he carefully walked in, placed a charge by the deep fat chip fryer, which he switched on and promptly left. At the same time, Smudger, who had taken the A13 to Pitsea, was doing something very similar in a takeaway behind the market.

They simultaneously continued on their routes with Tom taking a slight detour to targets in Brentwood and then Romford, while Smudger paid visits to takeaway branches in Grays and Dagenham, before meeting up in Manor Park, turning left off the Romford Road. They pulled into the driveway that ran behind the bakery, stopping at a loading dock. Smudger got out of his Range Rover Sport and climbed in with Tom. They had been chatting on the burners and agreed the gunman must have received a warning from the alarm at the storage unit and, with the bakery situated in a residential area, they were aware they had to be much more careful.

The bakery had been built just after the war as this part of East London had suffered heavily during The Blitz. Like the building in Southend, it was also single storey and had a similar alarm, but the difference was that this building had two roof lights. They used the ladder and foam again to silence the alarm bell. Taking a rope from the van, they climbed the ladder onto the roof of the building, then carefully crawling across the roof, Tom forced the roof light open. Tying the rope to the frame of it, he dropped the rope into the building and slid down it, followed by Smudger. They glanced around for any alarm sensors but couldn't find any, so hoped it was just the doors that were alarmed.

There was no doubt the building had been a bakery at some time in the past, but not any more. At first glance it just appeared to be a disused building until they opened a door that led to a staircase leading down to a basement. With their torches lighting the way, they turned at the bottom of the stairs into a large room, which they could tell instantly was a very similar set-up to Southend, with stacks of drugs packages. Keeping to the same plan, but with Tom setting a good many more but much smaller charges to avoid damage to the nearby houses, Smudger searched the building. Opening some double doors at the end of the basement, he stopped and whistled to himself. He called Tom and said, "I think you need to see this, Poacher!"

Tom ran over and stopped. Not only were there another eight boxes identical to the ones they had taken from Southend, but the wall was lined with a gun rack holding ten MAC-10 machine pistols, four H&K 9mm MP5s and two Mossberg 590 pump action shotguns, along with various boxes of ammunition.

Smudger shook his head. "Fucking hell, Poacher, what an arsenal! We can't leave all this here."

"Well, what we *can't* take, we will destroy; I don't want to chance the doors yet, so get these boxes up to the loading dock and I'll carry on setting charges. When we've done that we will see what we can take from here – weapons like this may come in very handy over the next week or so!"

They worked quickly and silently and soon all the charges were set with ten-minute fuses. The boxes were placed just inside the dock doors and they had taken both shotguns and cartridges, along with the H&Ks and four of the MAC-10s. To be on the safe side, Tom loaded a magazine into an MP5 and Smudger loaded a shotgun.

They then forced the loading bay dock doors open.

Pushing the rolling door up, Tom jumped down, scanned the area with his gun ready, but with no sight or sound of anyone, he opened the back doors of his Transporter as Smudger started to hand down the boxes to him. It took less than a minute to finish the loading and three minutes later they were back in separate vehicles, turning right to circle round onto the North Circular Road. They stopped shortly after to remove the cloned plates before turning on to the M11, where they had decided to take different routes back – Tom via the M25 and M1, while Smudger kept on the M11 and then the A14 and A43.

Tom called Dan who was waiting nervously to hear how things had gone. "It's far more nerve-wracking just waiting here than being out there in the action – I've hated it," admitted Dan.

Tom filled him in on everything including the gunman and the money.

"So, how much do you think there is?" he asked.

"At a rough guess, I would say possibly ten million quid."

"What the fuck? That's crazy. What are you going to do with it?"

"Well, that's up to us *all* to decide. It would be good to use some for our war chest; I am happy to pay out for all we need but it would be kind of fate to use their own money to beat them, don't you think? But after that, whatever you want… give it to charity, send some to the families of the officers who have died during this case, perhaps. I am happy with anything you want to do."

"OK, well, we have time to think it over, but I agree we should use it as our war chest."

It was just after 5 am when Tom pulled the van into the driveway and was followed ten minutes later by Smudger. Dan was waiting for them and helped them unload the boxes into the house and the weapons into the garage. Back in the house, Tom poured three very large Glenmorangie single malt whiskeys and they all toasted a mission well done.

Dan informed them that their mission was already in the news. "I kept updating Google News all night. At first, it was just an explosion in Southend and then another in Essex, but before long, more explosions were reported and they began to say it may be gang related and, although there hasn't been a statement from the police, papers are saying it's rival gangs fighting a drug war, which is just what we wanted – it gives us the perfect cover to continue with our plans and hopefully our man in Mumbai will have found out more about who is at the head of this. I'll check with him when I wake up."

Congratulating them both once more, Dan went to bed while the other two had a couple more Glenmorangies before turning in.

CHAPTER 53

It had been a nightmare couple of days for Agron Sefiri. His normal calmness had been replaced by anger and frustration. His plan to attack the convoy had failed miserably, with all his men dead and with no names released by the police of the dead and he had no idea if Hooper had been killed or not. It had caused a family rift with his brother Józef, who had been against it from the start and who was now questioning his mental state and leadership capabilities. He realised he had to put revenge to the back of his mind and concentrate on business. He knew Mehmet Ligor, the arrogant Turk, would also be stirring trouble, amongst other gangs he supplied, but knew that as long as he kept the supplies flowing, he would get through this. With that in mind, he had three large shipments to be sent over from Rotterdam later today, which would more than recover the merchandise lost in Yorkshire.

He hadn't been into his office for two days and had a lot to catch up on, so at just before 6 am, he left his mansion in Courtenay Avenue in his Rolls-Royce Phantom, driven by his trusty driver and bodyguard, Bato, for the ten-mile journey to Canary Wharf. He spent most of the journey catching up with files and e-mails that he hadn't bothered with for two days. Just as they passed the Leman Street Police Station, his phone rang. Checking the ID, he saw it was his brother, so he answered. Józef sounded worried and said, "Have you seen the news this morning?"

"No, not yet, I'm catching up on paperwork. What news?" Józef told him of the explosions. The Rolls had now turned left onto the A1230, known to locals as The Highway, and was approaching the Limehouse Link tunnel.

Agron was shocked and said, "They are all the Turks' places; have you spoken to him? He needs to know we aren't behind it."

"I have tried to call three times but no answer. I also called his right-hand man, Dost, but again, no reply."

The Rolls was now in the tunnel and, as Agron began to answer, a motorbike pulled up alongside with two men on it. The pillion passenger was holding a MAC-10 machine pistol and just as Bato yelled, "Boss, look out!" the gun fired, spraying bullets along the side of the car and the window that Agron was sat behind. Only a few close people knew that Sefiri had spent almost three million pounds having the Roller converted by the German company KLASSEN and that it had a Level-9 ballistic protection rating, meaning it was totally bullet-proof.

As the bullets bounced off the bodywork and windows, Bato swerved to the right, hitting the motorbike and crushing it onto the far wall of the tunnel, then pulling away to allow the bike to somersault through the air, smashing into pieces and sending both men cartwheeling back down the tunnel. Agron shouted at Bato, "Keep driving! Get me out of here quickly, we will be safer in the office!" He picked up the phone that had fallen onto the floor, telling his brother what had just happened and asking him to get some men to his office immediately with guns. He finished the call saying, "This could be war."

Within three minutes, they were entering the private underground car park beneath the thirty-two storey skyscraper in Churchill Place. The building was joint-owned by one of his companies and a consortium of foreign investors, as a way to launder money. It is thought that over one hundred billion pounds is laundered this way in the City each year.

His company occupied the top four floors, with the top floor solely for him, his brother and his PA. The lower floors were each rented out, bringing their international investors millions of pounds of 'clean' profits each year.

Taking his private lift from the car park to the top floor, with Bato at his side keeping very close and holding a Glock 19. In seconds, they were safely inside his office. Going straight to his desk, his first call was to his company lawyer, Andreas Kotsonaros, demanding he get to his office quickly, as they would need to inform the police of the attack and why they didn't stop. The lawyer said he would deal with the police and be there in half an hour. The next call was to his brother who was nearly at the office, saying, "We need to get more men on the street – I don't care what it costs and thankfully, they don't know where many of our businesses are, but we are under attack."

Józef replied, "I understand, my brother, but perhaps you should call Mehmet – it might not have been his men today and war is no good for anyone's business."

"It's a sign of weakness, but you are right – with everything else going on we don't want a war. I'll call him now."

Using his EncroChat phone, he called Mehmet Ligor and it rang so many times he thought it would go unanswered, but then the growling voice of the Turk answered, "Yes, Agron, can I help you?"

"My friend, I have only just heard your news and send you my deepest sympathy and the offer of any help I can give you."

The Turk growled again, "Do you take me for a fool, a jackass, *a budala?* Do you think I don't know that it was *you* behind last night's attack?"

"But, Mehmet, you have my word that it was *not* me or *any of my men;* I swear to you that is the truth. You know that I have been attacked as well – we talked of these a few days ago."

"Yes, we did, before you caused even more trouble with your failed attack in Essex, bringing even more attention from the police. The word is out that you are going crazy, *deli*, that you are too distracted. How can you prove to me that you weren't behind last night's problems?"

"Tell me how much merchandise you lost, I will replace it; tell me how many men you lost and I will repay their families. Someone else is behind this and they have been from the start. Together we must find out who it is; we must deal with them and then get back to normal – what do you say?"

The voice was even slower and deeper now, replying, "Do you want to pay back the millions of pounds I lost last night as well? I will think on your offer; give me time, I will be in touch." And with that the line went dead.

As he finished the call, his brother arrived by the private lift and so he told him of the conversation and Józef replied, "Well, let us see. I am sure they will do the right thing."

"You don't understand, do you, brother? The Turkish fuckers tried to kill me! When this is sorted they will be the ones to die."

Józef put his head in his hands and then looked up slowly. "What is wrong with you? How many times must I tell you that you need to get back to business?"

At that point, the intercom on his desk bleeped and his PA said, "Good morning, sir, Mr Kotsonaros is here to see you and with three police officers."

"Thank you, Selah; please show them in."

The lawyer and a detective were followed in by two armed police officers.

Sefiri smiled from behind his desk and said, "Good morning, gentlemen. Thank you for coming so quickly."

The detective walked towards the desk while the two armed officers stayed by the door, and replied, "Good morning, Mr Sefiri. I am DCI Quinn, we have come straight from the Limehouse Link tunnel, which I think will remain closed for the rest of the day while investigations are carried out. Could you tell me who is present here before we continue?"

"Certainly. This is my brother and business partner, Józef Sefiri, and that is my driver, Bato Dauti."

Quinn turned and asked one of the armed officers to take down the driver's details before continuing with, "Mr Sefiri, could you tell me what happened this morning?"

"Yes, of course. Well, we had travelled from my home in Harrow and I had been catching up on paperwork. We were traveling through the tunnel and I was on the phone to my brother, when a motorbike pulled alongside us and opened fire with a machine-gun. My driver, who is tactically trained, took defensive measures. The two men crashed off the bike and I told him to keep driving to get me out of there as quickly as possible where I thought I would be safer."

Quinn continued, saying, "I assume that your car is here and we will need to see it. I take it that it has been bullet-proofed; could I ask why you had thought you needed that and if you can think of anyone who would want to attack you in this way?"

He smiled again and replied, "Detective Chief Inspector Quinn, I am the head of many multinational companies with a turnover of billions and if I believe the press, I am amongst the most wealthiest people in this country. Do you honestly think that you can get to such a position without upsetting someone, somewhere? So, I have always taken my security very seriously, as do most people in my position."

"Thank you, Mr Sefiri. I completely understand. If you wish I could leave armed officers here."

"Thank you, but I am sure there is no need for that."

"In that case, we will be off. The Scenes of Crime team will want to inspect the car and will be here shortly. Oh, and just one more question – do you know a Reni Kotri?"

He realised that there was a good chance the police knew of the connection, so he nodded his head and replied in a sad voice, "Sadly, I do. I am his uncle and he was the son of my sister. It is such a shame, but over the past few years he fell in with, shall we say, the wrong crowd. We all tried to help him but that wicked evilness of drugs beat him in the end. We are all heart-broken at his death. It is tragic, don't you think, to see the damage that drugs are doing to the younger generations, Detective Chief Inspector?"

Without replying, the detective thanked him and they left.

Once they had gone, Józef was the first to speak. "They are getting too close to us, I can feel it; we need to be careful."

"You worry too much, but for the time being, both of us will only travel in three-car convoys; could you arrange it? Also, I need confirmation that the three Rotterdam shipments are on their way. You had best call them now."

CHAPTER 54

While Sue and Andy were up at a normal time, none of the men came down until after 9 am. Sue poured coffees for them all and while Dan and Smudger sat at the table, Tom took his up to his office. He quickly logged onto the dark web and was pleased when he checked the e-mail he used with Mongoose to see that he had received new files and a message. He opened the files and printed them off. Slowly reading through them, he realised they were a couple of steps closer to finding out who the ringleader was behind all of this.

There were more properties listed to various Albanian shell companies and more details of the Turkish connection. Mongoose had also uncovered details of secret bank accounts in various tax havens. Tom was busy checking all these details and mapping different venues when there was a tap on his office door and Sue poked her head round it. "I thought you might like some breakfast. How about a sourdough bacon sarnie with HP Sauce?"

"Sue, you are wonderful; that is perfect. Dan is a lucky man, thank you so much."

"You're very welcome, Poacher. Ah, hmm... I hope you don't mind me asking and I couldn't be more grateful for all that you are doing, but I don't even know your name. You are obviously very wealthy and I know that Dan trusts you completely, as do I, but it all seems so secretive. I hope you don't mind me mentioning it."

"Sue, bless you; of course I don't mind, in fact, I completely understand and thank you for trusting me. There are some bits for now that I would rather keep to myself, but my real name is Tom, but I would rather everyone called me Poacher. Dan and I go back a long way and it turns out also, with Smudger. If we could just leave it at that for now, but I promise when this is all over and the time is right, I will tell you more."

Sue smiled and said, "OK. I am hoping you're going to tell me you are a bit like a modern day James Bond."

Tom laughed at that as well and replied, "If only, but thank you for the breakfast, Miss Moneypenny."

Sue chuckled again while humming the 007 tune walking out of the office and Tom called after her, "Could you ask the guys to come up when they've finished their breakfast, please?"

Looking back round the door, she whispered, "Of course, Mr Bond," and promptly closed the door behind her.

Tom was excited by the new details; it would certainly give them more places to check out. He left the files to eat his sarnie and then realised he hadn't read the message from Mongoose, so he picked it up to read while he was eating. His chewing slowed down as he read further down the message. This was great, new information and he knew just what he would do with it.

At that moment, Dan and Smudger appeared at the office door. Tom looked up, just finishing the sandwich and said, "My man in Mumbai has done it again! Apart from a load more properties and bank accounts, he has been monitoring the EncroChat phone that this Józef was using. It would appear that there are three container lorries coming over from Rotterdam today, all going to their warehouse in Tilbury, to be distributed quickly because of stock they have been losing. I plan to tip off the police and customs and let them deal with it. He also heard the name Agron and it would appear that he might be the boss."

Dan butted in with, "Did you say 'Agron'?" which Tom confirmed, then Dan continued, "I have been looking at the news on my phone to see if there was anything from last night. There were mentions on the *Essex Live* and *Evening Standard* websites pointing to a drugs war, as we had hoped. But I have just seen a newsflash. It said that in the Limehouse Link this morning, Albanian billionaire Agron Sefiri's Rolls-Royce was attacked by two men on a motorbike; the car was bullet-proof so he wasn't hurt, but the men on the bike both died in a collision with the Roller, which continued to Mr Sefiri's office block in Canary Wharf."

As Dan was still talking, Tom was typing frantically on his computer. "Yes, I think we have found him. Wikipedia says: 'Agron Sefiri, shipping magnate, born in Tirana, Albania, in the top twenty of the *Sunday Times* rich list', and here is the slam dunk – he has a brother called Józef."

Smudger stood up and said, "That *has* to be him, doesn't it?"

Tom was still typing as Dan replied, "Yes, it has to be. No wonder they have thrown so much at stopping me; it would be peanuts to a man like that, but I doubt it would be easy to get to him – he must have lots of security and, as the paper said, even a bullet-proof Rolls. I would bet it was the Turks who tried to kill him, so let's hope they get him next time."

Tom looked over and added, "I don't intend to wait for the next time. I want to strike while the iron is hot; it's the perfect time because anything we do will be thought of as part of the gang war. I've just found out where he lives – Courtenay Avenue – the second most expensive street in the country, with security gates at the entrance and cameras everywhere."

Smudger shook his head and said, "Perhaps we will do better when he is at his office."

But Tom was already working on a plan. "No, I think the house is perfect, because of the private road and security – that's where he will least expect it. Looking around the location, it has Highgate Golf Course on one side and there is another road the other side, which might be a way in. Give me an hour; I want to try and find out a bit more, but I think it's doable and that we should try to strike tonight or, at the latest, tomorrow night."

Dan wasn't sure. "Poacher, I really appreciate what you're doing, but this isn't just big time, its mega big time and it can't be rushed."

But Tom was typing again and, as he finished, he looked over and said, "Trust me, let me work the plan out and we can talk it over, but I honestly think we can do it."

They left him to it and an hour later he came down, holding some papers and they made their way out into the garage workshop. He first laid out maps and screenshots taken from Google Street View – he had pinpointed the house, along with the golf course.

"As you can see, the good news is that there is a direct line of sight from the eighteenth tee of the golf course to the target. The bad news is, there are more than likely going to be more private, top of the range CCTV cameras around there than anywhere else in the country. So, getting in and out is the biggest problem."

Dan interrupted, "But, what good is being on the golf course, even if you have sight lines to his house?"

Tom signalled for them to follow him to the back of the workshop where he held his secret storage of weapons. Reaching in, he lifted out the long box he had got when he picked up the extra explosives.

"Just close the garage doors, please, Smudger," he asked. Once they were closed, he prised opened the box and when the others saw what was in it they both looked shocked.

As he started to lift the contents out of the box he explained what it was. "This is an L72A9 Light Anti-Structures Missile, better known as a LASM. It is, in fact, a 66 mm unguided rocket launcher. It's similar to the old M72 that you guys used in the Paras, but this carries a 1 kg warhead of enhanced explosives. Its purpose is to be used on bunkers and other buildings. It uses its kinetic energy to penetrate the outer walls of a structure before the high explosive warhead detonates inside. On the downside, it's a one shot system, designed to be discarded after launch, but I could only get hold of one, so we need to get it right first time."

Smudger took it from Tom and said, "Fucking hell, Poacher, how did you get your hands on this bit of kit? It's a beauty."

But Dan replied, "Yes, it *is* a beauty, alright, and might do some damage to his house if it hits it, but I'm not sure what that will achieve."

Tom replied, "You're right, but what if we follow up the rocket with the drone, either flying in through the hole or landing on the roof of the house with explosives? Obviously, it would depend on lots of factors – where the rocket hits, how much damage, etc. The least it will do is cause a bigger rift with rival gangs and perhaps get him to an easier location to actually deal with him, or the best is that we will kill him; either way I think now is the time to do it. It's a two-man operation. We can park on the far side of the golf course just off the A1, make our way in the cover of trees to the eighteenth tee, do what we need to do and then get the fuck out of dodge as quickly as we can. What do you guys think?"

Smudger replied first. "Well, I'm up for it. I think we need a backup escape route, just in case, but let's do it."

Dan was more hesitant. "The point is, guys, and I know I have said this before, I really appreciate all you have done for me, but the thought of you getting hurt or even worse really worries me, as does the fact that *I* should be doing this, not sat here waiting for you to come back."

Tom smiled and said, "Listen, mate, I was after these people before I knew of your problem with them, so I would have pushed as far as I could to get to the top man, on my own. These people are responsible for drugs, guns, human trafficking, prostitution, which is often under-age – they are evil bastards and we must remember we are doing the world a favour. It will either take his mind off you for the time being or end your problem with him. I am going to do it anyway, but it would be better to do it with your blessing."

"And, just so you know, I'm with Poacher, Captain."

Dan nodded. "OK, well, thanks, and good luck. What can I do to help?"

CHAPTER 55

They spent the rest of the morning and most of the afternoon talking through Tom's plans, all agreeing to take both cars, but they knew that using cloned plates once they got near London would be the right thing to do as this would give them two escape routes if needed. Tom would fly the drone and Smudger, to fire the rocket. They then made up the C-4 charges and attached them to a burner phone.

Tom took a break over lunch to send e-mails to the NCA Drugs Unit, as always, via a VPN chain where it bounced all around the world, making it impossible to link to his IP address. He gave all the details he had – where the shipments were coming from, where they were arriving and their destination address in Tilbury. He felt sure this would be yet another big problem for these Albanian villains.

Once the cars were loaded, they went back over the plan once more. They had decided against hitting the target in the early hours of the morning, fearing they would be more noticeable driving around at 3 or 4 am. Instead, they agreed to strike at 12.30 am, believing the target should be home at that time and they wouldn't look too conspicuous either, driving at that time. They had clocked the journey at about seventy miles, most of it on the M1, so decided to leave just after 10 pm. They both had a light dinner and grabbed a couple of hours' kip.

Dan watched them drive away with a heavy heart, wishing he were going with them, but knew he would only be a hindrance. Andy was already in bed, so he sat with Sue on the sofa, talking over the past week's events.

Although Tom and Smudger left at the same time, they didn't drive in convoy as Tom took the lead with Smudger dropping back as they drove along the Northamptonshire country lanes, then southbound onto the M1. The night-time traffic was still very heavy with lane closures near the Newport Pagnell services and then speed restrictions as they passed Luton. By the time Tom had turned off the motorway at junction 2 onto the A1, Smudger was only a few minutes behind. Both pulling into a small driveway to a sports field, they stopped and attached the cloned plates to their vehicles. At first, they kept to side streets, avoiding cameras, in case an observant CCTV worker noticed any change.

Firstly, they made their way to the far side of the golf course, leaving the Range Rover Sport in a side road. Smudger climbed in with Tom and they drove along The Bishops Avenue, turning right onto the A1 before pulling in behind a block of flats on Aylmer Road. The spot they had picked on Google Street View was perfect as it was hidden from the road and not overlooked. They quickly pulled on black overalls, balaclavas, night-vision goggles and gloves. Smudger took the rocket launcher, while Tom had the drone and explosives.

They entered the golf course from the car park, with Tom leading, via an allotment – not something you would expect to see in a part of London where land was so expensive. Once on the course, they followed the tree line around to their right, the night-vision giving them a green perspective of the area.

They had been walking stealthily for a few minutes when Tom raised his clenched fist as a signal to stop – he had heard something in front of them. Instantly crouching down on one knee, neither of them were moving, for quite a few seconds. Tom signalled to where the sound had come from, then with a rustle from the bushes, a fox walked out and stood innocently staring at the men, before turning and trotting off across one of the fairways. Both men nodded at each other and silently set off again. It took them almost ten minutes to get all the way around. Stopping deep in the trees for cover, Tom opened the drone and attached the explosive charge with its burner phone to it, with short bungee cords. There was no need this time to worry about shaking the charge off as the drone would be destroyed in the explosion. At the same time, Smudger was checking over the rocket launcher.

When both were ready, they made their way out from the shelter of the trees to the point where they could see the target. They both knew the plan of attack, so placing the drone on the eighteenth tee, Tom started it up and it lifted off the ground to about forty feet above their heads. Tom whispered into Smudger's ear, "Make it count, mate, we only get one shot at this."

He replied, "Don't you worry, I won't let you down." Standing with his feet apart and legs in a braced position, he aimed the weapon and once he found the right spot to hit, he fired. One of the advantages of the updated L72A9 was that it had virtually no back blast. The rocket flew with a whoosh at one hundred and thirty metres per second, between the trees that lined the Avenue and, in the blink of an eye, hit the first floor side wall of the target mansion, between two picture windows. The impact was shocking – first, the rocket pierced the outer wall making a metre-wide hole before it exploded in the building; and second, it shattered windows and created an even larger hole. The moment the rocket had fired, Smith was on his way back to his car, not even acknowledging Tom who was concentrating on bringing the drone back down from a height away from the blast, enabling it to fly through the dust and smoke and the now two-metre wide hole, right into the building. Watching carefully via the built-in camera, he could see the carnage the explosion had caused. Spinning it around, he could see the far wall of the room had collapsed, leaving a gaping hole onto a landing. Realising he didn't have much time remaining but wanting to cause as much damage as possible, he flew the drone as far as he could into the building. Leaving it hovering, he took the burner phone from his overalls pocket and, as he started to jog back into the trees, he pressed the 'call' button. It must have taken longer than usual to connect because he stopped and turned around, just in time to feel the ground shake and the huge front windows shatter, raining glass across the road and starting alarm bells ringing everywhere. People appeared from their houses to see what had happened.

But Tom was already on his way, the night-vision guiding him between the trees. The journey, which had taken ten minutes in, was closer to five getting out. Removing the goggles and balaclava as he got back to the allotment, he heard another explosion, which he guessed must be the gas main blowing. Thinking, 'Well, that was a bonus,' he casually walked back to his car. Checking no one was around, he removed the overalls, climbed in, started up and drove back out onto the A1.

As agreed, they would take different routes back, with Tom keeping on the A1 all the way to Huntingdon, before turning onto the A14. His only stop was to remove the cloned plates. Smudger was back in his car quicker than Tom, then he took the circular route out of London onto the A40, before taking the M25 and, again, back on the M1 also, only stopping once to change the plates. Tom thinking that this was surely becoming a habit, called home and brought Dan up to speed who, in turn, promised to have the whiskey ready for their return.

CHAPTER 56

After one of the worst days for some years, all Józef Sefiri wanted to do was have a quiet drink and an early night, but his brother would have none of it.

"I could have been killed today and you would have been either mourning or at war, but I am here and alive – work and worry can wait. Tonight, my brother, we celebrate me being alive. We will get our favourite girls here and have fun. I will get Bato to arrange the talent and get the little Japanese one with the big tits for you; it will be good to unwind.

Before the hookers arrived, the brothers sat down for their favourite dinner. They started with fresh Cornish Lobster Thermidor, followed by Kobe Wagyu beef fillet mignon with teriyaki sauce, washed down with a bottle of Krug Brut Vintage 1985. They both declined desert, with Agron having a very large glass of Rémy Martin Louis Xlll cognac.

Midnight had passed some time ago and the intimate party was well underway. Józef, who was still sober, was enjoying the company of Hitomi who was, by now, completely naked and riding on him as he sat on a couch, her massive 48DD breasts swinging in his face, while her hips ground into him, teasing him to near climax and then slowing down, before repeating the excitement.

Agron was sat naked in his favourite chair. He was in great shape for a man of his age, but having drank over half of the three thousand pound bottle of cognac and having taken (very rare for him) a couple of lines of the finest cocaine, nothing much was working for him in his nether regions, despite having taken two Viagra and his penis being massaged and licked by his two favourite, thousand-pound-a-night call girls. Both Anne and Marie were also naked apart from their Christian Louboutin stiletto heels and hold-up fishnet stockings – they were certainly working for their money tonight. Having performed a lesbian love scene for him, followed by some more oral, nothing was working, although they were far too professional to show it. Both were hoping for the night to end with or without a climax from their master for the night.

Hitomi was riding and grinding, faster and faster and Józef was about to reach his climax when the wall behind him exploded, virtually disintegrating both him and his Japanese courtesan, body parts flying everywhere. The rocket's path carried it further into the room before detonating, throwing Agron and the two naked women on their knees in front of him flying across the room, as the far wall and part of the ceiling came crashing down on to their motionless bodies. A few seconds later, the drone flew into the room, hovering before, that too, exploded with devastating effect, demolishing the floor and sending everything crashing to the ground.

Bato Dauti was in his own apartment in the staff wing at the back of the mansion. He was still on duty as he would have been expected to drive the hookers home later, a job he always enjoyed because he would sometimes get a free blow job. Sat watching porn on his laptop, he was stunned by the impact of the rocket hitting the building. He was instantly up on his feet, grabbing his Glock and running to the staircase as the next explosion blasted the house. Lights flickered on and off and dust and plaster fell from the ceiling. As he continued up the stairs, he was about to open the door into the kitchen to lead him through to the main house when the drone explosion erupted. The door was blown open, sending him tumbling backwards. He was quickly back on his feet though and through the door, choking with the dust and stumbling over the fallen debris – he was shocked by the carnage.

Searching through the rubble, he saw a man's arm poking out. Rushing to it, he lifted it but then recoiled in horror as he realised it wasn't attached to a body. He recognised the watch on the wrist as being the Patek Philippe belonging to Józef. Crawling over the wreckage, he spotted the naked body of Agron covered in dirt and rubble, with cuts and grazes all over it. Scrambling to free him from the rubble, he managed to lift him and carry his lifeless body back downstairs, taking him back into his own apartment, where the laptop was still playing porn and placed him on his bed.

As he laid him down, his boss started coughing, spitting out dust and then groaning as he held his head in pain. Bato grabbed a bottle of water, tilted his boss' head up and gently poured the water into his mouth.

Agron slowly came round and asked, "What the fuck just happened?"

"I'm not sure, boss; there have been three explosions. I think we've been bombed."

Looking very vague, no doubt due to the alcohol as well as the bomb attack, he looked at his driver and said, "What? I can't hear you!"

Bato realised the blast must have affected his boss' hearing, so he repeated it but much louder.

Agron answered very slowly, "How the fuck did that happen? Where's my brother?"

"I am sorry, boss, he didn't make it and I think we need to get you out of here. If it *is* an attack they may be coming in to make sure they got you too."

Still looking shocked and no doubt concussed, he looked into thin air, saying, "Józef, gone… I can't believe it, but you're right, we need to move. Could you get to my room? I need you to get me a tracksuit, grab a suitcase and open the walk-in safe – you know the combination – then fill the suitcase with as much of the cash as you can and get my passport and phone, but we need to be quick. Oh, and let me have your phone."

As Bato left to go back upstairs, Agron called the number for the pilot of his private jet. The phone rang a few times before he answered and Agron shouted down the phone, "Just listen, this is an emergency! I need you and the plane ready to fly me to Tirana in fifteen minutes. I don't care what it costs, just get it done!" and threw down the phone, before drinking more water.

The mansion had been built with a secret set of stairs that ran directly up to the master bedroom from the underground garage and, with the main staircase and half the first floor demolished, this was the route Bato took, running all the way. In less than a minute, he was on his way back down again and was told of the plan. Getting his own passport, a minute later he had helped Agron down to the garage and sat him in the back of the Rolls.

Pressing the remote in the car to open the garage doors, they sped up the ramp and out on to the Avenue, scattering bystanders who had come from their own mansions to see what was happening. Just as they reached the tarmac, there was another blast as the gas main exploded. Agron yelled, "Don't stop! Just get me to the plane!"

RAF Northolt, was fifteen miles away from the mansion, but with both the North Circular and then the A40 still busy, the journey took twenty-five minutes. The Northolt is both a military and commercial airport but is controlled by the RAF and is the home of The Queen's Flight. On arriving, all visitors must produce valid photographic ID for inspection at the Whitehouse Gate Guardroom and, at times, have their luggage searched, before going to the private terminal or direct to their plane. There were no such formalities for Mr Sefiri – as he was such a regular visitor, he was waved through without any inspection. Stopping the Roller next to his Gulfstream G650, the pilot and co-pilot, along with two attendants, came down the steps to greet him and help him on board while Bato parked the car. Agron was still finding it hard to hear and was very unsteady on his feet as he was shown to one of the two bedrooms where he lay on the bed, waiting for Bato to return.

As soon as Bato was on board, they prepared for take-off for the three-hour flight to the Albanian capital, leaving behind a wrecked mansion littered with dead bodies and a legal *and* illegal business empire tottering on the brink of collapse.

CHAPTER 57

By the time Smudger and Tom arrived back at his house, the Gulfstream would have been cruising at thirty-five thousand feet over the Austrian Tyrol.

As promised, Dan was waiting with large whiskeys for both of them. Smudger sat down with Dan, relaying all the details of the night, as if he was reporting back to his captain after a sortie in the Paras. But Tom preferred to take his whiskey up to his office for he had work he wished to get finished before the morning.

The next hour was spent collating the information he had received from Mongoose on Sefiri and his many companies, making sure there could be no link back to himself or his new friend in Mumbai. He then e-mailed all the documents to the National Crime Agency, the border controls and to Interpol at their headquarters in Lyon, France, as always, using his VPNs and Tor Browser. On having a second thought, he also sent them to a number of press agencies including Reuters, The Associated Press (AP) and Agence France-Presse (AFP) in Paris, knowing that, with the events being linked with the house's explosion, it should be headline news around the world the next day.

By then, the other two had called it a night so he also decided to turn in, looking forward to discovering what the next day would bring – hopefully the death or at least the demise of Agron Sefiri and his Albanian mobsters.

As it turned out, everyone was awake and up early the next day. It was agreed from the start to keep as much information away from Andy was possible, so Sue made coffee and bacon sandwiches for the men who had all settled in the office checking on the news, while she and Andy sat at the kitchen table. It was clear that Andy was beginning to go a bit stir-crazy and Sue hoped it wouldn't be too long before it was safe to return to their own home and to work.

The mood in the office was mixed; at first, they were elated watching Sky News and witnessing the damage to the mansion – the police, the fire brigade and all CSIs were there. The reporter stated that, at first, it was thought to be an explosion from a gas leak, in which at least three or four people had died and ten bystanders had received minor injuries from flying glass and rubble. But, if witness reports were to be believed, the gas explosion had followed two previous explosions, which had brought neighbours out onto the street. So, it was now being linked to the attack on Mr Sefiri's car the previous day and there were rumoured links circulating to a war between rival drug gangs.

But then, they were brought down to earth with a bang and were told it was believed Mr Sefiri had fled the scene as the building exploded and is thought to have left the country in his private jet. So far, there had been no statement from the police.

"For fuck's sake, the way the place went up, no one should have got out alive!" raged Smudger.

Tom commented next. "I shouldn't worry too much, mate; with all the evidence I sent to the police and press last night I think his reign as a master villain has come to an end. It will be interesting to see what the next day or two brings."

Dan agreed and said, "Yes, with a bit of luck we could be leaving you in peace in the not too distant future."

"To be honest, it's been good having you here," stated Tom. "I haven't felt this much camaraderie since I left the regiment, but one thing we need to do is agree on what we do with the money."

"Yes, we do," agreed Dan. "I like the idea of giving something to the families of the coppers that died, but it's a tricky situation. Let's be honest, how can you put a value on how much a police officer's life is worth? In the families' and our minds, it's priceless. It might be better to donate it direct to the Police Benevolent Fund; I think we need to look into it. Poacher, you should take whatever all this has cost you and Smudger, I think, should have a share of it."

Smudger shook his head. "To be honest, Captain, I'm not short of a few bob and when the time comes, I have no one to leave it to. Like you, Poacher, this has been the most I have enjoyed myself since I came out; it certainly beats all the shitty private work I've done these past few years. I have a fair idea of what you've been doing and if you intend to carry on, mate, I would be happy to join you."

Tom stood up and held his hand out, which Smudger took. "That would be brilliant, mate, yes – there are certainly enough adventures waiting out there."

It was now Dan's turn to stand and conclude the conversation. "Well, I think that sorts it; use it for your war chest, but do what we can to give a good amount to the right charity. I would like to call Bronco – have you a burner I can do it on?"

CHAPTER 58

Tom handed over the phone and Bronco was pleased to hear from him. He asked if Dan had seen the news as everyone at the nick was wondering if there was any link with Dan's case, but Dan played that down. He was then told that the date had been set for Chief Superintendent Jackson's funeral in five days' time. Dan said immediately that he wanted to be there, but Bronco's reply was that the word from the top was that he shouldn't attend in case he was targeted again. Dan understood that and said he would think on it for a day, hoping to himself that, with Sefiri gone, he shouldn't have to worry any more, but he asked if Bronco could contact AC Harris again and arrange another video call. Telling Bronco he would call him back the next day, Dan ended the call and returned the phone to Tom.

All men decided it would do them good to get some fresh air so, keeping all eyes on Dan, they followed Tom through the village and onto a series of footpaths that led them to the edge of the Althorp estate. It was a route that Tom often used on his runs, but thought his visitors would like a chance to see the final resting place of Diana, Princess of Wales. They stood by the beautiful, black wrought iron gates, set perfectly between two brick gatehouses, looking down the long driveway and, although unable to see either the house or the late Princess' memorial, they couldn't help but feel wrapped up in the area's wonderful tranquillity.

Throughout the majority of the walk, Tom and Smudger

had been in deep conversation, no doubt talking more about working together, which suited Dan as it gave him some special time with Sue and Andy. He was amazed how well Sue had dealt with all the trauma of the past week and still keeping her wonderful sense of humour, constantly teasing him and making him laugh. In the fresh Northamptonshire country air with the sun shining, it also made him realise how lucky he was to have got through all of this more or less unscathed.

By the time they stopped off at the local pub for some lunch, they had taken just over an hour to walk three miles. Dan was starting to feel fit again and the rest of them were the most relaxed they had been for some time. There was an Amazon parcel waiting for them when they got back to the house, which, after checking it carefully, Tom gave to Andy who looked confused. Upon opening it he was very excited as he saw it was the latest Xbox, including five games.

"I thought that might cheer you up a bit, Andy. I know it's not been easy staying here and missing your mates. I hope you like it," said Poacher.

"*Like* it? It's *brill*iant, Poacher, thanks so much!" and with that they gave each other a hug.

Sue smiled as she watched. "That's so kind of you, thank you," and she kissed him on his cheek. Tom put his arm around Andy, leading him into the lounge. "Let's get it set up, shall we? Perhaps we could have a competition later," he suggested, at which point they all laughed.

The rest of the day was spent between challenging Andy and watching the news in the office, where more of the story was breaking. The BBC announced there would be a *Panorama* special about foreign billionaires behind crime in this country. Questions had been asked in Parliament about how such a high profile businessman could be a major figure in organised crime and the Home Secretary was due to make a statement later in the day.

The R&R continued throughout the day; it was as if a weight had been lifted off their shoulders, but after so many stressful days it was an early night for them all, wondering what the next day would bring.

CHAPTER 59

Dan was the first up and, using the same burner, he called Bronco who informed him that AC Harris would be available for a video chat at 9.00 that morning. Dan thanked him and said he would send on the link and let him know the outcome. He then knocked on Tom's bedroom door who was already up as he opened it straight away. Dan set up the black sheeting in the office while Tom sorted the link.

It was just after 9.00 when Dan clicked on the link and, after a couple of seconds, the face of the assistant commissioner appeared and then a couple of seconds later the audio was connected.

He could see that the AC was sat alone in her office at New Scotland Yard and she smiled as she began to speak. "Good morning, Dan, it's good to see you looking so well. How are you feeling and how is Sue?"

Dan thought how nice it was that she was keeping it on first-name terms. "We are both fine, thank you, ma'am. I am feeling much better and looking forward to hopefully returning home again soon."

She raised her eyebrows as she replied, "Really – do you feel safe enough to do that?"

"Well, I was hoping to hear some news from *you*, ma'am; obviously, I have seen the news about this Albanian and his link to Kotri, but was hoping you may have had some joy finding the mole?"

"Yes, well, there *is* good news – we have arrested a

sergeant here at the Yard and he has admitted to it, claiming that his family had been threatened. We are still looking into that but, in the meantime, he is in custody with a twenty-four-hours-a-day guard. Investigations are still underway regarding Mr Sefiri, but it may take months and months to wade through all the information we now have, but his empire appears to have crash-landed, at least for the time being."

Dan felt relieved. "In that case, ma'am, I think we would like to move back home as soon as we can; I'm told it's the Chief's funeral on Friday and I intend to be there."

The AC shook her head and said, "I really don't think you should; it will be a big public event and if there is anyone still after you, it would be dangerous for Arthur's family as well as all the other mourners."

"Ma'am, I completely understand your comments, but this man died because of *me* and there is no way I will not be there to pay mine and my families' respects."

"And if I were to order you to stay away?"

"Then, in that case, I would have no hesitation in resigning from the force, ma'am."

"It really means that much to you? Well, they are the last things I want to happen, you being vulnerable to threat and/or resigning, so let me think on it and we will find a way to do it. But, I will insist on an armed guard at your house and will send in our technical team first to set up an alarm with CCTV and a panic button, just to be on the safe side until we have more information about how much of his organisation is still operating. I hope you won't oppose that?"

"No, ma'am. That's fine, thank you."

She smiled again and said, "That's good. Now, just one more thing… Through the dealings you have been involved in on this case, do you think that this is gang war? As you have no doubt seen in the press, there has been a huge amount of highly secretive and incriminating data sent to the police and press regarding Mr Sefiri and no one can find where it had come from; in fact, our best IT experts can't even trace the e-mails. What are your thoughts?"

"To be honest, my main thoughts have been about looking after my wife and stepson and keeping safe, but obviously I have been wondering myself. It would appear that Sefiri was after me because of the death of Kotri, but at the same time another gang or, more than likely, an international criminal organisation had fallen out with him or just wanted to take over his business. It has to be an organisation with a lot of clout to be able to do both the technical IT stuff and the attacks. It almost smacks of a paramilitary set-up, to me."

"Yes, that is something we are looking at, as are MI5 and the National Counter Terrorism Security Office (NaCTSO) and SO15. Well, I must get on; I will liaise with you through DS Laine and no doubt see you at the funeral. Take care and stay safe."

"Dan grinned and replied, "Thank you, ma'am, you too."

With that, the link ended.

Dan made his way down to the others in the kitchen and relayed to them the conversation and how he would be attending the funeral, at which Sue also said she would and, although Dan wasn't happy, she was as determined as he was to go. He made them laugh when he told them of his comments about the attack possibly coming from a paramilitary group, but as the laughter died they all realised that they had to be careful on so many fronts because of the police and any other government agency that may be investigating and any of Sefiri's organisation who may still be operating.

It was decided that they would stay for one more night at Tom's, but that Smudger would meet up with Bronco and Tish, along with the team installing the alarm, to do a recce of the area to ensure everything was safe for their return.

Sue couldn't wait to get home, but Andy was having the time of his life and didn't want to leave and was even happier when Tom told him he could take the Xbox with him. Dan was quiet for most of the day, his mind on the funeral, what they had all been through and what might lie ahead for them in the coming weeks, but mostly, about how lucky they were to still be alive.

He also thought how hard this must have all been for Sue after the horrific event she had witnessed, Dan's hospitalisation and whether he should indeed resign from the force to give her less worry. He promised himself he would discuss it with her when they were back in their own home.

CHAPTER 60

Bronco called late the following afternoon to tell Dan that all the alarm work was finalised and that they could make their way home. Smudger was going to drive them and stay for the next few days. Tom was to follow at a discreet distance, but it was agreed he shouldn't spend much time in the area in case anyone recognised him from the vigilante murders.

It was dark by the time they got home. There was an ARV parked outside the house with two officers in who got out and introduced themselves to everyone. Dan explained that Smudger was staying. Tish and Bronco had filled the fridge with food and Sue was happy to be back in her own kitchen, quickly preparing a meal for the four of them. It was agreed that Andy could take the next day off school and, when he did go back, Smudger was to accompany him there and back. They all decided that an early night would do them good and Sue couldn't wait to get Dan into bed.

As soon as they were in the bedroom, she threw herself on the bed, smiling seductively at Dan. "Right, you handsome hunk of a detective chief inspector, I want you and I want you now, so come here!"

Dan smiled but looked a little embarrassed. "Sue, darling, I am a little bit worried as to whether I am up to it yet, after the injury and everything, and you wouldn't want to take advantage of an injured man, would you?"

Sue grinned and replied, "Wouldn't I? Are you really asking me that? Well, up *to* it, Mr Hooper, I will get you up *for* it and then *we* can get up to it. I don't expect you to do any of the hard work; you can just lay there and let me take charge – I can be your dominatrix." After that the pair of them burst out laughing.

But Sue continued through a fit of giggles. "I am not joking – get your kit off, get on this bed and get yourself ready to be ridden like a Grand National winner."

Dan just thought he had better do as he was told and, boy, was he pleased he did.

The next two days were spent resting. The news carried extensive information about Sefiri and his fall from grace. More questions were being asked about human trafficking and money laundering. Interpol had released a statement about raids throughout the Netherlands, netting millions of pounds of drugs, along with money, firearms and numerous arrests. Dan made a brief visit to the nick and was met first by Tish who ran up to him, throwing her arms around him and kissing him on both cheeks.

"It is so good to see you, Guv, we have all really missed you." This was followed by Bronco and Stan Jones, along with a few other officers. Tish asked about Sue and he brought them all up-to-date and was pleased to tell them that he would be at the funeral the next day. They spent the next hour sharing their own memories of the Chief Superintendent, before Dan returned home to Sue.

CHAPTER 61

It was a grey, misty morning as the funeral cortège left the Union Street police headquarters. Three police motorbike outriders led as the black Jaguar hearse slowly pulled away, followed by four matching Jaguar limousines containing family and, finally, senior officers from various police forces. Such was the feeling of loss within the police community that officers had travelled from all parts of the country to pay their respects. The role of arranging officer had been given to Superintendent Terry Ward who had worked alongside Chief Superintendent Jackson for many years, before retiring with ill health following a heart attack whilst on holiday the previous year.

The procession drove silently and solemnly through the town centre and continued the 20-minute drive to Chelmsford Cathedral. Dan was waiting there with Bronco and Stan, all dressed in full uniform as they were to be pall-bearers, along with the Chief's son, Richard, and two other former officers.

Dan was nervous about meeting Richard as he still felt himself to be responsible for his father's death. He needn't have worried as, as soon as he got out of the limousine, Richard walked directly to him, shaking hands first before hugging him.

"My father thought the world of you, Dan, and thank God both you and your wife are safe. I hope you aren't putting yourself at more risk being seen in public again."

"Thank you, Richard, that means the world and, no matter what, I wouldn't have missed today. I am sure all the people behind this are either now dead or have fled the country, so I am not worried."

Afterwards, they lined up to carry the police flag-covered coffin with the Chief's hat laying atop it, into the cathedral slowly and in perfect step – six men all in mourning and all scared to put a foot wrong. To the sound of Schubert's *Ave Maria* they made their way down the nave under the beautiful gilded and engraved roof. Once the coffin was in place at the altar, Richard took his place with family members at the front while Dan and Bronco moved further back with colleagues from their station.

A huge police presence surrounded the cathedral as everyone came out following the service. Dan and Sue were chatting in a group which included Jane Roberts, who had returned from her new posting for the day and Callum West, who had travelled up from Wood Green along with Tish, Julie and Jimmy Edmunds. They were interrupted by the assistant commissioner. Ms Harris thanked them all for their hard work and asked to have a private word with Dan. She smiled and said, "Well, Dan, it's good to meet you in person and I just wanted a quick word to say thank you for being here today, it was the right thing to do and I was wrong to have thought otherwise. I have no doubt you will continue to rise quickly through the ranks and I am sure we will be meeting again soon." With that, AC Harris turned to walk back to her car and head to London.

The wake, or 'funeral reception', as it was printed on the order of service, was being held at a large country house hotel just off the A414. Over one hundred people attended and the atmosphere was understandably very serious; however, the team from the Union Street nick sat together with Stan Jones who was, as always, trying to lighten the mood. Richard and the rest of the family arrived back from the private burial and thanked everyone for being there. Soon afterwards, Dan and Sue said their goodbyes and travelled back with Bronco in his car, followed by an ARV with two armed officers. It would be the first of five, albeit smaller, but no less emotional and poignant funerals that he would attend over the next week.

CHAPTER 62

THREE WEEKS LATER

Dan had been back at work now for ten days. As each day passed, the mood of the station seemed to lift. With everything getting back to normal, the armed officers had stepped down from guarding the house and everyone was feeling more relaxed. Smudger had returned to Leytonstone but was going to keep popping back. Work had been quiet as if the town's villains were also in mourning and keeping on the straight and narrow. Tish and Stan had been dealing with a domestic abuse case – a repeat offender – who, once again, had put his wife in hospital after a drunken attack. He had foolishly tried to take on Tish when she attempted to arrest him resulting in a dislocated shoulder for him, along with a strained neck, which meant also being charged with assaulting a police officer and resisting arrest. Hopefully, this would lead to a custodial sentence.

Bronco had been in court dealing with a man caught with a cannabis farm in his garage. His defence was that forty plants with a street value of almost fifty thousand pounds was for 'personal use'.

Dan was still going over old e-mails when his phone rang. "Is that Mr Hooper? It's Dyson's Garage here, sir; we have a problem. You left your Freelander here this morning in our car park; well, we went to do the service just now and it's gone. You didn't come back for it, did you?"

"No, I didn't, that's *not* good news. Has there been anyone hanging around or has this happened before?"

"We *do* have a problem, mainly with teens taking cars and joyriding, so it's more than likely that, but we didn't see anything."

"OK, I'll get someone onto it from this end and be in touch."

As he was concluding the call, PC Jimmy Edmunds appeared at his office door. "Jimmy, come in; what can I do for you?"

"Sorry to trouble you, Guv, but did you know that your car is parked on the street outside? It's got a parking ticket on it."

"Well, that's good timing. I had left it at the garage for a service this morning, but they just called to say it has gone missing. At least it hasn't got far. Let's hope there's no damage; I wonder if the thieves somehow got the keys from the garage?"

"Do you want me to bring it into the car park for you, sir?"

"That would be great, thanks. I have a spare set of keys here somewhere for emergencies," he said, while looking through his desk drawers. "Yes, here they are; make sure you wear gloves, we may get prints off it."

"No worries Guv, of course I will."

Dan resumed the task of deleting old e-mails when, suddenly, the building shook with an explosion, shattering some windows. He ran to the corridor to look out though a cloud of rising smoke and dust onto the street, to see his car destroyed. With pieces of it strewn all over the street, there was also glass from smashed shop windows littered everywhere and bodies lying on the ground.

Dan screamed as he ran down the stairs. "No! No! Not Jimmy." He ran straight to the largest piece remaining of the vehicle, which was part of the chassis, and stood looking around for Jimmy's body, but all he could see were body parts. It was a scene of mayhem and destruction. Bronco soon joined him and Dan breathlessly explained about his car and Jimmy.

The entire station was soon out with officers attending to the injured and others closing the street. It was quickly confirmed amongst the fellow officers that Jimmy *had* been in the car. In a couple of minutes, ambulances and fire engines began to arrive, as did two ARVs, soon to be followed by two more. Within twenty minutes, both the army's bomb squad and the NaCTSO were on the scene with the latter taking control.

Once it was explained to the armed response officers whose car it was, they told Dan he should leave the scene and go back into the police station. He felt sick and was in shock – for, as much as he had witnessed colleagues die in the past in combat, this was so different. At least when Arthur Jackson and the armed officers were killed in the ambush they were at work, albeit protecting him. But this was young Jimmy, a brilliant lad with so much potential and so much to look forward to. Dead because he was doing a favour. Sue was stood by the front door of the nick and as he walked back she reached up, they hugged and she began to sob. Keeping her close to him, they turned, walked inside and went up to his office. The sobs subsided as she began to speak. "It's awful, Dan. Will this ever end? I'm heart-broken for Jimmy, he was such a lovely boy, but that bomb was meant for you – it could have been both of us in there or even with Andy. I'm sorry, but I'm scared shitless; what are we going to do?"

At that moment, Dan's phone rang and he noticed it was Tom. "I've just seen the news of the explosion. What's happened?" Dan explained it all to him and then Tom said,

"Right, I'm coming down to get you and the family – you can't stay there."

"Thanks, mate, but I can't be seen to be running away; the young officer who was killed was a good lad and it's down to me to be here for the rest of the team. I am sure they will increase the guards again. Listen, I must go, it's like a war zone here at the moment. Talk soon."

CHAPTER 63

Over the next two days, the area was virtually completely sealed off, with security checks on anyone arriving and leaving. Some of the country's top forensic explosive experts were painstakingly going over the area with a fine tooth comb, in a bid to find and re-build the parts of the bomb to try and identify the bomb maker. Every part of the Freelander had been photographed, numbered and taken away to a nearby warehouse that the police had commandeered, where they would slowly re-build it.

After that, Dan, Sue and Andy were escorted everywhere by at least two armed response officers and Smudger had moved back in with them.

The press had a huge presence again and a press conference had been arranged in the function room of a local hotel, with press officer, Megan Barrett, and the Chief Constable, Sir Norman Evans.

A team had checked CCTV and had spotted a car near the garage before the Freelander was taken, but that car had been found burnt out in a country lane six miles away. Dan was stood in the main office looking through CCTV pictures when his phone rang. It was Tom.

"I need to see you; I'm across the road but can't get any closer because of the security. Could you get out for a couple of minutes?"

"OK, but it won't be easy. If you don't want to be seen, go down the alleyway between the shops; there are garages at the back and I'll be there in five."

As Dan turned around he realised that Tish was standing right behind him. "Are you alright, Guv?"

Dan stood there for a second wondering what she may have heard. He replied, "Yes, yes, I'm fine; I have to pop out for a bit, won't be long," and he promptly turned and left. Tom was waiting at the end of the alley and Dan beckoned him to go around behind a fence at the rear of a shop.

They exchanged greetings and Tom continued, "I wanted to see you face to face, Dan. We need to talk this through – I don't think you are safe here and, to be honest, I don't think you will *ever* be safe while Sefiri is still alive. We need to cut the head off the serpent; it's the only way to ensure you, Sue and Andy are going to remain safe. If only he had died when I attacked the house, the rocket Smudger fired was spot-on and the drone worked brilliantly, but he must have nine lives – I really thought we had him! Thanks to my man in Mumbai I have a very good idea where he is hiding out in Tirana. I've talked to Smudger and we are going to put a plan together to go out there and finish the job, once and for all."

Dan thought for a second before replying, "In that case, I am going to come with you. This can't go on any longer, with others dying because of me. I thought that, after we had killed El Boushi and his evil son and gained justice for Catherine, I would eventually be able to go back to a normal, law-abiding life, but you're right – that's not going to happen while Sefiri is still at large, so count me in."

At that moment, Tom looked over Dan's shoulder. Holding up his hand to stop Dan talking, he said, "Can I help you?" to Tish who he suddenly realised was standing there.

"Tish, what do you want?"

She looked deadly serious. "Well, if I could ask for an explanation of what's going on here, that would be great. I followed you because I thought you might be in danger, but after all that I've heard, I guess no explanation is needed. I take it you are Poacher?"

Tom just stood and looked from Tish to Dan and back again, but didn't reply.

Instead, Dan attempted to respond with, "Tish, I don't–" but she put her hand up to stop him.

"Guv, don't say a word, I heard everything and it all falls into place now. Your mate here blew up Sefiri's house with the help of your other mate, Smudger, and I would guess that you, Poacher, were the vigilante."

Dan spoke louder this time. "Tish, you don't understand enough of this."

"Excuse me, Guv, but I think I do. Between the two of you, you are guilty of a string of vicious murders and, if convicted, neither of you will see the outside of a cell again in your lives."

This time, Tom responded. "Tish, you really need to know the full story before you decide if you're going to turn us in, but let me make one thing clear – I will plead guilty – *I* am the one who undertook the killings. Dan had nothing to do with it, but it will be impossible to prove otherwise."

Tish looked from one to the other before replying, "Yes, well, in that case, let's get one more thing clear. I am proud to be a good copper and believe in upholding the law, but what I have seen recently and what I've just heard puts a different light on things. So, here is the deal… I won't turn you in, on one condition, and that is that I come with you on the mission to kill Sefiri and, before you say anything, that's not negotiable. You know I can handle myself better than most men – I'm firearms trained and I want this all over and done with as much as you two do."

Dan really didn't know what to say, so Tom replied, "If you are sure, I think it could work, but it is going to be very dangerous. He is going to be well guarded and it won't be easy getting the fire-power we need into the country or out again once we have taken him out. If you agree… Dan, I think we all need to have a meeting to brainstorm this and you need to talk to Sue and see how she feels about it before you go any further."

Dan agreed and Tom said he would be back in touch later in the day as he wanted to set up a local, safe place for meeting. Tish and Dan walked slowly back to the nick, "You don't have to worry, Guv," she said, "I won't let you down. He will be blaming you for all that is wrong in his life and won't rest until you're dead, so it has to be done and it's not something the authorities will do."

"It's not you I'm worried about, Tish, it's what Sue will say when I tell her. It won't be an easy conversation after all she has been through."

Dan couldn't have been more wrong about Sue's reaction to Tom's idea – the death of Jimmy Edmunds, which was meant for Dan, was obviously the final straw. As soon as Dan told her, she agreed immediately. She said, "Obviously, I'm not happy about you going and putting yourself in danger, but the fact is, *you* are in danger here and I think you always will be while that monster is alive, I trust you to be careful and take care of yourself, but don't you dare get hurt, else you will have *me* to answer to!" She put her arms around him and they kissed. They had just finished hugging when Tom called, giving them the address of an Airbnb a few miles away in the country that he had just rented. He asked them to meet him and the others there at 8 pm that night, so they could begin to put the plan together.

CHAPTER 64

Cantley Lodge was a six-bedroomed, grade two barn conversion, set in fifteen acres of rolling Essex countryside. It was new on the market and Tom had been able to rent it for the next two weeks, with a further two if required, using the cover of a TV company using it as a base for a documentary. It was well after midnight by the time the plan was finalised and the logistics agreed. Tom calculated it would take a fortnight to put everything into place and, after taking pictures of Dan, Smudger and Tish, they said their goodnights and left with new burner phones to keep in touch, only using WhatsApp messaging unless in an emergency.

Tom's first two jobs were to book a flight to İzmir, Turkey, to get new fake passports for the others, then to sit down with Smudger to work out what armaments they would need and put the order in with his Irish supplier.

The next day he checked in at Stansted Airport, with only hand luggage and using fast-track at security. He was soon at the gate for the three hours and forty-minute Pegasus Airlines flight to İzmir Adnan Menderes Airport. From the airport he went straight to the office of Mecho, his contact for any kind of fake ID. This was now their fourth meeting and Tom was greeted like an old family friend. He then caught a taxi to the Ramada Plaza Hotel opposite the Luna Park, where the first time he came here he had broken both arms of two muggers who thought he might have been an easy target. He spent a quiet night at the hotel and was back to see Mecho first thing in the morning, before taking a taxi to return to the airport and then his flight back to Essex.

They all met at Cantley Lodge again that evening and Sue had arrived early to cook them all a meal. Dan had spent the day at the nick and the good news was, thanks to the painstaking forensic work, the net was closing on the bomb maker and MI5 were now dealing with it. As soon as dinner was over, Tom began to explain the logistics of the mission.

"In three days' time I will drive my van with everything we need in the hidden compartment, to Dover, then take the ferry to Dunkirk. Once there, I will drive to Calais and meet with Smudger who will have travelled using one of the false passports, by train on the Channel Tunnel. We will travel first to Ghent, where I will rent another van, leaving mine there. We will spend the next twenty-four hours driving to Tirana. In five days' time, Dan, again using one of his two false passports, will fly from Stansted to Istanbul, staying over for one night at the Yotelair Hotel, which is airside at Istanbul Airport, before flying on the next day to Tirana. Tish, again using one of her two false passports, will fly in six days' time from Luton Airport on Wizz Air direct to Tirana – it takes just over three hours.

We have a three-bedroomed villa; Smudger and I will share in Farkë, which is in the hills overlooking Tirana and about three miles away from our target. Although I have recced the place on Google Maps, here are some images." Handing out pictures to everyone, he continued, "We will need to spend some time there doing a proper recce, before deciding on the final plan. Ideally, it would be good to get him away from the villa, but that might not be possible. We should hire a couple of motorbikes for surveillance and we will have the drone as well. If all goes as planned for our exit strategy, we have open-ended BA tickets from Tirana to Heathrow for both Dan and Tish. Me and Smudger will split – him going to Skopje and flying to Luton and me to Thessaloniki, flying to Brussels, where I will rent a car to take me to Ghent, get my van and travel back from Dunkirk to Dover. Any questions?" They all shook their heads. The plan was a good start and they agreed they would know much more once they were on the ground in Albania. The evening ended soon after and the next day, everyone at the nick was preparing for Jimmy Edmunds' funeral.

The City of London Cemetery and Crematorium dates back to 1856. It is the final resting place of many famous and infamous people, including Catherine Eddowes and Mary Ann Nichols, both victims of Jack the Ripper, Joseph Merrick (the 'Elephant Man'), Dame Anna Neagle and Bobby Moore. It stands in two hundred acres next to the A406 North Circular Road. Jimmy's funeral was attended by all of Dan's team and other officers from Union Street, along with ex-station sergeant, Dave Reeves, and his wife from Jimmy's digs. They were joined by old school friends and Jimmy's mum, but his dad who now lived in Canada with his new wife, however, hadn't returned for the service. Dan had been asked to do the eulogy and spoke of what a fine and intelligent young officer Jimmy was and how he would have gone far in the service. Afterwards, Jimmy's mum thanked Dan and said how proud Jimmy was to be working with him. Dan couldn't help but think that if he hadn't been so close to him he would still be alive. All the party were invited for drinks at a nearby pub but declined as they had to return to the station.

CHAPTER 65

So, it was early on the Sunday morning that Tom set out for Dover. The traffic was light and his journey took him down the M1 onto the M25, over the Queen Elizabeth II Bridge and then onto the A20 heading towards Dover, before the two-hour crossing to Dunkirk.

Smudger had taken the Central line tube into London, changing at Liverpool Street onto the Metropolitan line to King's Cross St Pancras. After passing through security trouble-free, he was on the Eurostar for the journey to Calais-Fréthun station, which took less than an hour. He was quickly off the train and pleased to see Tom waiting for him outside in the van. Within the next hour they had parked close to the Europcar depot in Sint-Denijs-Westrem, a suburb of Ghent. Tom checked in at the reception using one of his false IDs and collected an Iveco Daily van. Larger than a transit, it would be plenty big enough for their needs. With Smudger driving Tom's VW Transporter, it only took a few minutes to drive to a secluded country lane where they transferred everything into the larger van, hiding it in two wooden crates he had obtained from the Irish arms dealer – they were what he used for bringing weapons into the country and appeared to be filled with tins of paint but had large false bottoms, which he assured Tom would work well.

The journey to Tirana clocked almost fourteen hundred miles and over twenty-four hours on their satnavs. Tom was happy to take the first shift at driving as it was agreed they would do three- to four-hour sessions each, giving the other time to rest. Soon they joined the European route E40, Europe's longest road, almost five thousand miles long from Calais to close to the Russian-China border in Ridder, Kazakhstan. Fortunately for them they weren't travelling that far on it by passing around Brussels, then on into Germany, crossing over the Rhine on the Cologne Rodenkirchen Bridge, before turning south, the Autobahn making the driving fast and easy, so in under four hours they reached Frankfurt where, after a very quick toilet break, Smudger took over the driving. Tom had brought some Ration-X 24 hour ration packs to keep them fed on the journey. As they continued south, passing Nuremberg, Tom slept while Smudger kept to a steady 80 mph all the way to the Austrian border. After nine hours and six hundred miles, they took their time to refuel the van, have another toilet break and stretch their legs.

Like all good servicemen, both had the ability to sleep anywhere at any time and, after eating his rations, Smudger was asleep in seconds as Tom set off on the next leg that would take them through the beautiful scenery of the Bavarian Alps. Sadly though, at night, there was very little of the snow-covered peaks to see. As the miles swiftly flew by they were soon crossing the border into Slovenia and then on and into Croatia, finally stopping outside Zagreb. After a toilet break, Smudger took over the driving again as Tom slept, the route this time turning west towards the Adriatic coast, then virtually following the coast south into the region of Dalmatia, passing the town of Split and finally stopping after four solid hours of driving. After topping up with fuel again, Tom took his turn for the next part of the journey, crossing borders into Bosnia and Herzegovina, as the dawn broke over the hilly countryside, then to Montenegro, before entering Albania after a twenty-minute wait in the queue at the Muriqan-Sukobin border crossing. The final part of the journey took under three hours and, by just before midday, their satnav had led them straight to the villa in Farkë.

As they were arriving at the villa, Dan was being dropped off at Stansted Airport by Sue. He had taken compassionate leave following all the events over the last few weeks, with Jimmy's death being the final one. They parked in the short stay car park and Sue came with him to the check-in. Dan only had hand luggage on him and they slowly walked hand in hand towards the fast-track passageway. Placing his rucksack on the floor, Dan took Sue in his arms who felt a little anxious, and said, "Please don't worry, darling, this will all be over in a few days and we can get on with our lives together."

With tears streaming down her face, she quietly replied, "I know you will be fine; don't worry about me. Concentrate on what you have to do. I can't believe I am saying this, but deal with that evil bastard and get back to me safe and sound as soon as you can. I love you and need you."

With that they kissed and Sue turned and walked away, beginning to sob. Dan watched her go, his heart pounding – he knew he was doing this for her and for their future together. Quickly making his way through security and straight to the gate, he was pleased to see his Turkish Airlines flight was on time. Just over four hours later, but by local time seven hours later, he was checking in to the Yotelair Hotel at the airport. Ordering dinner from the room service menu, he called Sue to let her know all was well and went to bed knowing he had an early start the next morning. Istanbul's location straddles the Bosporus Straight, separating Europe from Asia, which makes the airport one of the world's busiest aviation hubs. With that in mind, he left plenty of time to find the correct gate for his flight to Tirana. Dan was deep in concentration for most of the 90-minute flight and by the time he was approaching passport control at Tirana airport, he was worried because it was the first time his false passport had actually been checked. He felt nervous about it, but knew he had to look relaxed. He was waved through and was relieved it was straight forward and was soon in a taxi heading for the villa.

Tish had been uncertain how much to tell Julie Burton. They had met just over six months ago when they were both on a course and it had been instant attraction. From their first date it had quickly blossomed into a full on relationship and Tish had now moved in with her. They had no secrets but knew she couldn't be totally honest about this. She had told her that she had to go away for a few days and would be out of contact for most of that time. She informed Julie it was linked to work and she asked Julie to trust her, which she agreed to do.

Julie had dropped her at Luton Airport four hours ago and, like Dan, her mind had been filled with thoughts of the mission. She was still deep in thought when the seat belt warning lights came on as the Wizz Air Airbus A320 prepared to descend into Tirana Airport.

CHAPTER 66

An hour later Tish found herself with the others at the beautiful villa with an infinity pool and south-facing views over the Albanian hills and mountains – it really was luxurious, but more important for them – secluded. Luckily, it was also close enough to the town and Sefiri's villa.

Tom and Smudger had worked non-stop since they arrived, stocking the house with food and drink, hiring two motorbikes and buying helmets and clothing. They had both done drive bys, getting as close to the villa as they could and had also flown Tom's new drone high above, filming the layout of the grounds and surrounding area.

The four of them were sitting in the lounge drinking mugs of coffee and, after talking over their journeys, Tom started up his MacBook Pro. Pressing 'play' on a video, he began to speak.

"As you can see from the drone video, the villa is in an area of other high end villas, all with the kind of security you would expect to find for such properties. Sefiri's stands in about two acres; it's surrounded by a high wall topped with razor wire – the only way in or out is through the front electric gates, which are worked from the gatehouse. There are lots of CCTV cameras and armed guards patrolling inside and out – we don't know how many, but they all appear to be living on site. We think they also have a couple of lookout vehicles parked a short distance away, monitoring traffic in and out of the area.

"My man in Mumbai has been working hard for us, he sussed after we hit Sefiri's place who we were after and, after researching all that has happened, he wants to help us. He is working on hacking into their CCTV and hopes to have that done later today. He is also trying to get the building plans for the villa; it would seem that Sefiri is keeping a very low profile and as far as we know, he never leaves the place, which is not what we had hoped for. Despite the extradition treaty between the UK and Albania, very few criminals have ever been extradited. He no doubt has police and politicians on his payroll, but there are many in the government trying to clean up corruption here, so that may be the reason why–"

Dan interrupted, "What about deliveries?"

Tom continued, "From what we can gather so far and the feedback from Mumbai, there aren't any – all supplies are brought in by his men. Two of them go out every day in a van and collect what's needed."

It was Smudger's turn to speak. "I followed them yesterday; they made two stops. One was at the Interspar supermarket at the Tirana East Gate shopping mall where they parked the van in the multistorey car park, but then they disappeared into a bar/restaurant place and had a couple of beers and a burger–"

Then it was Tish's turn to interrupt with, "If they do that every day, I could bump into them in the bar and chat them up, see if I can get any info. At the same time, is there anything we can do to the van?"

Tom replied, "That's a great idea, Tish, and yes, if nothing else we can put explosives on the van, if only for a diversion if we need one. It wouldn't hurt for you to visit the bar today anyway to give you a feel and perhaps chat with the staff – that way you will fit in better when the men are there. If Smudger takes you, then Dan can come out on the bikes with me to give him an idea of the area.

Dan and Tom were the first to return and Dan had a few thoughts about the location. "My first question is 'where do they get their electricity from?' and my second is 'do they have a backup generator?' because if we are going to go in it needs to be in darkness and we would need to knock their power out. My other question is, 'are any of the neighbouring villas available to rent?' Where we are is perfect for what we need now, but that would at least get us in closer and give us an FOB, a Forward Operating Base."

Tom agreed. "I will check that out and if Mumbai gets the plan of the villa, we might see where the generator is – they *must* have one."

They were still talking as Tish walked in and Tom smiled. "How did it go?"

"Very well," and then in an American accent, she said, "Meet Tori McMahon – how y'all doing, folks? I am a writer for the Lonely Planet and am researching western food in Albania; could I ask you some questions?" They all laughed as she continued, "I think the manager, Emal, who speaks good English, fancies me and so I will keep playing up to him to keep him sweet."

Tom and Dan both continued laughing as Smudger walked in. He was the first to comment. "I know, she's got more front than Marks and Spencer; I couldn't believe it when she told me."

Tish answered, "Well, I just thought if I tell them that, then I can interview customers. I've arranged to go back tomorrow when, hopefully, these guys will be in and I can find out something useful."

Dan congratulated her and Tom said he would take Tish in the next day. He then went on to bring her and Smudger up to speed on his latest plans.

CHAPTER 67

Tish arrived at the restaurant just before noon. She chatted with Emal again and when she started to interview customers, he acted as an interpreter when needed. When the two guards arrived, they were welcomed as regulars by the staff and Tish asked Emal to introduce her to them. One spoke a little English, but one spoke much more, so she concentrated on him. Soon she got into the swing of chatting generally, her talking about America (which she only really knew about from films) and eventually they talked about themselves.

Tom had been in the supermarket when Sefiri's men had arrived earlier. Watching from a distance as they did their shop, he noted carefully what they purchased, then when they went into the restaurant, Tom checked out their van in the multistorey.

As much as the men were enjoying chatting with Miss Tori McMahon, they had to get back to work and left. Tish interviewed another couple, just to give cover to her story, then thanked Emal and left.

While this was ongoing, Smudger and Dan bought twenty burner phones and five chargers, only purchasing the one in each shop and travelled all over Tirana doing this to avoid any suspicion. When the whole group were back, Tish passed on the info she had gained. They both seemed genuinely nice guys – they worked preparing food for the twelve guys working there, but not for Sefiri – he has his cooked by someone called Bato. She finished with, "They're all living on site at the moment and they only get out each day for the supplies."

Dan said, "Bato… must be Bato Dauti, his bodyguard, driver and personal assistant. We think it was him who got Sefiri out of the house and to his plane at Northolt."

It was then Tom's turn. "If that *is* him, he must be good at his job and we need to look out for him. I checked the van over; it will be easy to plant a charge on it and easy to get in through the back doors. Knowing how many men are in there and seeing the food and water they've bought, it's obvious they don't keep a stock but use it daily. They bought four dozen bottles of water today which makes me think… if we get into the van while they are in the restaurant, we could spike the water and, if it comes to it, some of the food. I'm sure I can mix up something that might not kill them, but will certainly lay some of them out, making the job a bit easier. I need to check in with Mumbai but, if we can, let's get all our ducks in a row today – we could go in tomorrow night. If you guys could start making up the charges with the C-4, I will contact Mumbai."

Dan and Smudger showed Tish how to deal with the explosives, while Tom was contacting Mongoose on his MacBook, but again through a series of VPNs. When he finished he said he was going into town on the motorbike as he had a few things to get.

Smudger was the first to finish working on the C-4, so he went to the kitchen to prepare a curry for everyone's dinner. Once Tom was back, he told them about the news from Mumbai and what he had bought.

"Well, I have great news from Mumbai. He has got the ground plan of the villa, can patch us into their CCTV and take it out if necessary. He can also take out their power or, if we wanted, *all* of Tirana's power. I've also heard back from the letting agent and there is a villa available two plots away from Sefiri's, which we could rent for a couple of days as a film location, if we think it will help. I've brought various bits from a few chemists and some fine needle syringes to inject into the bottles of water and clear superglue to seal them afterwards.

After a short discussion it was agreed to rent the villa as an FOB. Tom immediately contacted the agent and paid for it on a credit card. It was agreed they would pack all they needed in the van that night, get into the new villa first thing in the morning, then be back at the restaurant by lunchtime. Tish would keep the men talking until the others had planted the explosives on the van and spiked the water and food. They would then spend the rest of the day making final preparations and they planned the attack for 3 am the following morning.

Everything went smoothly the next day; the new villa was perfect, its high walls giving security from prying eyes, but in a brilliant position to attack Sefiri. The food and water had been spiked and the bomb was attached to the underside of the van.

By 7 pm, everything was ready for the mission; plans had been checked and re-checked as had weapons and explosives. Mongoose had been able to link up to their coms headsets via Bluetooth so Tom could call for action on power and alarms. Tickets had been booked for Dan and Tish on the first flights out in the morning and it was time to get a few hours' rest before starting the mission. But first, Dan asked Tish to come out onto the veranda for a chat.

They sat down overlooking the plush grounds and Dan began to speak. "Tish, I just wanted to say to you that, if you have any doubts about taking part in the mission, you are welcome to walk away and none of us will think bad of you. People will die – we won't be leaving any witnesses and you may find that you will need to kill and I know what a quandary that must put you in."

"Guv, thanks for that, but I know what I'm doing and we both know it needs to be done. Trust me, I will do whatever it takes." With that they both stood up and Tish gave Dan a hug. "Let's make this count, Guv, then we can get back to whatever 'normal' is in our job." As she walked away he was thinking just what a remarkable woman Tish was and then he thought of Sue and how he hoped this would lead them to a normal life together.

CHAPTER 68

They were all up by midnight, hardly talking to each other, in anticipation of the events to come. After washing and each getting dressed into the combat clothes Tom had got them, he brought them each a strong coffee. The clothes consisted of a pair of Oakley Elite assault boots, combat trousers, black, long sleeved combat T-shirts with hard plate bullet-proof vests fitted with heavy titanium plates. Gloves, balaclavas and night-vision goggles completed the attire. They were also armed with Glock 19s fitted with silencers and each of them with four spare mags, apart from Smudger who always preferred his Beretta M9. Tom and Smudger had M4 carbines while Dan and Tish preferred Heckler & Koch MP5s. All of them were carrying stun grenades and the men all carried F1 fragmentation hand grenades and, like Tom, all were armed with Fairbairn-Sykes knives.

Tom checked in with Mongoose who reported back that the spiked food and drink was working as some guards were either unconscious, vomiting or in great pain.

The night was pitch-black, which suited them. Tom nodded to Smudger who was the first to leave, slipping out of the gateway and heading away from the villa to take care of the guards who were acting as lookouts in the two cars back down the street. Both had one man in them and both men had their throats cut with a single strike. As soon as Smudger was back they left in pairs on either side of the street. As they approached the target, Tom told Mongoose to take out the CCTV and then ten seconds later to open the gates. The guard in the gatehouse was busy trying to get the CCTV to work. As Tom was the first through the gates, he opened the door just as the guard turned around and double tapped him, the 9mm bullets almost silently piercing his chest and blowing a hole in his face.

The other three were right behind him. Spreading out, their night-vision covering the villa with a green hue, they looked across the circular drive with a large fountain in the centre, to the villa with a garage block and what they now knew to be the staff quarters to the left.

They heard a door open in the villa and spotted two men holding torches in one hand and pistols in the other, who came out running towards the gate. Dan shot one while Smudger shot the other – three down, nine to go. Tom was quickly making his way to the generator room but wasn't there in time as the power cut had started it up, bringing lights on everywhere. For a second their night-vision goggles blinded all of them, but they quickly moved them onto the top of their heads and carried on. In a couple of seconds they were able to put them back on as Tom had reached the room and managed to turn it off before placing one of the charges on it, which was linked to a burner.

Dan and Tish replaced their goggles and were covertly making their way to the villa. As they passed the fountain, a man stepped out onto the first floor balcony, shining a powerful flashlight. As he swept it over the driveway, it picked out Tish, instantly blinding her and she instinctively turned away. He lifted a pistol to fire at her but was too slow – Dan fired at him. The first shot went high, but two more hit him, sending him tumbling headfirst over the balcony and onto the drive. Dan ran to the body and fired again twice. As Tish caught up with him they approached the front door of the villa together.

Smudger joined Tom outside the staff quarters' door. As Tom began cautiously to open the door it was pulled from his hand when a guard came rushing out, bumping into him and making him stagger back. The guard yelled something and reached for his gun in his belt but he didn't have time to draw it as Smudger used the butt of the M4, knocking him back against the wall and then drew his knife, placing his left hand over the guard's mouth and stabbing him twice in his stomach. The yell had alerted any remaining guards who hadn't been affected by the poisoning. As Smudger attempted to open the door again, a hail of bullets smashed against the woodwork, making him dive for cover. As Tom witnessed what had happened, he opened fire with the M4 before diving to the floor near Smudger. Grabbing a fragmentation grenade from his belt, he pulled the pin and lobbed it to the end of the room. The explosion rocked the building, throwing bodies into the air. As the smoke and dust cleared it was obvious the grenade had done its job; there were bodies that had been torn apart lying across the room. They both climbed off the floor and slowly walked forward. There was no movement from any of the guards so, covering the room with their carbines at the ready, they quickly checked each one was dead, counting the bodies at the same time.

Tom was furthest into the room when the toilet door burst open and a man in just his underpants appeared, firing a Kalashnikov AK-47. Smudger had his back to the door and didn't see him coming. He had no chance – at least four bullets ripped into his back; two hit the back plate of his vest, but one had gone through his pelvis and one through his neck. In a heartbeat, Tom turned and fired a volley, hitting the man repeatedly and dropping him to the floor.

He ran to Smudger and, seeing the blood bubbling from his neck, he tried to stem the flow, but it was just too much.

Smudger opened his eyes and coughed but more blood escaped down his chin. In a weak voice he said, "I always thought I had eyes in the back of my head, I guess I was wrong."

Tom was holding his torso off the ground with one arm and his chin with the other. "Hang in there, mate, we will get you out of this. You're a tough old fucker – this won't beat you."

But Smudger shook his head, speaking slower with every word. "Nah, this is it… it's a shame we never… got to carry out… all our plans… but don't you ever give up. Tell Hoops I'm sorry, I real…" and he coughed again and died in Tom's arms.

Tom held him close for a second or two, the blood soaking his left arm, when he heard gunfire coming from the villa. Laying Smudger down, he turned and made his way towards the sound.

CHAPTER 69

Dan opened the front doors to the villa; both him and Tish had their Glocks at the ready, carefully scanning the area for any movement when they heard shouting from upstairs. Dan signalled for them to make their way up. They were almost halfway when a man appeared on the landing and fired his pistol, hitting Tish, sending her tumbling backwards down the stairs. Dan returned fire, hitting the man and knocking him backwards. He hit the wall and slid down to the floor. He wanted to go back and care for Tish but knew he had to continue and find Sefiri. As he reached the top of the stairs he realised that the shooter had been Bato Dauti, the driver bodyguard. He looked at him and, without a second thought, fired two shots into the man's head.

Quickly re-loading the Glock with another magazine, he opened one of the double doors that Dauti had come out of; he was certain that this was where the shouting had come from, but the room looked empty. It was a large lounge with a huge TV, three long sofas and a bookcase filled most of one wall. He looked out on to the balcony but still no sign of anyone. As he stepped through the door though, he was hit hard on the back of his head, knocking him down onto the floor, his gun skidding under a sofa and his night-vision slipping off. He rolled over to see Sefiri himself standing over him, brandishing a pistol. Looking up at him, Dan began to speak. "So, finally, we meet."

"What do you mean, 'finally, we meet'? Who are you?

Who sent you?"

"No one sent me, I am the man you've tried to kill time and time again. You have been behind the deaths of many good, honest men, some good friends of mine and I have come here to kill *you.*"

"You're Hooper? The man that killed Reni and no doubt behind the death of my brother, Józef. Stand up slowly and take that mask off – let me see you before I kill you."

Dan eased himself up onto his feet and as he reached for his balaclava there was the sound of an explosion from the staff quarters. This startled Sefiri, enough for Dan to dive at him, knocking the gun out of his hand and landing on top of him on the floor. But even though he was in his seventies he was still as strong as an ox and knew how to fight. Using the heel of his hand, he aimed to hit Dan just under his nose, which would have driven it back into his head, but Dan turned at the last second, the blow catching him on the side of his jaw, knocking him off to one side. Sefiri instantaneously locked his arm around Dan's neck, trying to choke him, but Dan managed to turn and reach up to the older man's face to stick his thumbs into his eye sockets, making him break the hold. But Sefiri wouldn't stop charging at Dan. With all his strength, they hit the bookcase so hard, it rocked. Dan brought his knees up into Sefiri's groin, making him double over and yell, backing away in pain, but as Dan stepped after him the bookcase began to tip forward, crashing on top of him and knocking him to the ground.

It had knocked the wind out of him, but he pushed himself to his knees and began to crawl out from under it. He was almost out when he was kicked hard in his head, once again almost knocking him out. But, although he remained conscious, the damage may have been done, because for the first time since the ambush his head began to spin the way it had in hospital and he lost all sense of balance. Putting his head in both hands to try and clear the spinning, he was kicked hard in the ribs, sending him tumbling over and making the dizziness worse. He looked up to see Sefiri standing over him again. He had picked up his gun and was holding it in two hands.

Sefiri laughed and said, "Finally, I can pay the debt of *kanun* to my family. Your death will be rejoiced – then I will find your wife and I will let my men rape her time and time again and then kill her."

With that, he slowly lifted the pistol. Dan so longed to just get up and fight, but his head was still spinning like a top. He could hardly focus on the man, let alone the gun and in that instant he knew it was over.

They say that when you are dying your life flashes before you and at that moment it did for Dan. Images of his life were exploding like rockets in his head… Catherine's face, her death, Sue smiling at him and Tom and him driving over the Imam and his evil son. It was like a slide show that took minutes, but it was less than a second. He heard the voice of Sefiri like it was in a dream: "Now, you will die!" And then a single gunshot.

He must have just passed out as, sometime later, he opened his eyes as he heard a familiar voice say, "Guv, are you OK? It's me – Tish."

Looking at her, he whispered, "But Tish, you're dead… I saw you get shot and tumble down the stairs."

"Nah, the bullets hit the vest and knocked me down the stairs. I must have banged me head and was out for a bit, but when I heard the noise up here I ran in and saw him with the gun. But it's all over, he's dead – I just killed him."

Dan's head began to clear. He was also in awe of what Tish had just told him. As she was helping him up, he explained about the bangs on his head and the dizziness and then he asked if she was OK.

"Yeah, I've got a headache and my tits are killing me, but that vest saved my life."

Tom frantically ran in and asked, "What's happened? Are you OK, Dan?"

"I've been better, but it's over thanks to Tish – she just saved my life."

He reached out to hug her and she hugged him back. "We did it, Guv! We did it and it's over." Dan smiled at Tom and asked, "Where's Smudger got to?" But Tom just looked back at him and shook his head.

Dan asked again, "Where is he… what's happened?"

"He didn't make it, he's in the staff quarters," and he went on to explain what had happened.

They were all in shock. Dan had known him the longest and losing yet another comrade made the hurt all the worse. He finally spoke, exclaiming, "We aren't leaving him here. I don't care how we do it or how much it costs – we get him home and give him a *proper* burial." Tom couldn't agree any more.

They all returned to the staff quarters where they wrapped his body in a sheet. Dan picked him up in his arms and they all set off to the other villa. Tom said he would be back there shortly and asked for everyone's C-4 charges in the meantime. Tish looked at her watch and realised that all this had happened in less than fifteen minutes, which seemed impossible.

They all cleared their belongings out of the villa before they began the mission and, once they had laid Smudger's body in the back of the van, Tom was back and they started to drive to their first villa. Driving for about five minutes they heard an explosion and saw a glow in the sky behind them. Dan and Tish glanced at Tom who said, "Let them search the rubble for him – it's the only tomb he deserves.

CHAPTER 70

Back at the villa, they allowed themselves a minute to brew a coffee and they made a toast to Smudger. Tish started to wipe down all the surfaces with bleach, while Tom and Dan began to work out a plan to repatriate Smudger. Their first task was to get Tish booked on to a flight home. Tom's concern was that the Albanian authorities would have knowledge of Sefiri's problems in the UK and if they knew that the demolished villa was his they may well be taking a close look at passengers flying via BA. So, it was agreed that Tish would take the same route that Dan had flown out on. She would take the 8 am Istanbul flight and have an hour's stop-over before flying on to Stansted.

Dan said he would stay and travel in the van with Tom, having hidden Smudger's body in one of the crates, their remaining weapons in the other. They both agreed it wasn't ideal, but they were determined to get him home and this looked like the best way. By 6.00 they were packed and ready to go. Dropping Tish off at the airport, they urged her not to call Julie until she got to Istanbul. Taking the same route back as Tom had taken, they were crossing the Albanian border before 9 am, relieved to get into Montenegro and on their way home. Dan couldn't wait to call Sue and the relief in her voice was plain to hear. He thought it was better to wait to tell her the sad news until he saw her.

The return route actually took a couple of hours longer, mainly due to heavy traffic. They took frequent stops as both were tired and feeling the after-effects of the adrenaline rush from the mission and the pain of losing their comrade.

It was almost noon the next day before they arrived at Tom's own van. They transferred the crates over but placed the body along with the weapons in the secret compartment and drove to Calais, where it was agreed they would separate – Dan taking the *Eurostar* to Ashford International station in Kent where Tom would pick him up after he took the van on Le Shuttle.

They were back at Cantley Lodge by 7 pm where Sue and Tish were waiting for them. As soon as they pulled up, Sue ran out to greet Dan and said, "I am so relieved to see you, it's been horrible not knowing how you were. Promise me you will never leave me again."

"I promise, darling, I promise, but first I have some sad news."

EPILOGUE

TWO WEEKS LATER

It was a beautiful spring morning as they made their way to the woodland burial site near Epping Forest. Dan had managed to acquire a forged death certificate sent from Meko in Turkey, giving cause of death as a heart attack. The wicker coffin had been sealed and was placed on a low wooden cart with flowers decorating it. Dan visited Smudger's flat where he found his red beret, which was now in place on top of the coffin. Dan and Tom slowly pulled the cart, followed by Sue and Tish, the only mourners, from the main building to the plot in the woods. Daffodils were in full bloom and the birds were singing a welcoming chorus.

There was to be neither a religious representative nor celebrant – it had been Smudger's last wish in the papers, along with his last will and testament, Dan had got from his flat leaving everything to the Army Benevolent Fund. Instead, he had asked for his former Captain to lead the service. Dan spoke of how he first met John 'Smudger' Smith, how he became his trusty Staff Sergeant and good friend, saying he was one of the bravest, kindest men he had ever met and how he owed his life to him many times over – a debt he was never fully able to repay. The coffin was lowered into the grave and each took turns to say a final goodbye, sprinkling a handful of soil onto the coffin. Two cemetery worked arrived to fill the grave, but Dan turned them away as he and Tom took off their jackets, picked up spades and filled it themselves.

As they turned to walk away, Dan stopped. He turned back, walking to the edge of the grave and saluted, tears running down his face.

The small procession walked solemnly back through the woods and were about to climb into Dan's new Mercedes GL 3.0, which he had just bought to replace the destroyed Freelander, when the door of a Bentley parked opposite opened and a man Dan thought he recognised got out and called to them.

"Gentlemen, may I have a word with you, please? Do excuse me, ladies, I shan't keep them long."

They both looked at each other before walking over to him.

"Detective Chief Inspector Hooper, you may remember me, we met after the unfortunate death of your fiancée, Catherine Raye. I'm Commander Timothy Blair, you came to my office at Thames House."

He then turned to Tom and said, "And you, of course, are Thomas Windsor, former trooper in the SAS, AKA the Vigilante Murderer."

Tom began to speak, but Blair held his hand up to stop him. "There really is no need to deny it, I have followed both of you closely since you dealt with that evil Islamist, Abdelhay El Boushi, and his son, Ayaan. I must say, it did present a bit of a problem at the time, but you more than likely saved my department a job as he wasn't giving us anything worthwhile. But enough reminiscing, I would like you to meet me at my office at midday tomorrow. I have moved from Thames House to somewhere more discreet and will text you the details. I have an offer to make to you that I think you will accept; the alternative would mean I have to hand my findings over to the National Crime Agency. But, I am sure when you hear what the offer is you will willingly accept, as you both obviously have such a fearless quest for justice.

THE END…

…for now, but the story continues in Book Three of the Hooper/Windsor thrillers,

ULTIMATE JUSTICE

CHAPTER 1

Dan Hooper and Tom Windsor had found themselves in many dangerous situations in their adult lives.

Both had killed enemies while in the service of the Queen…

Dan, as Captain in the 1st Battalion, Parachute Regiment (1 PARA).

Tom, as part of the 22nd Special Air Service Regiment (SAS).

And both had killed terrorists and gangsters…

Tom, as a member of various private military companies (PMCs) and, more recently, in his unflinching quest for justice.

Dan, as a police Detective Chief Inspector and, more recently, in protecting and finding justice for his family and loved ones.

But throughout all of that, although neither would have admitted it to the other, they had never felt as nervous as they did now.

They walked up into the bright daylight from the subway of Leicester Square's tube station in London's vibrant West End, turning left onto the busy pavements of Charing Cross Road, before turning left again into the quiet pedestrian street of Cecil Court. This was often nicknamed 'Booksellers' Row', where the Victorian frontages of the twenty or so shops haven't changed for over a century.

The text message received the previous evening from Commander Timothy Blair had instructed – almost ordered them – to be at Appleyard Books & Antiquities, 18A Cecil Court, London WC2N 4EZ, at 12 noon to meet him.

The shop window was overflowing with a plethora of old books, militaria, coins and stamps. They had hardly spoken since they got off the tube, but turned and looked at each other in anticipation, both taking a deep breath and raising their eyebrows in unison before Dan pushed the door open.

For just how full the shop window appeared from the outside, the inside was a hundredfold; the full length of one side was overtaken by bookshelves, some modern but many very old. Glass cabinets on the opposite wall contained everything from toy lead soldiers and military badges, to Dinky Toys, Hornby train sets and even a signed picture of Winston Churchill. The shelf above had a selection of military headwear including a white pith helmet with brass spike on top, reminiscent of those worn in the film Zulu, depicting the Battle of Rorke's Drift.

A large, bearded gentleman greeted them, wearing dark brown corduroy trousers, a cream shirt with what they both recognised as a Grenadier Guards' tie, and an unbuttoned tweed waistcoat. He was sat in a wingback chair with a book in his hand. Looking up at them over the top of his half-rimmed reading glasses and taking his unlit pipe from his mouth he spoke with a cockney accent. "Ah yes, gents, you are expected. Could you both confirm you have signed the Official Secrets Act?" which they both confirmed they had. "Thank you; in that case, can you please make your way down the staircase," he requested, using his pipe to direct them. "Someone will be waiting for you."

They made their way down the narrow steps, both noticing the small camera above a large oak door at the bottom, which opened as soon as they reached it.

A smartly dressed, forty-something man with the look of a former rugby player, greeted them. "This way, please, gentlemen; you are expected."

Following him through another door and then down a cast iron spiral staircase, he took them to a subbasement, which, in turn led to a metal door with a keypad and biometric retina scanner. The man placed one eye over the scanner and typed in a six-digit pass code, which neither of them could see. He then led them through the open door, into what could only be described as a mini version of Houston's Mission Control. They were both astounded – the longest wall was actually one huge screen showing dozens and dozens of feeds, some of traffic, some from the air and some of people walking or of buildings. Facing it were twelve computer terminals, all occupied by a mixture of men and women of various ages and race.

Commander Timothy Blair was standing by one of the terminals as they entered. He walked towards them, shook both their hands and asked them to follow him to his office.

As they entered it was as if they had stepped back in time, going from the high tech control room, back to a gentleman's club of the 1930s. The walls were covered in oak panelling, there was a bookcase filled with old leather bound volumes, an antique mahogany desk with a red leather embossed top was stood in the middle, behind which was a classic oxblood red, high back Chesterfield Queen Anne wing chair. On the wall behind that was a large picture of the Queen in an ornate gilt frame. As they quickly surveyed the room they noticed that the only links to the 21st century was another large plasma screen, a 27-inch Mac desktop and three telephones.

"Take a seat, gentlemen," pointing to the two oak Carver chairs. "We could have met at Thames House but I thought it would be good for you to see where most of my department's work is done." Promptly moving on, he continued, "I won't offer you tea or coffee at this moment; to be honest with you I am unsure how long you will be staying here, so let's get down to business." He produced two large, brown files from the desk drawer and dropped them onto the desk with a thud. "Well, here it all is, gentlemen. Shall I start with you, Mr Windsor?"

Opening the file and lifting the index page out, he said, "Let us see what we have… Thomas Charles Windsor, date of birth unknown as you were a foundling, but birth date given to you by the staff at Dr Barnardo's Homes, Barkingside, is 17th February 1967. They also gave you your name as both parents unknown. Attended Mossford and Fairlop schools. Joined the Royal Anglian Regiment, good service record; after two years were accepted into the Special Air Service; again, a good record. Upon retiring, various private military companies, ending up in Baghdad for Coeus, a front for our American friends at Langley and one of the CIA Special Activities Center's nastier black ops. The only details missing are what happened the night their base blew up and you obviously survived –perhaps, one day, you may want to tell me how."

Pausing briefly to look at Tom, the Commander continued.

"You next turn up in Turkey where you set up home and then finally return to Blighty where you set out on a murder spree, culminating in the death of the Imam and his son, which, as I have already told you, was what brought you to my attention. You may be pleased to know that Major General Grover J Buchanan retired, met an untimely death soon after returning to the USA when he was killed in a drive by in a rather shady part of Washington DC. Ten kilos of cocaine were found in his car and even more was found in a trunk at his house. Anyway, moving on… it would save time for you to just believe me when I tell you I have details of your recent missions targeting human trafficking and then assisting DCI Hooper in bringing down the biggest Albanian czar in the country, before going to Albania and killing him."

He paused again for a reaction but got none so he continued.

"You may think you can deny anything of what I have just said, but I would advise against it as I haven't even yet mentioned your house in Northamptonshire, various accounts in banks from Turkey to Grand Cayman and, of course, the Julius Baer Bank in Zurich."

Following another long pause where Tom looked at him, unflinching, he turned his attention to Dan.

"DCI Hooper or, indeed, Captain Hooper, there is no need for me to go through any of your records; they are mostly all public knowledge, apart from the aforesaid killing of Abdelhay El Boushi and son and then your trip to Tirana to deal with Mr Sefiri. I am fully aware of the injuries, trauma and personal loss you have been through, especially in the past few months, but obviously your willingness to take part in such activities could easily result in an extended stay at Her Majesty's pleasure, or possibly something far worse."

Dan nodded his head in acknowledgement, but didn't speak.

"So, let's be clear… I can arrange for these to go to the NCA today, in fact, it will only take a signal to the hidden camera on the wall behind you, to have you arrested now.

"That obviously isn't why I have asked you here today, but before I move forward, I need to make something very clear to you both. What I am about to tell you goes way above your security clearance. Once you have heard it, if you decide not to accept my offer, the consequences may be far worse than prison. Do you both understand and do you wish me to continue?"

They looked at each other again and Dan replied, "I don't think we have much of a choice, sir, do we?"

To which Tom agreed.

CHAPTER 2

"In that case, if you're sure, I will continue. What you have seen here is the main operations room for an elite, covert intelligence unit, formed to work with all of MI5, MI6 and SIS, the Secret Intelligence Service, with the title of Joint Special Services Operation Group. We are only answerable to the highest level of government and civil service, with a remit to operate anywhere in the world, and to do that we have an unlimited budget.

"This control room operates 24/7, three-hundred and sixty-five days a year, along with an elite Cyber Forensics Laboratory (CFL) and a team of mobile surveillance officers, or MSOs. I could go on and on but, suffice to say, we are the 'dog's bollocks' of covert security. We currently have eight front line field operatives, all recruited from the security services, so therefore, I can imagine you are both thinking 'Why bother with us?'

"So, let me cut to the chase and I remind you, again, this is way above your security clearance. Five days ago there was a ransomware cyber attack on government Internet network servers, which has obviously been kept from the press and all but those at the highest echelons of government. We believe it came from a foreign state, either China or Iran, and that the ransomware was a cover to extract sensitive information. A deeper search has revealed that it is possible details of all our field operatives may have been taken, putting them in grave danger.

"Sadly, such attacks are becoming commonplace these days, almost in the same way during the Cold War we would take it in turns arresting each other's field agents. But it has presented us with a major problem that I want to deal with in-house rather than via SIS.

"I would like you two to take over a mission that two of my men would have been starting this week, but given the current circumstances, it is now not possible. It is imperative that it's carried out quickly and successfully to avoid a major terrorist attack in this country. If you agree, you will join my team in the first instance on a short-term basis with DCI Hooper, using the cover of being seconded to MI5, whilst you, Mr Windsor… or we could go back to calling you Mr Greensted if you wished, become a freelance agent for us, thus allowing you to carry on with your own personal crusade and still having full use of your various bank accounts.

"If you both agree, every detail of your previous escapades will be removed from all records and you will be free to continue with your private lives.

"I assume you would like to think it over. I will leave you in here and you have my word I will turn off all the cameras and recording equipment."

They both agreed and the Commander left them to chat.

Speaking quietly, secretly fearing a video recorder was left on, Dan asked, "What do you think? I can't see we have much of a choice."

Tom smiled and replied, "Honestly, I am gobsmacked that they know so much about us, but I don't care, I would love to work with them. For me, it looks like a dream job. I would be worried for you and what Sue would think though."

"Yes, I thought that, but she'll understand, I'm sure she will."

Tom went to the door and called the Commander back in.

They all sat down again and Tom spoke. "Thank you, sir. For me, it's a no-brainer; it would be an honour to work for you. Obviously, I have no one to worry about but myself, but Dan has, so it may be different for him."

The Commander looked at Dan, who said, "Well, I don't think I have much choice and if it is to deal with a terrorist threat, of course I agree."

CDR Blair stood up and walked over to shake both their hands. "Thank you, gentlemen, you will be doing your country a great service. It's time I told you more about the mission.

"It is to locate and terminate Abdullah Al-Mughassil, number two on the world's most wanted terrorist list, who we believe is recruiting British jihadists to carry out a poison gas attack on the London Tube network. He seldom moves from Northern Iraq or Syria, but we have been given information that he will be in Dubai for five days of secret talks, arriving in two days' time. It isn't the easiest place to carry out such a mission, but we may never get the chance to get him again.

"You will spend the next two days here working with our team who will bring you up to speed on the plans, you will then fly to the UAE where the local MI6 will contact you.

"Dan, or Number Eight, as you will now be known, I am sure you need to get back to your wife to explain what's happening. Number Nine, you are welcome to stay here and we will provide you with a hotel room or you can leave as well, but we want you both here at 7 am tomorrow morning."

Tom replied, "If it's all the same to you, sir, I will leave with Dan; I'm sure we have lots to discuss, but I will see you in the morning."

"Yes, of course, Number Nine, I quite understand. If you can both be under the next train display sign on the westbound platform at Leicester Square station at 06.55, someone will meet you and bring you in the tradesman's entrance. But before you go, I would like to introduce you to someone who will be working with you, another new recruit who joined us this morning – meet Number Ten."

The door opened and both their jaws dropped at the same time as Tish walked into the office.

"Hi, guys, it looks like we are going on another adventure!"

ACKNOWLEDGEMENTS

Thanks.

No one is more amazed than me that I have been able to finish my second novel, and it would be very easy to sit back and take all the credit, but the truth is I have so many people to thank, without whom I would never be writing this.

First and foremost I must thank my wife of fifty years, Jill (she says it seems longer). She is the person I turn to so many times during the day to ask for words that I cant find in my head, to run plot twists past her, and to do the first edit of the manuscript. She is also an expert at dragging me out of my office, to get fresh air and clear my head when words just won't come. I know I could never have done this without her.

I must once again thank the excellent team at Spiffing, especially Gabriel for putting up with my impatience, and Caroline for her brilliant editing.

My deepest thanks go to you, yes that's you!, the reader for taking the time to read this book, and for those of you who have followed me from book one, Time For Justice, special thanks for your wonderful reviews and kind words of encouragement, which really do give me the confidence to continue writing.

As I mentioned in book one, if I could ask you one favour, it would be, could you please leave a review. Reviews are like gold dust for authors, especially for new ones, and it really would be a great help if you could find time to do so, and even better if it's a positive one. You can do this by going to this books page on Amazon.

If you would like to know more about future books, character backgrounds and other interesting projects, please check out my website www.neilsandsbooks.com, you will also find me on Facebook, Twitter and Instagram at NeilSandsBooks.

Last but certainly not least, is my wonderful family. The New Zealand wing, of Jemma, Grant, Myla, Riley, and the Surrey wing of Jamie, Laura, Autumn and Rex. Who bring constant joy and happiness and make me believe that grandchildren are Gods greatest gift.

Thank you all so much.

Neil,

Pinewood, Suffolk, England

About the Author

Hello, I am Neil Sands, I was born in Ilford Essex, but have lived in Suffolk for over 40 years.

To say I have had a varied background would be an understatement. From getting my first guitar and singing on stage when I was just eight years old, to leaving school at fifteen with no qualifications. My first job was a £5 a week messenger boy on the London Stock Exchange, while at night playing guitar in many local groups, during the swinging sixties.

Since then I have been a transport manager, window cleaner, debt collector, sales rep, bouncer, fitness instructor, professional wrestler, publican, stand-up comedian, and for the past twenty years a theatrical producer. My life has certainly been diverse, with many ups and downs, but unquestionably always exciting and never dull.

My love for reading really started soon after I started work in the city, travelling on the tube every day, it not only passed the time, but opened my mind to another world inspired by many great authors.

Since then I have always been an avid reader, be it at home reading every night before I go to sleep, and often well into the night when I can't sleep, and on holidays where it's almost a book a day, on my trusty Kindle. My favourite genres have always been action crime thrillers, and I must have read thousands over the years.

Often, driving back home after a wrestling show in the

1970's, anywhere from Plymouth to Perth, I would make up plots in my head, and think how I would write them. The idea never went away and back in 2012, I finally sat down to write a book for the first time. In a few weeks I had written the first 15,000 words, but work took over again with my touring theatre shows really taking off, so it was put to one side, but never forgotten. I would think about it constantly, and add bits here and there, when I had time.

But then the lockdown happened! A week before the start of a 40 date tour, all theatres closed.

So for all the worry and stress, it has also been a blessing for me, because I was able to not only finish my first book Time For Justice, but finish this my second one, Pursuit Of Justice, and have already started on book three of the Hooper / Windsor Thrillers.

Writing has given me a release for any artistic talent I may have, in fact my wife says its kept me sane during lockdown. I realise that I have much to learn as an author, and I will work hard to learn my trade, hopefully with each new book, being better than the last.

I sincerely hope that you can join me for my journey with Dan and Tom, and that together we can travel through some exhilarating tales with the rest of the series.

Kindest regards,

Neil,

Pinewood, Suffolk, England.

Printed in Great Britain
by Amazon

81346068R00174